I0739023

New England Mysteries

Book #1 - **A Cold Morning in MAINE,**
  published in October, 2014.
  ISBN 978-0-9962397-0-7

Book #2 - **A Quiet Evening in CONNECTICUT,**
  published in April, 2015.
  ISBN 978-0-9962397-1-4

Book #3 - **A Bad Night in NEW HAMPSHIRE,**
  published in November, 2015.
  ISBN 978-0-9962397-2-1

Book #4 - **a PIZZA NIGHT in the BAHAMAS,**
  published in November, 2016.
  ISBN 978-0-9962397-3-8

Book #5 - **A Hot Afternoon in MASSACHUSETTS,**
  published in May, 2017.
  ISBN 978-0-9962397-4-5

Bookstores, kindle and amazon – audio books
available from audible.com and iTunes.

www.nemysteries.com

A Rainy Weekend in
RHODE ISLAND

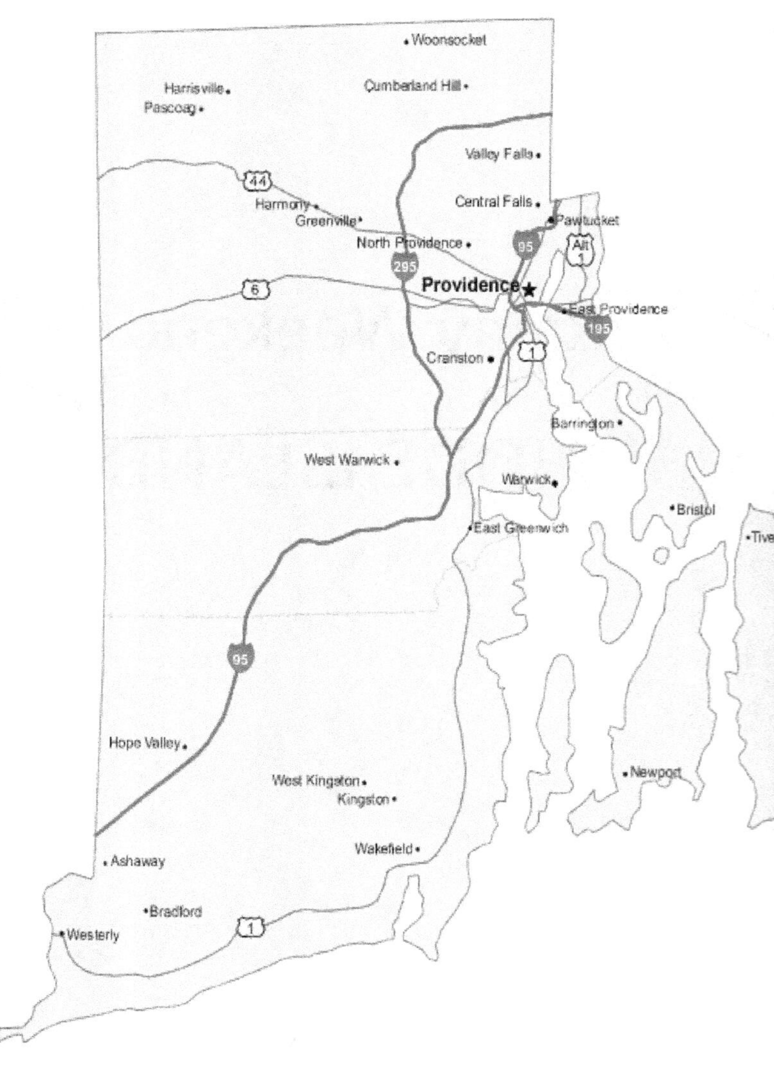

Woonsocket
Harrisville
Pascoag
Cumberland Hill
Valley Falls
44
Central Falls
Harmony
Greenville
Pawtucket
North Providence
95
Alt 1
295
6
Providence
East Providence
195
1
Cranston
Barrington
West Warwick
Warwick
Bristol
East Greenwich
Tiver
95
Hope Valley
Newport
West Kingston
Kingston
Wakefield
Ashaway
Bradford
1
Westerly

A Rainy Weekend in
RHODE ISLAND

Terry Boone

ISBN 978-0-9962397-5-2

First Paperback Edition: November 2018
10 9 8 7 6 5 4 3 2 1

Published by
THREE RIVERS GROUP

Cover photo by the author.

A Rainy Weekend in

RHODE ISLAND

This is a work of fiction. Names, places, events, timelines, distances and other information have been adapted or created entirely by the author. While some aspects of the story were inspired by career experience as a broadcaster, far and away much of what you will read in this book is made-up. Any similarity to real people and real events is coincidental.

Published by **THREE RIVERS GROUP**

Contact: threeriversgroupvt@gmail.com

Dedicated to all of the good reporters, then and now; all of the good cops, now and in the future; and a lot of very talented, devoted chefs and food people in the state of Rhode Island.

One

"**On average,** Providence gets less than four inches of total precipitation in the month of October," the man said, the information offered with understated authoritative certainty in a soft spoken delivery.

I was about to take a seat at the bar, this guy was getting up to leave. I had asked him if he thought the downpour would let up anytime soon. Idle chatter about the weather, even though practically everyone had a smartphone app that could tell you the precise minute when the rain would stop. And when it would start again.

Shrugging his shoulders, he pulled the zipper up to the collar of his jacket, started to head for the door, then stopped. He turned back and gestured at me with his travel umbrella.

"Of course, you could hunker down right here. Ask Pauly to make up a pitcher of Dark 'n Stormys," he said, tipping the umbrella at the man behind the bar who was fiddling with an automatic coffee maker.

"Good idea," I said. "Might have to call a cab to get back to the hotel."

The man smiled, nodded, then turned to step out into the rain.

I pulled my slicker off, shook it and hung it on the

back of the bar stool.

"Be with you in just a second," the bartender said.

"Take your time. I'm OK," I said, taking a seat on the stool next to my coat.

According to an eyewitness, a man with an umbrella had been walking west and had turned onto Union Street. A couple of seconds after he turned the corner, the witness said, "Pop, pop. Sounded like firecrackers."

The reliability of the 'eyewitness' could be an issue. Known to many as a harmless old wino who spent most of his time walking the streets in this section of downtown, Billy 'Quick Whistle' Woodson was also well-known to city police.

The body being loaded into the emergency vehicle would come in as the ninth homicide of the year. With another two months plus on the calendar, there was a possibility that the year-end total could follow a recent pattern of being *below* the five-year average.

The official code 09A – Murder and Nonnegligent Manslaughter – had a weighted annual average of 12. But the stats were down now, by more than a third, from the high of 20 recorded back in 2014.

A small crowd stood across the street from where the shooting had occurred. A couple of people had umbrellas, others wore rain coats with hoods. One teenage boy straddled a bicycle, a dark green plastic trash bag made into a poncho draped over his upper body. The kid watched the Freigthliner ambulance pulling away, almost silent save for the sound of the tires moving slowly through a skim of water in the street.

Police had taped off the area. They were placing small plastic markers on the sidewalk where the man went down. Billy Woodson, wearing a soaked trench coat and an old, faded black Providence College baseball cap, head drooped forward, stood with his back against one of the cruisers. He might have been asleep.

Two

Columbus Day Weekend and we had come to check out the Rhode Island Broadcast Pioneers annual exhibit of classic old radios, as well visiting some of the restaurants.

'We' being myself, Michael Hanlon, sole proprietor of a Private Investigations/Background Security service based in Vermont, and my pal, Louis James Ragsdale, long-time undercover drug cop. Known to friends as 'Louie', he routinely stayed under the radar, domiciled with a wife and two dogs and living just off an unpaved back road deep in the hills of Vermont.

Common interests made the connection for us: a shared enthusiasm for fly fishing; watching certain professional sports, in a stadium or on TV; and yanking each other's chain when discussing politics or current events. We each had some early in life broadcasting experience, both having been bitten by the radio bug when we were kids. I'm a former news reporter, while Louie had done a long gig in college as an oldies DJ. Eventually, we gravitated to different vocations and first met a few years ago while working on a kidnapping case in Maine.

Another mutual interest we had discovered was an appreciation for old radios, as in pre-digital, pre-stereo, even pre-hula hoop. The flashy art deco Bakelite tabletop models scored high on our lists and we knew that there would more than a few at this show. Louie's wife, Becky, was accompanying us but planned to skip the radio exhibit.

I looked down at my phone to see if Ragsdale had sent a text. Nope.

"What can I get you?" the bartender asked. He was tall, thin, brown hair brushed straight back, high forehead. Maybe mid-fifties but looked younger.

For a few seconds I held the thought about the Dark 'n Stormy. Instead, I ordered a pint of Leaning Chimney Porter. A bit early in the season for a dark beer, but I liked the name and the brief description written on the chalkboard behind the bar.

The bartender placed a basket of nacho chips and pretzels in front of me and came back with the beer. Chocolate brown with a creamy tan head to the brim of the glass. I lifted it and took a sip. Nice.

Simply called *Paul's*, this establishment was small, perhaps maximum legal seating for 30 people. Glancing around the room, there was just one couple in a booth near the back. No one else was at the bar. Early. Or, maybe the place only got a later crowd. Maybe the rain. Fine with me. The concierge at the Hilton Providence had said that it was quiet and unpretentious. He was right on both counts.

Outside the rain was still at it. Not really a deluge, but steady.

I placed my phone on the bar, took a pretzel from the basket and had another sip of the beer.

The driver's license identified the victim as one Clifton A. Torres of Parsippany, New Jersey, DOB Mar 10-53. The license photo made the man look heavier than he now appeared there on the gurney.

The EMT had said the man had two gunshot wounds, both from the back; one below his left shoulder and another at the base of the skull. Not much blood from the head wound, but a large dark red stain covered the back of the man's tan colored windbreaker. The guess was that he'd been face down for maybe five minutes before the police arrived. Pretty certain that he was dead with the second, close-range headshot.

A green and white travel umbrella was upside down and blown against the building only a few feet from where the body was found. The police had retrieved the umbrella after some photos had been taken. One of the small yellow markers had been put in its place for the forensics team.

"Billy. How 'ya doin?" one of the cops said.

Billy looked up. It was Phil Dyer, a veteran detective Billy had known for a long time, back to the days when Dyer was just learning the ropes with the Providence PD.

"Hey, Detective," Billy said, extending his right hand. "I'm OK. How are you doing?"

Shaking hands with the old timer, Dyer shrugged,

removed his own baseball cap, snapped it twice to shake water off, then put it back on his head.

"Let's get out of the rain, huh?" He motioned to his unmarked car parked at an angle across the street. Billy followed Dyer who opened the front passenger door for him. He slid in and the door closed.

Three

Nathaniel had convinced himself that the cops would think it was mob hit. I mean, *come on*! We're talkin' Providence, for Christ's sake.

As an insecure teenager, during the summer months, occasionally hanging out with guys he rarely saw between September and May, Nathaniel Crane, II was always quick to make wisecracks about mob families that were getting a lot of ink in the newspapers and extended coverage on TV.

He disliked 'small brained gangsters' and resented the endless harassment that he had endured as a 14-year-old during his first year at St. Paul's School in New Hampshire. Fifteen years later, some of the acerbic jokes volleyed by older boys had stayed with him.

Most vivid among the taunts was that of one fucking senior who had dismissed Nat's waspy surname. In a rather pathetic parody of Pee Wee Herman, the asshole had told a group of other students that the name Crane was most likely changed from Cranucci. Or, more likely Cranatelli. Occasionally, changing voices to sound like a hick, the senior called him 'Natty Bumpo'.

Nathaniel had not forgotten the kid. He knew where he lived today, what his profession was and more than a little about the guy's family.

However, Nathaniel's focus at present was lasered on how to maneuver 8.6 million dollars in his direction. The money, approximately one-third of his late grandfather's estate, had been left to his mother. Unfortunately, his *mother* – Sophia Crane of East Greenwich, Rhode Island – had died in a boating accident just a year ago. Nathaniel, on the other hand, had survived that accident. He was still here.

Still here also were his mother's two sisters, the other beneficiaries of the estate. And that got us to tonight. A guy out walking in the rain and shot on a side street in downtown Providence.

It didn't take large portions to feed Nathaniel's paranoia. The latest example being his need to find the man who was trying to find him. This required a total, no holds barred surveillance of his least favorite of the two aunts, his mother's youngest sister, Lisa, who lived in California.

A little help from a hacker buddy in LA had produced copies of emails and text messages that gave Nathaniel all the confirmation he needed. It proved that his Aunt Lisa was dead-ass serious in her threat to expedite legal proceedings against him. He also knew that she now had his other aunt, Sandi, on board embracing the belief that not only had he killed his own mother, he probably was involved in the death of their father, his grandfather, who died three years ago from cardiac arrest.

Why Lisa had engaged Clifton Torres from New Jersey

to come check on Nathaniel, who fucking knew? Maybe there really *was* a mob connection. In any case, Torres no longer posed a threat. He was outa here and Nathaniel was preparing to take it up a few notches. He had hired his own fucking lawyer. 'Bring it on,' the voice said.

This was only the latest in the rapid-fire conversations that he frequently had with himself, presently driving through the rain back to I-95 south.

Contact with the New Jersey State Police and law enforcement officials in Parsippany would lead the Providence police to any next of kin for the victim. The information could be back before morning, maybe even tonight.

After the crime scene clean-up was finished, the area would remain taped-off at least through late morning tomorrow. Patrol cars would rotate at the scene to be sure that no one messed with anything, accidentally or on purpose.

Maybe the rain would stop later tonight. Or not.

Four

My pint was down to about eight ounces, still no word from Ragsdale. Two men entered the place and stood at the door for a couple of seconds, then started toward the bar.

The guy in front, late forties I guessed, wore a black lightweight jacket that was soaked. His black cap had an insignia that I couldn't make out. He took off the cap first, then the jacket. And just as I had done earlier with my rain slicker, he hung the jacket on the back of a stool. Behind him, the older guy, wearing a well-used tan trench coat and a Providence Friars cap, climbed on a stool and removed his cap. He kept the coat on.

Could be father and son, I thought. The old guy had thinning gray hair, two-day growth of whiskers and was a couple of inches taller than the younger guy, maybe six feet. I spotted a black leather holster on the young guy's left hip.

"Hey, Mister Paul. Long time, huh?" the young guy said, reaching across the bar to shake hands with the bartender.

"Indeed, Nice to see you," the bartender replied. "See you're in good company. How's the mayor doing this evening? No games tonight, Billy."

The old guy smiled. "Two weeks. Opener against UConn. Mohegan Sun."

"How 'bout some coffee?" the younger man said.

"Good night for it," Pauly said, turning to pull two mugs from under the bar.

Louie and Becky Ragsdale walked the three blocks from the hotel to meet Hanlon. Never mind the steady drizzle and cars splashing from the street. Louie was enabling Becky's recently introduced plan that 'we need to walk more often'. Okay.

They nearly passed the entrance. From the sidewalk, in the dark, it could've been mistaken for an insurance office or maybe some counseling service. One small window next to a solid wooden door with an even smaller window. But glancing inside, Becky spotted Hanlon seated at the bar. She tugged her husband's arm.

Louie stopped, peered through the window, then looked up. Above the door was a greenish blue neon sign - *Paul's*. Becky went in first, Louie collapsed the umbrella and followed.

"Damn near missed this place" Louie said as Hanlon turned to greet them.

"Yeah, sorry. I shoulda' texted again after I got here," Hanlon said.

Becky stepped in and gave Hanlon a peck on the cheek. "Michael, how are you?" she asked. He returned the greeting with a light kiss to her left cheek.

"Good. A little wet, but I'm good."

The Ragsdales removed their coats. Hanlon got up from the bar, picked up his beer and pointed at one of the tables. He motioned to the bartender that they were moving.

After they were seated, Becky ordered a glass of Pinot Grigio. Louie said that he would have a pint of whatever Hanlon was drinking. The bartender went to get the drinks.

"And you found this place *how*? Louie asked.

"It was on the cover of a recent issue of *Hard to Find Pubs in The Northeast*. Goes back to the days of the temperance movement, here in the US, anyway, during the 1920s," Hanlon said. He held his glass up to look at the dark liquid. "Half full," he added.

Ragsdale gave an eyeroll response and looked around the room to check out the place.

Pauly was back from getting drinks for the couple who had just arrived. He leaned on the bar and resumed the conversation with Detective Sergeant Phil Dyer of the Providence Police Department.

"You said he'd been in every night for the last week. Anyone ever join him?" Dyer asked.

Pauly shook his head. "Nope."

"Did he talk to other customers? Or was he a loner, one of those quiet drinkers kept to himself?" Dyer followed up.

"Oh, he was friendly enough. Quiet, yes. But he didn't

ignore people. In fact, I would say that he was observing everybody who came and went. He just wasn't all that gregarious, I guess you could say."

Dyer stared at Pauly, then turned back to Billy Woodson. Billy was looking around the room, at the ceiling, the door, the people seated at the table a few feet away.

"You said that you never spoke to him," Dyer said to Billy, which seemed to startle him.

"No, no. I never talked to him," Billy said.

Hesitating for a second, Billy added, "He nodded at me once." Squinting and pursing his lips, Billy twitched his mouth and nose back and forth, then added some more. "Wednesday. I was listening to Mut at Night on WEEI." He pulled a small pair of radio earbuds from his coat pocket and held them up.

Now Dyer stared at Billy.

"Honest. I never talked to him," Billy repeated.

"You said earlier that you always saw him around the same time coming up the street."

Billy was nodding vigorously in the affirmative. He pulled the left sleeve up on his old raincoat and looked at his watch. He tapped the face of the watch.

"Just after six," Billy said. "They do their station identification and a bunch of commercials. That's when I take a breather. Stop for a minute and rest."

Pauly was smiling, looking at Billy. "You're still doing the power walking routine, mayor?"

"Twice a day," Billy quipped. "From the river, out Richmond Street, past City Hall, then back again. One hour and twenty-nine minutes."

Dyer got up, placed a ten-dollar bill on the bar, put his right hand on Billy's shoulder and motioned with his other hand toward the empty coffee mugs.

"Why don't you stay here until the rain lets up," Dyer said. "Take care of him, Pauly." He shook the bartender's hand again and pulled his jacket on. "Probably gonna see me again real soon," he added. "See if you can think of anything else."

Pauly held up a finger for Dyer to wait. He motioned for him to come to the other end of the bar, then pointed at the two men and the woman seated at the table.

"Guy over there, with the yellow coat on the chair," Pauly said, gesturing with his head. "I think when he first came in tonight he spoke to the man for a minute or two."

Dyer looked toward the table, then back to Pauly. "Guy with the beard?"

Pauly nodded. "I was over getting water for the coffeemaker. Didn't hear the conversation, but they were talking."

Five

Louie was seated with his back to the wall. He watched the man approaching their table and knew that he was a cop. Becky and Hanlon were talking about restaurants.

"Excuse me," the man said. Hanlon turned to look at him. It was the same guy that he had noticed wearing a gun on his left hip when he sat at the bar. Now he pulled a badge and ID from his belt. "Detective Sergeant Phil Dyer, Providence Police. Sorry to interrupt, but I'd like to ask you about a man who was in here earlier," he said to Hanlon.

Becky was watching the policeman, then turned to look at her husband. Ragsdale was showing the beginning of a smirk. Or at least his trademark, thinly disguised expression of self-satisfaction.

"Sure," Hanlon replied.

"Pauly says that you spoke with a man who left here," Dyer looked at his watch, "maybe 30 minutes ago."

"Yeah. The tall guy. Wearing a heather tweed driving cap and tan colored windbreaker," Hanlon said. The cop nodded.

Now Hanlon was looking at his watch. "I came in a couple minutes before seven," he said. "He had just pulled his jacket on and was getting ready to leave. He had a travel umbrella."

"That's the man," Dyer said. "What'd you talk about?"

"The rain," Hanlon laughed, gesturing toward the door. "I asked him if he thought it would let up."

The cop nodded again. "He have an opinion?"

"Not really. Just smiled and said something about Providence only gets an average of around four inches of rain in October."

"Anything else?" Dyer asked

"He joked that I might be better off just staying here for the evening. Have a 'pitcher of Dark n' Stormys'."

"Probably not a bad idea," Dyer said.

"Is there some problem with the guy?" Hanlon said.

"Not now. Somebody put a couple bullets in him," Dyer said, motioning with his head toward the street. "Just around the corner, half a block from here."

"He's *dead*?" Hanlon said.

"Afraid so," Dyer said.

We talked with the detective for another minute. He asked for my name and I gave him a business card. *Private Investigation/Background Security Services*, then my name, cellphone number and email address. He studied the card for a few seconds.

"Private Investigator." he said. "Were you a cop?"

Ragsdale snorted before I could reply. Dyer gave him a bemused look.

"No, I've never been a cop," I said.

"What brings you down to the Creative Capital of New England?"

"My personal assistant here," I said, nodding to Louie, "and his better half, are going to take me to some 'outstanding restaurants'," and offered air quotation marks with my fingers.

Now Dyer was giving Ragsdale a closer look. "Personal assistant, huh?" he said.

Louie pulled out his own ID handing it across the table to Dyer. Unlike my plain vanilla card, I knew that Louie's included a photo and his affiliation with the *Joint Northeast Counter-Drug Task Force*.

Once he'd absorbed Ragsdale's info, Dyer handed the ID back. "Thanks for the work you guys do," he said. "It's a big help," he added. Louie nodded, putting the ID back in his pocket.

"Sorry. I don't have a card," Becky said, extending her right hand to Dyer. "I'm Rebecca Ragsdale."

When she said this, Louie's eyebrows went up and he gave me the look.

"Nice to meet you," Dyer said. "You folks enjoy your stay," he added. "The rain will clear out soon enough."

"I hope so," Becky said.

Dyer gave me one of his business cards. "Cell number on the back. Call if you think of anything," he said. "And," he added, "you might try Los Andes, over on Chalkstone Ave. If you can get a table."

"It's on our list," Becky said, holding up a sheet of paper she had printed before leaving home.

Dyer went back to the bar and the older guy he'd come in with.

"You know, Hanlon," Louie said, "do you call *ahead* and tell people you're gonna' be in town? Maybe set up a little... Bang, bang! Okay, who got whacked *this* time?"

"What're the odds?" I said.

Louie turned to his wife, tilted his head and held his palms up. "*Rebecca*?"

"I was nervous," she said, punching his shoulder.

Six

US boating fatality number 503 for the year. That was Sophia Crane, age 66, when her body was not recovered from an 'accident' nearly a hundred miles from shore. That was more than a year ago, in August, 2017.

Sophia's only son, Nathaniel, showed up on a life raft, when he was spotted by a fishing boat off Martha's Vineyard. According to his story, there had been an explosion and fire on the boat, he never saw his mother go overboard and was barely able to launch the raft as the boat was sinking.

The insurer for the boat – a thirty-foot Pearson P303 – has yet to settle Nathaniel's claim, which is one piece of the ongoing exploration of what actually occurred. Some pieces of the boat were found, not all. Despite multiple interviews with the US Coast Guard and investigators working for the insurance company, Crane has not wavered in his account of what happened out in the ocean.

The latest development was, as far as Nathaniel knew, still within the family. It boiled down to a charge from his Aunt Lisa that he not only had staged the boating accident that killed her sister, but that his actions in the company of his grandfather three years earlier had caused the old man to suffer a sudden cardiac arrest that led to his death.

During a tense, voluble and increasingly loud altercation at his mother's home in East Greenwich six weeks earlier, Lisa had declared her intention to engage an attorney. His other aunt, Sandi, had been non-committal in his pleas for support. She said that she understood his grief over losing his mother and, more-or-less, dismissed his concerns over Lisa, saying that 'some family wounds take a long time to heal.'

Cliff Torres was a quiet, gentle, intelligent man. When he learned of the death of Sophia Crane, a month after the boat accident, he was able to locate her youngest sister, Lisa, now living in southern California.

Lisa had bittersweet memories of his acquaintance from when she was a young girl. Cliff had been a friend of her sister and brother-in-law. She had seen Cliff seven years ago at a memorial service for Sophia's husband, Steven, who had died at fifty-nine from prostate cancer. Now Sophia was gone, as well.

Cliff had called Lisa again on the first anniversary of Sophia's death. That call occurred two days after the confrontation with Nathaniel and Lisa had shared her misgivings. By the time the phone call ended, Cliff had offered to help. Lisa suggested a face-to-face meeting when she was going to be in New York in early September. That meeting had proved to be both therapeutic and productive; Cliff volunteered to go up to Rhode Island for some discrete surveillance of Nathaniel Crane's activities.

Now, Cliff Torres was dead at the age of 65. This information had not yet made its way to Lisa Bryan in San Diego.

Seven

Saturday morning, 6:30. Gray overcast sky and still a light mist outside the hotel window. Tapping the Weather Underground app on my phone I studied the screen as though positive thinking would make the blue arc collapse and a sunny icon just suddenly appear and change the forecast.

It wasn't happening. The graph indicated precipitation in gradual peaks and valleys for the next three days. Fortunately, the heaviest rain seemed to be behind us.

Louie, Becky and I had walked back to the Hilton the night before and had dinner downstairs in The Vig, a casual, small restaurant inside the hotel. Becky had gone back to their room early while Louie and I watched a baseball playoff game on one of the TVs at the bar. We packed it in just after 11 o'clock and agreed to meet for breakfast before heading to the Convention Center and the antique radio show.

After a shower, I made coffee, pulled on my pants, a long-sleeved tee shirt, socks and all-weather waterproof sandals, then sat next to the window. Our rooms were on the 14th floor and I was looking down at the roof of the

Dunkin Donuts Center and the Providence Journal building farther up the street.

Two taller buildings stood directly ahead. A parking garage and a Macy's blocked the view of the state capitol building with only the dome visible. Off to my left was traffic heading north on I-95. Slow going in the rain on a Saturday morning, not the usual commuter rush that radio folks think of as 'drive time'.

On my smartphone I found the Providence PD web site. Scrolling through the Investigative Division, I saw that it included eight separate units: Detective Bureau, Youth Services Bureau, Narcotics Bureau, Bureau of Criminal Identification, Intelligence and Organized Crime Bureau, Cold Case Unit, Gun Task Force and School Resource Officers.

There was a color photo and contact info for the Commander of the Division, as well as names and contacts for six officers assigned to head the different units. Nothing listed for Detective Phil Dyer. When I clicked on the *Reports* section, I was given a choice of languages – English, Khmer, Portuguese and Spanish. Out of curiosity, and ignorance of what to expect, I selected Khmer. I did know that Khmer was the primary language of Cambodia, but I had no idea what the alphabet and script looked like. I was impressed by the city's attention and efforts to make the website widely accessible.

I heard someone knocking. I closed the link, got up and went to the door. Louie and Becky greeted me with a copy of USA Today and a paper cup of coffee.

"Thanks," I said, taking the coffee and the paper. "You ready to get breakfast?"

"No, we came by to see if you wanted to come over to *our room* and watch QVC TV?" Louie replied.

"Let me pull on a sweater."

A minute later, we were in the elevator, Becky rummaging through her handbag for something and Louie, eyes toward the ceiling, with only a mild smirk. I hit the button for the lobby, the doors whispered closed and we began the descent.

Washing his face and hands, Billy Woodson's mind settled on mortality. He had witnessed death several times in his 78 years. As a college student working construction during summer months, he had seen an iron worker fall more than 200 feet onto a concrete slab, and a carpenter who died from an accident that had ruptured his spleen. While he had only heard the shots last night and *then* saw the body on the sidewalk, it was that cold finality of a man face down on the pavement that took him back 43 years.

Before the booze, the countless times in and out of jail for drunken behavior, the mocking and humiliation from words and actions by too many people, *all* of those wasted years, Billy's own near life-ending experience came in the summer of 1971. His wife and eight-year-old son had died in a car crash. He survived, but blamed himself for the accident.

He had been waiting at the airport for his wife and son to pick him up after returning from a NCAA Basketball Officials clinic in Columbus, Ohio. He was tired. He asked his wife to drive. Later, he told police that he'd fallen asleep on the drive home and did not remember the crash, only regaining consciousness two days later in the hospital. And *that* was when he learned of the horrible accident that claimed his family. Also killed was a man driving the car that crashed into them at an intersection.

Still young, with a promising future as both a life insurance agent and highly respected college basketball referee, Billy never regained reasonable control of his life. There were emotional breakdowns, binge drinking, rehab, relapses and a recurring cycle that usually dumped him on some street late at night with no idea of where he was.

The pattern continued for more than 30 years. He only managed to bring marginal stability to his life, selling newspapers on the streets in Providence when people still did that, and later working as a janitor for a local church.

Gradually, with occasional tumbles off the wagon, he transitioned from full-time drunk to most-of-the-time Good Samaritan.

Billy would help anyone with anything. He ran errands for a priest and many of the parishioners; washed windows, raked leaves, cleaned out garages and cellars. And for more than ten years, he had not had a drop of alcohol.

The highlight of his life activities now was officiating in a men's amateur league, running a youth basketball program and listening to almost any kind of sports on the radio. Occasionally, he would watch a game on TV. But he preferred the crowd noise, the sounds of the game and allowing his imagination to create the game in his head. He particularly loved the Providence College basketball team, The Friars.

Today, early on this wet Saturday morning, Billy finished his cleaning chores at the church and set out for one of his twice-daily walks that lasted 90 minutes. He no longer sold newspapers, but every day he read a paper, purchasing a copy of The Providence Journal. At the end of his walk, he would go to a restaurant, or back to his tiny efficiency apartment, settle in and read.

And he read every page, including the classifieds.

Eight

Nathaniel Crane called another friend. Probably a good idea to disappear for a while. If his aunts really were moving forward with legal action, or possibly ready to go to the police, he wasn't going to make it easy for them to find him.

It was one thing to have his lawyer fighting with insurance companies over the settlement for the boat and his mother's whole life policy. Being accused of murder would take the family squabble to an entirely new level. As confident as he was that he could stick to his story about the boat accident, he was not sure that he was prepared to go deeper with the police. He needed more time.

"Chad. It's Nathaniel Crane. How ya doin?" he said, placing the phone closer to his ear. Chad Williams, a friend from their prep school days, was a mid-level program analyst working for the Social Security Administration in Silver Spring, Maryland.

"Nathaniel Crane 'The Deuce'. What's up, man?" Chad answered.

"Not much. Thought I'd give you a call. It's been a spell."

"*Yeah*. Coupla' years, at least," he said. "Where are you these days?"

"Right at the moment I'm back at my mother's house in Rhode Island. I don't know if you may have heard about it. A year ago my boat caught fire and my mother was killed."

"Christ! I am *so* sorry. No, I did not know that." Chad was trying to recall if he'd seen anything on facebook from mutual friends. He was drawing a blank. "Were *you* hurt?" he added.

"Crazy. I was thrown back to the stern, knocked unconscious. Then I couldn't find my mother. I was lucky to get a raft into the water. It was late in the afternoon, no other boats anywhere near where we were sailing. There was no wind at all. I'd just started the engine a minute earlier."

Chad was silent listening to this. He'd only been a guest on another friend's boat in the Chesapeake Bay a couple of times and knew next to nothing about being on the water, sail boats or otherwise.

"Don't remember much of anything. I was picked up by some fisherman off Martha's Vineyard."

"That's *horrible*. I am really sorry about your mom."

"Thanks," Nat said.

"So now you're like me. Both parents gone, bumps you up on the list. Makes you think about what you're *doing* with your life."

"Yeah. Focus on a career, like some of our buddies.

And you. Or still searching, like me," Nat said.

"It's gotta' be right for you, man. You'll find it."

"Chad, have a question for you. Actually, it's the reason I called. Do you still have the chicken coop up in Vermont?"

"Yeah, but I haven't been there for coupla' years now. Still paying the taxes. I keep thinking that I'm going to sell it. Place needs a *lot* of work."

"It was in pretty rough shape when we went there in college," Nat said.

"Started out as my grandfather's hunting camp. Then my parents used it some for family ski vacations. It was never really big enough. My dad did a little work on it, added the bathroom and that room with two beds."

"Turk and I slept in there when we went up with you and Mouse."

"Yeah. You know that Mouse is living in Colorado now?" Chad said.

"Didn't know that."

"Hooked up with some cowgirl this summer. Decided to go west."

"So, the chicken coop. Any chance I could rent it from you? Just for a couple months, maybe."

"Why not?" Chad said.

"You'll have to do some cleaning. Hell knows what critters might be living there."

Another five minutes on the phone and Nathaniel had a deal with his old pal that would allow him to stay in a two-room camp off a dirt road in southwestern Vermont. He also got the name of the nearest year 'round neighbor, a warning about the old plastic water line that froze up early and where to find the key. He told Chad that he might even help with a little repair work while he was there.

He could pack his car and be in Vermont by nightfall. The drive, even in the rain, would not be much over three hours.

Nine

"Becky has some exciting news," Ragsdale said, as we walked into the hotel restaurant. I looked at Louie, then at Becky.

"Let me guess. You're getting a new puppy." I waited for confirmation. Zip.

Becky stopped and turned to face me. "Thank you again for the book." She put a hand on my left arm and looked at me. "I had no idea what to expect by the title. *The Art of Racing in The Rain* and all about an old dog! It's a wonderful story," she added.

"Nah, we're gonna wait a while," Louie said. "Bucky was special. I've had a lot of dogs, but none like him."

"OK, *what* is the exciting news?" I asked. We were waiting to be seated for breakfast. Becky was shaking her head and giving Louie the 'you are such a smartass' look.

"There's a club down the street featuring an oldies band tonight. Only a five-dollar cover," Louie said. I waited for the punchline but got only the smugness. He arched his eyebrows. "I'm serious," he added.

"Thought we were here for the *food*. I'm not sure I can take the atmosphere of a club," I said.

"Hanlon, you are *so* quickly becoming an old fart."

"Hey, I like live summer events. I like the concerts in halls that have comfortable seats and good acoustics. I am no longer crazy about small, noisy clubs."

The hostess led us to a table, gave us menus and said that our server would bring coffee and take our order. Or, that we could enjoy the buffet breakfast.

"Think I will have an omelet," Becky said, closing her menu and placing it on the table. Louie was still scanning the choices. I decided to go for French Toast. Our server, a middle-aged woman, arrived with a pot of coffee and filled three of the four cups already on the table. After taking our food order, she collected the menus and went back to the hostess station to tap a computer screen entering the selections.

I turned to Becky. "What's your plan for the day while we go look at antique radios?"

"Maybe a little shopping. There's an art glass boutique a friend told me about. Not very far from here. And I'm going to the RISD Museum this afternoon. What time do you think you will get back?" she added, looking at her husband.

He shrugged. "Most likely 3:30 or 4."

"I might use the hotel fitness center when I get back," she said.

"Great. Do maybe a few minutes on the treadmill for me," Louie said.

"Where'd you hear about the oldies club?" I said.

"Becky saw an ad in one of the entertainment guides back in the room. The Parlour. Says it has live music every night. Listed all the bands they've booked for the month," Louie said.

"And the band that's playing tonight?"

"Are you ready for this? The Bonnevilles. How's that for 1957?" Louie held his left arm up to make a muscle.

"I think there's a British band called The Bonnevilles," I said. He was shaking his head.

"Maybe. Don't think that's what we have here. The ad said Original Rock 'n Roll."

"Becky, what time is our dinner reservation?" I said.

"Six o'clock. If the rain stops, maybe we can eat outside," she said.

"Always the optimist. Don't count on it," Louie said.

Detective Sergeant Phil Dyer sat in his car watching pedestrians with umbrellas. The rain *acted* like it wanted to let up – the overcast was perhaps a shade lighter – but it never really stopped completely. Light drizzle.

NOAA, or the National Oceanic and Atmospheric Administration, was predicting up to ten inches of rain across the state for the weekend. Might seem like a lot, but short of the record. 6.38 inches in a 24-hour period set on October 15, 2005. During that previous storm, the National Weather Service reported that 7 to 9 inches of rain had fallen between October 13th and 15th.

Dyer put his hat on, got out of the car and moved quickly to the back entrance of the Providence Public Safety Complex on Washington Street. He was in his office on the third floor two minutes later. If you're gonna' be stuck indoors, better that it's not sunny and bright outside.

No useful info on the shooting victim from last night. Cops in Jersey had confirmed the address from the driver's license, but nothing yet on relatives or employment. No social media presence for Cliff Torres. Next step was to speak with neighbors down there. Might have something later in the day.

Clifton didn't really match up with Torres. Maybe the guy had changed his name. Maybe his parents had some particular reason for choosing that name. *Maybe* it was bullshit, a phony ID.

The ballistics report indicated the slugs were 9-millimeter. The lab would be more specific when the full summary came up. Cause of death almost certainly was the shot to the base of the skull.

Dyer opened a file on his computer that held short summaries of murders in Rhode Island for the past 10 years. Every cop in the state knew that according to recent FBI statistics, Rhode Island has the highest per capita murder rate in New England, 2.7 per 100,000 people.

Massachusetts is not far behind, with 2 per 100,000; Connecticut and Vermont each had 2.2 per 100,000; Maine with just 1.5 per 100,000; and New Hampshire 1.3 per 100,000. Veteran law enforcement officers also knew that compared to the national murder rate of 5.3 per 100,000, that it was all relative.

Providence, RI – 10/5/18 – Clifton Torres would make a slight bump in this year's numbers from the Ocean State.

Ten

A below the fold headline in The Providence Journal read, **Man Shot Downtown**. The story ran 144 words and did not identify the victim.

Billy Woodson read the story and tried to think of anything else that he might have seen. He was certain that no one had been running. Sure, there were cars, but he hadn't paid attention to the traffic. It was dark. And raining.

Like he told Detective Dyer, he had seen the man at least twice previously but had never spoken with him. Now he racked his brain trying to recall if he'd ever seen anyone *with* the man, or talking to the man, or *following* the man. Nothing was coming up. Just the guy out by himself, walking in the opposite direction. Billy had liked the tweed cap the man wore.

Despite all the hours he'd spent cleaning the church and running errands for Father Mike, Billy never went to mass. As shaky as it was, he kept his faith to himself. The priest allowed him that space and not once had he ever made Billy feel guilty about not attending services, confession, or church functions that might be awkward for him.

Even the death of a stranger could stir up a mixture of pre-existing guilt and a lot of sadness. That's what was happening this morning. One good way to wring it out was to go to the church gym and be with the kids.

Refereeing men's games was fun, but not the same as being around the U10 youngsters. Billy got his court shoes, his whistle and a bottle of water from the fridge. He locked the door and went up to the street for the two-minute walk to the gymnasium.

Louie pointed at the street sign when we turned on Broadway. "The Drifters, 1963. Phil Spector on guitar!" he said. "Big hit. Just slightly over-produced. *Way* too much with the strings."

We were walking from the Hilton Providence to the Rhode Island Convention Center. Still light rain, but only a three-minute stroll. Becky was off somewhere and likely enjoying a break from us.

"George Benson did a cover version, yes?" I said.

"1978. One the few recordings *ever* that is actually better than the original. Much better intro. And George Benson *can* 'play this here guitar."

When we got inside, it became clear that the Broadcast Pioneers gathering was only a side event with dealers and booths assembled in a smaller breakout room. The main exhibit hall apparently was occupied by the much larger annual conference of the New England Independent Booksellers Association.

Multiple lobby signs directed us to **RADIO Collectors Do It with More Frequency**. Okay.

While Louie was paying our admission, ten bucks each, I scanned the room. Maybe 2,000 square feet with individual tables set up for display of radios, old tubes for radios, journals and periodicals on radios, a variety of electronic equipment, antique microphones, headsets, schematics for radios, faux soda cans that were actually transistor radios with tiny speakers on top of the can.

"Hope you have your AMEX Black Card," I said. Louie handed me a copy of the room layout listing all the exhibitors and the booth numbers.

He put his left hand on my shoulder. "Tell you what, Anderson Cooper," he said. "You find a FADA 200 Bullet in *mint condition*, or an Emerson FC 400 Patriot, I'll cover ya. No matter what it costs."

"Right."

After checking out most of the exhibits, we didn't find a mint FADA in the sweet yellow cabinet style, with red knobs and handle. There *was* a marbleized dark blue model with pumpkin trim, priced at just $5,000.

I did come across a 1967 First Edition of *Encyclopedia of Radio and Television Broadcasting* by Robert St. John. The cover was faded and it had a small stain on the sp ne, but the interior looked clean and no pages seemed to be missing, so I bought it for $20.

40

Eleven

Checking the front door to his mother's house in East Greenwich, Nathaniel went into the kitchen, stood and looked around. Satisfied that there was nothing else that he needed, he set the security alarm and went to the garage.

The garage door was open and he walked to the rear of the house beyond his mother's perennial garden and began to unroll the heavy-duty mesh fabric cover for the 40-foot inground swimming pool. He would not take time to clear the leaves that had begun accumulating. He secured the cover at the far end, went back to the garage, got in his car and slowly backed out. A two-year old Subaru Outback that had belonged to his mother was still parked inside.

He tapped the button attached to the sun visor and the double-wide door began closing. The last thing he noticed was his mother's golf clubs in the nearest corner next to the door. He had a flash memory of her taking the clubs from her car and placing the bag where it now stood.

Following Shallow Brook Drive out to Tillinghast Road, he turned left in the direction of I-95. He would be on the interstate heading north in minutes, bypassing Providence. The directions on his trip planner app showed that he would be in Worcester, MA in one hour, then head west on Route 2. His thought was that he would stop somewhere to eat and shop for a few basic provisions before proceeding on to Vermont.

No one else knew his plan. No one else *needed* to know. There was no reason to check in with his lawyer. If his two aunts actually followed-through with the court threat, he would know soon enough. And with his Aunt Lisa's friend Cliff now out of the picture, that offered the possibility of both confusing and delaying any immediate action from her.

Regardless of what happened next, he believed that he could remain out of sight and away from imminent danger, whether it came from the court, insurance investigators, or any police investigation of a drive by shooting.

Lisa Bryan sent a short email to Cliff. It was 10 o'clock in San Diego, 1 PM in Rhode Island. She was puzzled that he had not been in touch since their exchange of text messages two days earlier.

In any event, she would hold off until Tuesday – Monday was a holiday – to talk with her attorney, even if Cliff had nothing of interest to tell her. The information from the previous email was that Cliff had followed

Nathaniel twice into Providence. At least one of those trips appeared to have been to a lawyer's office located downtown. The other trip, he had gone to an apartment complex, according to Cliff. He did not follow Nathaniel into the building. That was Wednesday, Cliff reporting this to her on Thursday morning.

Logging off her computer, Lisa got up, adjusted the window shade, closed and locked the office door and headed for her car. She planned to meet briefly for latte with a colleague, shop for groceries, then spend the afternoon at her health club. Later she would have dinner with a friend, maybe go see a film.

Seated behind the wheel of her 2015 Porsche Boxster, Lisa waited for the top to settle into place in the boot. She heard the click, saw the light on the dash go out. Just as she was about to pull out of her parking spot, an old man was crossing the street at the corner. He reminded her of her father. She lost it.

Shutting off the ignition, Lisa rested her arms on the steering wheel, dropped her head forward and began to sob. Her father had been dead for three years now. Heart attack at 85. But the memory of him riding with her in this car when it was brand new, just a month before he died, was as vivid as yesterday.

He'd loved the racing yellow exterior, the leather seats, the dashboard with the red tachometer and all the different little engine indicator symbols, the audio system and the built-in Bluetooth phone connection.

Lisa did not tell him what she'd paid for the car and he had not asked. She was pretty sure that it wouldn't have made any difference. He was proud of her, as he was of both her sisters. But as the baby in the family, Lisa always got a little extra slack from him, if not from her sisters.

Getting her emotions back in control, she now felt the anger. Not only did she believe that her nephew had killed his own mother, but that he had in some way taunted and provoked his grandfather the night the man died.

Nathaniel had brushed away the accusation and it was virtually impossible to prove. But she would never forget it. And when the current legal action was fully engaged and she had her day in court, Lisa would make certain that her attorney would force Nathaniel Crane, II, to answer in front of a judge, under oath.

Twelve

The investigation of the street shooting was gathering momentum. Detective Phil Dyer believed that they were seeing the beginning of a profile of the victim and now had details on a vehicle owned by the man.

According to information coming back from New Jersey, Clifton Torres was a recently retired polymer engineer who lived alone. Neighbors claimed not to be aware of relatives or close friends, stating that Torres seemed to be a private man and had only recently moved into the condominium listed as his current address. The Providence PD was searching for a 2014 Toyota RAV4 with New Jersey plates. It had not been found on the streets; hotel parking lots and garages were next.

Being a federal holiday weekend, Dyer knew that obtaining useful information from either Torres' former employer or from the Social Security Administration would move slowly. But one development came from an email exchange and text messages discovered on the dead man's cellphone. Dyer told the Jersey cops about this and requested details of anything they discovered on Torres' computer once they had searched his condo.

In the meantime, Dyer had sent his own message to a woman named Lisa – email address lisab1030@gmail.com. No reply as of the moment. More promising might be the text messages if the receiving phone could be traced.

The woman had been corresponding with the victim as recently as two days ago when he told her about being in Providence and 'keeping an eye on NC'. Most intriguing was the last message Torres' had sent saying that he would stay in Rhode Island through the weekend.

Who is Lisa B? And who is NC?

Most of the kids in the church gym had more energy than they had athleticism. They were all 10 years old and under. A few of them had some basketball moves and showed promise.

Billy worked with three high school students, members of the CYO, who served as team coaches and chaperones for the rowdy youth, while he ran up and down the floor as the lone official keeping the game moving along.

The teams were mostly boys, with only a few girls participating, depending on time of the year. This morning there were three girls present. All the kids wore different color pinnies; red, green, yellow, purple, blue. Billy had donated some of his own cash to help purchase the pinnies. Some of the players were so small that the pinnies came down below their shorts, nearly to their knees.

After two hours of round-robin games, Billy was beat. He stood talking with one of the high school students, Abeo, who was wearing a Catholic Youth Organization tee shirt from Nigeria. It had a faded gold and green logo showing two hands releasing a peace dove with olive branch over the words *Let Your Light Shine*.

Abeo was tall, quiet, big smile and a favorite with the kids. He displayed impressive basketball skills all the kids tried to emulate. But he'd confided to Billy that what he *really* loved was soccer.

"You should take some of the soccer officiating classes," Billy said. "Help you earn spending money when you go to college next year."

Abeo gave the smile and rolled his head like he was loosening up for a game. Billy wondered if it was a natural move or something he'd picked up from watching athletes on TV. He put a hand on Abeo's shoulder and added, "I'll put you in touch with a man I know at URI. He can help get you started."

A minute later, Billy was headed back for his apartment. He'd barely left the gym when he felt the rain and his thoughts were back on the shooting incident from the night before.

Too much violence, too many guns, too little consideration for human life.

Billy willed his mind back to the scene he'd just left. The sounds, the faces, the eagerness of a bunch of youngsters up and down the floor; Abeo and the two other teenagers patiently working with the kids, instructing them and trying to direct the enthusiasm.

Despite his own life experiences and the skepticism he held about many things, Billy had previously concluded that Father Mike, and others like him, should get the Nobel Peace Prize or *any* humanitarian awards available. Plus, maybe their non-profit community organizations could get just a *fractional* percentage of all that money sloshing around in everyday life in America.

Thirteen

Ragsdale was seated at a table with two paper cups of coffee when I came out of the restroom. He was thumbing through the book I'd just purchased from one of the antique radio dealers.

"Look at these photos," he said, shoving the book across the table in my direction.

I picked up the book and it was open to a collage of old photos of long dead news reporters; Eric Sevareid, Howard K. Smith, Bob Considine and Walter Cronkite. All radio or print guys who made the transition to television and eventually became household names by the end of their careers.

"You think Cronkite would have a facebook page. Or a *Twitter* account?" Louie said.

"Maybe not himself, but one of his associates might goose it a little. Gotta' stay in touch with your audience, eh?"

He reached for the book and started flipping through the pages again, stopping at a photo of Eddie Cantor holding a bouquet of flowers and standing next to an ancient radio microphone. Louie tapped the photo with his right index finger.

"Look at that mic. It's the size of a friggin' *toaster*," he said.

"Hey. That was state of the art in what, *1928*?"

Louie closed the book, placed it on the table and took a drink of coffee.

I took the lid off my cup to be sure that he hadn't put in too much cream. It looked OK. I sipped it to test how hot it was. Fine.

Louie tapped my arm. I looked up and he pointed to the crowd moving along the exhibit booths.

"Isn't that the guy from the bar," he said, indicating a man talking to one of the dealers.

"Yeah. Paul. Or, Pauly as everyone seems to call him." It was the bartender from last night, the man of few words. Then again, he was more talkative with the cop and the old guy in the trench coat. Just as this thought zipped through my brain, he turned in our direction. We made eye contact.

A glimmer of recognition and Pauly stepped toward our table.

"Hey, gents," he said. "You old radio buffs?"

"Yeah. It's one of the reasons we came to town," I said.

He gestured over his shoulder at the man he'd been talking with. "My cousin. He's a ham radio operator. Been collecting this stuff forever. I just came down to say hello to him." He pulled out a chair and sat across from me, next to Louie.

"Those ham guys are pretty serious," I offered. Pauly nodded.

"You're tellin me," Pauly said. He pointed at his cousin in the booth, who was now talking with one of the other exhibitors. "Andy was building his own sets and doing Morse code when we were kids."

Louie gave a snort of laughter. His eyes brightened and he leaned forward.

"You remember the Jean Shepherd show he did about learning code?" Louie said.

I laughed. "Yeah. When he was in the army."

Louie nodded. "That's the one. He told about his buddy out at The Presidio who could do 60 words a minute. But they were screwing with the army instructor and pretending not to be able to get *any* of it." He laughed, then imitated Shepherd's radio voice, "I can teach code to a *dog*!"

"Where you fellows from?" Pauly said.

"Vermont," I said.

"Nice. I dated a girl from Burlington years ago," Pauly said.

"Up north on Lake Champlain," I said. "I live in the east central part of the state, near White River Junction." Pauly nodded. "The ambassador," I said, pointing at Louie, "lives with his wife and dogs in a wooden shoe up in the hills."

"Did your old girlfriend tell you that Burlington really *isn't* Vermont?" Louie said.

Pauly shook his head. "Didn't last that long."

We yakked for a couple of minutes, Pauly stood, shook our hands and invited us to come back to his bar.

"I'll fix you one my new special cocktails. Has maple syrup in it," he said. "On the house."

Finished chatting and comparing some notes with her colleague, Lisa checked messages on her phone. Among the new emails was one from Detective Phil Dyer in Providence. She didn't recognize his name. He provided his contact information and asked her to call. No explanation regarding the reason.

She walked back to her car, put her handbag on the passenger seat and prepared to make the call. Waiting for the connection, she wondered if there was some new wrinkle in the boating accident investigation, if police had new information about her sister's death. The US Coast Guard had declared months ago that the body would not be found. But what involvement could the Providence police have?

Cliff. Perhaps he had been in touch with this Detective Dyer. But he would have spoken with her before he did that.

"Phil Dyer," the man answered.

Fourteen

When Dyer finished explaining how he'd obtained her email address and why he wanted to speak with her, Lisa felt a chill. She knew that what came next was not going to be good news.

"Mister Torres was shot last night. I'm sorry to tell you that he's dead," Dyer said.

"My God," Lisa whispered into the phone. "What happened?"

Dyer spent a minute recounting what had occurred the previous evening, adding that police in New Jersey were trying to find any relatives Torres might have, but nothing so far.

"Reading the messages you exchanged, it seems that he was working for you, is that correct?"

"Not really working for me. He was a friend of my sister and her husband from years ago," she said. "My sister died last year in a boating accident. Cliff was trying to help me get more information about her death."

Dyer was silent at the other end of the call. When

he'd concluded that she was not going to say more, he asked, "So he was here in Providence to do what, exactly? On your behalf."

Deep sigh. "I think that my nephew deliberately caused the accident that killed his mother. Her body was never located. The Coast Guard says that it is extremely unlikely that they will *ever* find it," then she added, "Investigators for the insurance company have not been able to show that anything 'intentional' caused the accident."

Dyer maintained his silence, allowing her to offer more.

"I have been working with an attorney in Woonsocket in preparing to bring a suit against my nephew. We hope to gather enough substantive information that a judge will allow the case to move forward. And that law enforcement in Massachusetts, and the Coast Guard, will pursue the case."

"The accident that claimed your sister, that was in Massachusetts?"

"Yes. A few miles off Martha's Vineyard," she said.

Dyer had a dim recollection of a news story from a year earlier when a woman from Rhode Island went missing in a boating accident. "When did this happen?" he said.

"August 29th, 2017," she said. "That's the day my nephew was found by fishermen."

"Tell me about your nephew. His name, and does he

live in Rhode Island?"

"Nathaniel Crane. He's been staying at his mother's home on and off ever since the accident."

"And where is that?" Dyer said.

"East Greenwich."

"Can you give me the address for your sister's home?" he said.

By the time she ended the call, Lisa Bryan's heart rate was likely spiking near 80, more than a third higher than usual. She took deep breaths and tilted her head back. After a few seconds, her pulse began dropping back to its normal range.

When she had composed herself, she contemplated a call to her lawyer in Rhode Island. She had not told him anything about Cliff Torres. And she hadn't told her sister Sandi, either. Now Cliff had been murdered.

Not a coincidence.

It was 11:45, or 2:45 on the east coast. She found the lawyer's contact on her phone and tapped the green call icon.

Dyer placed a quick call to the PD in East Greenwich. He gave a summary of the case and told about the possible connection to the son of a woman who recently lived there and that he would like to schedule a visit.

The on-duty Sergeant told Dyer that he would make the arrangement and that as soon as Dyer knew when he was coming, to call back and confirm the time. One of the East Greenwich officers would escort him to the Crane home.

Billy Woodson went to check on the church before the five o'clock mass. The cleaning and vacuuming that he had completed earlier that morning was the most time consuming of his Saturday routine.

One of the recurring thoughts Billy had had throughout his sober years was how his wife, Dorothy, might be today if she were alive. Would she have become a more religious person? They were not Roman Catholic, she had been raised Lutheran and he came from a family that attended Presbyterian services once a year at Christmas. Their son, little Billy, had been baptized as an infant and his mother later had taken him to services on an irregular basis.

Moving through the nave of the church, everything was in order. Billy adjusted the lighting for the sanctuary, organized some pamphlets placed on a table in the church vestibule and made certain the area rug near the entrance was straight. He knew that Father Mike and the altar boys would be arriving soon. His work was done until later in the evening when he would return and vacuum once more for the Sunday morning services.

Putting his coat on and picking up his cap, Billy set out for the evening walk. Maybe the rain would take a breather.

Fifteen

The rain falling on much of the southern New England coastline was a mix of wet snow in western Massachusetts and into southern Vermont. It was unusually early, but not unheard of, and would melt in a day or two.

The slush on Route 2 east from Fitchburg – all the way to the Berkshires – was keeping traffic below the speed limit. That included Nathaniel Crane, drumming his fingers on the shifting lever of his Mitsubishi Eclipse. The car in front of him was going about 40. Nobody had their winter tires on yet.

After more than a half-an-hour of this nonsense, he took a backroad shortcut in the town of Erving that would take him through Northfield and get him to I-91 and into Vermont. He wanted to make it to Chad's camp before dark.

On a section of road leaving state forest land and coming over a rise, there was a one-ton dump truck that had gone sideways and spilled most of its load of firewood. Two men were standing next to the truck. They had put out a flare and appeared about to begin clearing the wood from the snowy pavement.

Nathaniel geared down and stopped a few feet from the flare.

We took a taxi from the hotel to Los Andes. Becky had managed to get a reservation, but we had to be there by six. The concierge assured us that it was less than ten minutes away when he got us a cab.

A small, unpretentious, brick façade on a street corner in a mixed-use neighborhood. Blue awning, a couple of unoccupied outdoor café tables, umbrellas cranked down in the rain. The restaurant was at street level of a triple-decker. Maybe apartments on the floors above. The cab stopped at the curb a few feet from the entrance. I paid the driver and got his card to call him back later.

Authentic Bolivian & Peruvian Cuisine, so read the sign in a side window. There was a short line of people on the sidewalk standing beneath an extended plastic-covered canopy. We joined the cue. I looked at my watch; three minutes to six. I went to the front of the line to check in with the hostess. After asking my name, she looked at a list in front of her, glanced around, then said that we could be seated next. I went back to get Becky and Louie.

The hostess took us to a table near the center of the room. I was scoping the place out and calculating the seating capacity. Best guess, maximum 100 people. And it looked as though every table was filled, including all the booths along the wall. South American music coming from the speakers in the ceiling. The bar was busy, too. I couldn't see any empty seats there. We had indeed lucked out.

"Hey, gaucho," Ragsdale said. "Let that beard grow a little longer, get one of those hats. You'd fit right in." He pulled on my chin whiskers and gave me the kiss, kiss sound.

"They start rounding up recruits for the next cattle drive, I think *you* are the more likely candidate." I flicked his squared-off van dyke with the back of my right hand as though I were brushing away crumbs.

"I have a beautiful poncho from Argentina," Becky said to me. She turned to her husband and added, "Be nice to me Louie, I might let you wear it." He gave her the kiss, kiss.

We hadn't opened the menus before a young man in a white shirt with a skinny black necktie was at the table pouring glasses of water. He introduced himself as Aaron.

We ordered a medium-priced bottle of Malbec then focused on the menu. It took me less than a minute to zoom in on the Pique A Lo Macho, strips of sirloin sautéed in a mustard/wine sauce, served with raw onions, jalapenos, tomato salsa and hard-boiled eggs on top of steak fries.

Becky went for Paella served with saffron rice, Louie ordered the Ceviche Clasico that came with sweet potatoes. We ate more than we talked, and the music was at the right volume to make it more enjoyable. But the place absolutely hummed with energy.

The smell of all the spices coming from other tables and from the kitchen was incredible. By the time we'd finished our meal, the idea of *another* restaurant tomorrow night was a little frightening. I might not eat for another week. Nobody in our party could even think about dessert.

"Okay, Becky. Scale of zero to 10, this place pulls down a 9.5," I said. "And *you* get an 11 for finding it."

"Thank you. Glad we came," she said.

"Hanlon. Wanna' borrow the poncho before you sign on for the round up?" Louie added.

"Isn't there some good fishing in Argentina?" I said.

"There's a thought," he said. "What, it's springtime there right now, correct? Let's book a trip."

"But you don't like to fly," I said. "Long boat ride."

"I'm sure we can figure something out."

As Louie faked enthusiasm for a South American trip, Becky was shaking her head. Her expression conveyed, 'Don't buy the tickets quite yet.'

Sixteen

The snow had changed to a light freezing rain when Nathaniel arrived at the Jacksonville General Store, his first stop in Vermont. Leaving the I-91 in Brattleboro, he followed Route 9 west, then south on 100. It was 6:55 PM.

One thing he hadn't yet purchased was propane. Chad had told him that he would need it for the combo portable grill/stove at the camp.

He parked off street at the side of the store. There was a propane tank display cage next to steps at the front entrance. Inside, Nat paid $60.41 for a new tank as he did not have a tank to swap out. The man behind the counter went outside, unlocked the cage and lifted out a squat, fifteen-pound Blue Rhino tank and handed it to Nat.

After he placed it on the floor next to the passenger seat, Nat went back to the porch of the store to look at notices on the bulletin board. Items for sale, lost pet photos, a poster for a Candidates Night for the upcoming state legislative race, musical instruments for sale. Nothing too exciting. He went back inside and bought toilet paper, a box of large kitchen matches and a six-pack of Long Trail IPA beer.

Ten minutes later, making his way in the dark, west then north, he found the unpaved turn-off that would take him another four-and-a-half-miles to a dirt turn-off into the woods, and eventually to the camp. Chad told him to watch for a weathered four-by-four post inside an old rusted milk can, which marked the turning spot that would lead through the trees. Nathaniel vaguely recalled the milk can from his visit seven years ago.

Standing at the edge of the road, next to the milk can as though guarding the place, was a whitetail deer and twin fawns from the previous spring. Nat braked. The deer froze in place.

He flashed his headlights. The big deer twitched its tail, jerked its head to face the car, then leaped into the woods with the two younger ones following.

Welcome to Vermont.

A little shy of three-thousand miles away, in the Pacific Time Zone, Lisa Bryan left her health club feeling worse than when she had arrived two hours earlier.

The bar bell squats, the pull ups, the stretching, the spinning, all great. Her body was as toned and fit as any woman she knew. But her mind was rattled and quickly going off the rails.

It was anger. At first, despite the music in her ear buds while she was on the bike, the anger began seeping in and pushing thoughts around like a pinball machine.

Bing. Bing. Bing. And bing again.

Her father, her sister. And now Cliff Torres was dead. The crying in the shower after the workout gave only temporary relief. She was now just about ready to rip out that psychopath's heart.

Where did someone like Nathaniel Crane come from? It had to be something in the DNA from his father's genes. But his father had been a nice man. Loving and kind. And dead too young. Was *that* it? Nat's twisted personality got worse after his father died? How do you *become* the kind of person who hounds your own grandfather until he has a heart attack and dies in front of you? How do you find the cold, maniacal determination to kill your *mother*?

Lisa wouldn't wait for another phone call from the police in Providence. She would fly to Rhode Island, meet with her attorney and move this case forward. She didn't care if the lawsuit dragged on for years. She didn't care if her sister Sandi had the stomach for it or not. There had to be justice out there somewhere. Let that monster spend the rest of his life fighting and appealing. Let him die an old man, tortured and shriveled in some jail cell.

She called her friend to beg off their dinner plans. She needed to get home, get online now and find flights from San Diego to Providence. She could be ready to leave the next morning.

But she couldn't shake the image of her nephew. He would not get a *dime*.

Seventeen

Dyer was finished for the day. Or, so he thought. New information; a phone call from 'someone' who thought that she might have 'seen something' related to the shooting on Union Street last night.

According to the dispatcher who took the call, a woman had seen a report on the Channel 10 *News at Six* about the shooting. She said that she had been leaving a Dunkin Donuts near where the shooting reportedly had taken place. She saw a car pull out and speed away. The car splashed her as it went by.

Dyer had the woman's phone number and he tapped it into his cellphone. When she answered, he identified himself and asked if she could repeat what she'd told the dispatcher. She went through the bit about the car pulling out and causing water from the street to spray onto the sidewalk.

"Can you describe the car?" Dyer said.

"It was black. Or dark blue, maybe. It had one of those things in the back. Like a NASCAR racing car," she said.

"A spoiler," Dyer said. "Raised up in the back?"

"Yeah. Curved. An arch across the trunk."

"How about the license plate?"

"It looked like a Rhode Island plate, sort of. Except it had a dark stripe on the bottom," she said. "I didn't get the number."

When he'd finished talking with the woman, Dyer placed a second call to the East Greenwich PD asking them to relay information about cars found at Sophia Crane's home. An earlier check with Rhode Island DMV did not bring back any vehicles registered to a Nathaniel Crane.

Dyer scribbled a note to himself, then went online to a data base that showed updated variations of license plates for all fifty states and Washington DC. A quick scan showed that five other states had plates that could be considered similar to Rhode Island's basic wave plate, colors of light blue on white background with dark blue numerals. Two of the similar plates had a darker area on the lower section; Michigan and Wyoming.

Then there were a variety of other plates to consider; veteran's plates, special design charity and conservation plates, lighthouse and sailboat plates. Red Sox Foundation and New England Patriots plates. You really needed the plate *number*.

How many cars out there had spoilers? There had to be a dozen American and foreign auto manufacturers that produced a model with *some* variation of the aerodynamic device designed to help cut down turbulence, or 'spoil' unfavorable air movement across the body of the car. Certainly, tens of thousands of cars on the road today.

The RI DOT – Rhode Island Department of Transportation – maintains 31 cameras in and around Providence, 5 of those are close to the downtown. There are no municipal cameras in the city and none of the DOT cameras are located precisely in the area where the shooting occurred on Friday evening. Police would seek images captured by privately operated surveillance cameras from area businesses.

Video monitoring and recording throughout the US has grown exponentially over the past twenty years. Just in the years since the Boston Marathon bombing in 2013, surveillance equipment has become more sophisticated and the increasing expenditures by local, state and federal government agencies are measured in the billions of dollars, not including the money spent by private citizens and businesses.

After the 9/11 terrorist attacks of 2001, when four fuel-loaded commercial airliners killed 2,977 people in three separate locations, the industry serving the needs of domestic security in the US has dramatically changed how most people live. A 'camera on every corner' may be virtually true in urban areas of the country, if not in the smaller towns and cities. But the simple vehicular traffic monitoring by video cameras is not foolproof.

A black or dark-colored car with *possibly* a Rhode Island license plate, speeding away from a parking spot in downtown Providence on a rainy evening? Maybe.

Eighteen

It was 8:20 when we got back to the hotel. Louie and Becky wanted to go back to their room early. Maybe it was the Peruvian spices. Who am I to be nosey, eh? I wanted to walk back over to Paul's to have some port.

"Breakfast at 8:00?" Becky said.

I pointed across the hotel lobby to the entrance of The Vig. "Whoever comes down first gets a booth, yes?"

"We can come down earlier Hanlon, make a special request to have 'em turn on ESPN," Louie said. I shook my head and held up my phone. "I'm good. I'll check scores before I go to bed. We can watch the highlights tomorrow night."

They went to the elevator and I turned back to the revolving door and went back outside. The rain had stopped but the air was damp, possibly what it feels like in London on damp foggy nights. Although as I stood in front of the Hilton looking around, no fog. But a comfortable temperature, so I took off my rain slicker.

I watched the traffic for a minute. Headlights reflecting on pedestrians, buildings and street signs; the sound of tires on wet pavement in front of me and over the embankment on the highway; people out walking on Broadway and on both sides of Atwells Avenue.

Turning right, I went up the street in the same direction I'd gone before. It was only two blocks to Paul's, probably easier to spot without the rain from last night. While I hadn't brought it up again with Ragsdale, or Becky, for fear of the unending razz that Louie could put on me in a heartbeat, I wanted to find out if there was anything new on the guy who'd been shot.

Maybe you live in a city like this and you grow accustomed to shootings and stabbings and street crime. Not that it doesn't happen up in the woods where we live, but when it does, there's generally a momentary pause in community activities. At least I'd continued to convince myself of that every time we had something out of the ordinary.

Inside Paul's there were more people than had been here last night. Couples seated at the few tables and a cocktail waitress serving drinks and appetizers. At the far end of the bar were three women, in their forties, I guessed. One of the women was waving her arms around while the other two were laughing at whatever she was saying.

Three remaining empty seats at the bar and I took one at the opposite end from the women.

Detective Phil Dyer met with Patrol Sergeant Christopher Ballan in the rear lot of the East Greenwich Police Station before they drove to the home on Courtney Drive, the address given to Dyer by Lisa Bryan. They shook hands and Dyer gave Ballan a quick summary.

"The woman who lived there, Sophia Crane, died in a boating accident last year," he said. Ballan nodded. "One of her sisters," Dyer went on, "told me that the deceased woman's son has been staying there." No response from Ballan.

"We had a shooting last night downtown. The guy's dead. The late Mrs. Crane's sister, who lives in California, knew the victim. She's given us some information and we'd like ask a few questions of the son."

"You have a name?" Ballan asked.

"Yeah. Nathaniel Crane. Nathaniel Crane the second."

"It's less than ten minutes. You want to follow us?" Ballan said, pointing to a patrol car that already had another policeman behind the wheel.

"Appreciate it," Dyer said, then climbed back into his own car.

The two cars turned north onto First Avenue and started the drive to the woodsy section of town three miles west.

"How's it going," Pauly asked, placing a drink coaster on the bar in front of me. He was wearing a short-sleeved teal colored Hawaiian style shirt which I thought had the usual floral print. But as he stood in front of me, I could see that there were different fish all over it.

"*Great* shirt," I said.

He looked down, took the spread collar in both hands and pulled the shirt away from his chest. "Yeah. My daughter gave it to me for Father's Day."

"Are those trout?" I said.

"Rare and endangered trouts of the world," he said. 'It's an old Limited Edition Patagonia shirt she found on eBay."

"You a fisherman?"

He shook his head. "Not really. I sometimes go out with a buddy who has a boat on Narragansett Bay" he added.

"But you're not a hardcore *trout* fisherman. One of those TU guys?" I said.

"Nah. She just bought this for me because I have a buncha' Hawaiian shirts I like to wear."

"It is one cool shirt," I said.

"Thanks. What can I get you?"

"Ah-h, I already had a couple of drinks at dinner. I better amp it down a notch. Have any port?"

Pauly swung around and looked at bottles lined up on the shelves behind him. He stepped toward them and tapped a shelf in front of different bottles of port.

"Looks like we have three here," he said.

I leaned to my right and stretched forward to see the choices. "How about a glass of the Broadbent Madeira?"

He picked up the bottle and studied the label. "Ten years old. Must be good," he said, reaching for a port glass in the rack above the bar.

"I've had it before. It's pretty nice."

While he poured the wine, I scoped out customers at the tables, then glanced back at the three women at the other end of the bar. They were having a *good* time.

Pauly placed the glass on the coaster in front of me. I held it up. "Good health," I offered, taking a sip. Yes, it was a nice port.

"So, you hear anything new about the shooting?" I said, putting the glass down.

He shook his head and came back to stand across the bar from me. "Nothing. There was a story on the front page of the Pro Jo this morning. TV crews are all over it."

It took me a second. "Pro Jo. Providence Journal, yes?" He nodded.

"Who was the guy with the cop last night?" I said.

"Billy. The man in the Columbo trench coat?"

"Yeah."

Pauly leaned on the bar, crossed his arms, then raised his right hand to support his chin. He looked directly at me, shook his head slightly while holding his fingers over his lips as though he wanted to keep them sealed.

"A sad story that has actually started to get a little better. At least in recent years," he said. My brain was functioning enough to relay the message, 'Keep your mouth shut Hanlon. *Listen*.'

"Sweetheart of a guy. Had went through a horrible tragedy when he was a young man. Almost finished him off," he went on. "Wife and son killed in a car accident. He survived. Developed a bad drinking problem and stayed in the bottle for too many years."

"Umh," I grunted, shaking my head.

"Yeah. But he's turned it *around*. Maybe nine or ten years ago. A local priest helped a lot. Got him a place to stay, found some work for him at the church. He's a different man today than when I first saw him on the streets long time ago."

He glanced around to see if any customers or the waitress needed his attention. Everything was under control, he turned back to me, folded his arms across his chest, stood upright and went on.

"The story has it that back in the day, Billy was an *up and coming* college basketball ref. All over New England, in New York and out to Pennsylvania. Then it all fell apart."

He held his hands up in a 'whatd'ya know' gesture and added, "But since he's been on the wagon the past few years, he's back working in a men's basketball league and does a lot of youth games. They love him."

Pauly laughed, then went on, "Some of the macho types who spend too much time running up and down the court, NBA wannabes, a few of those guys give him some shit on his calls. They dubbed him Quick Whistle."

Now I laughed. "You watch any sport these days, especially on TV. Somebody's *always* got a beef with the officials," I said.

"My impression last night, "I added, "was that this Billy guy knew the man who was shot, yes?"

Pauly was shaking his head. "No. He'd *seen* the man a couple of times. Billy does an evening walk, covers ten or twelve blocks in his regular loop. He was coming around the corner when he heard the shots."

I nodded and took another sip of the port.

"That's the first shooting around here in a while," Pauly said. "There's some gang stuff in other parts of town now and then, but downtown's been reasonably quiet."

"There must be surveillance cameras around," I said. "Has to be video somewhere."

Again, Pauly gave me the head shake. "Nope. No city cameras."

"Really?"

"The DOT has cameras at some interchanges. Maybe a couple of street level speed trap cameras. One of those was stolen last year. Police said it cost about seventy-grand. But, unlike some other places, Providence has *not* put up a whole bunch of cameras," he said, shrugging his shoulders.

"A citizen's right to privacy question, huh? No spies on us."

"There you go," Pauly said, walking over to check on the three women.

I sipped my port and thought about a few towns where I *knew* they had multiple cameras scattered around. Some clearly visible, others only if you knew to look for them. Made me think that I wanted to go talk with the detective who was here last night.

What's he gonna' do, run me out of the city?

Draining the last drop of port from my glass, I signaled Pauly that I was done for the night.

Nineteen

Two minutes at the front door, another five walking around the house and the covered swimming pool and it was obvious that nobody was home. At least no sign of activity inside, no one coming to the door. A couple of lights on, probably on timers.

Dyer and the two East Greenwich cops stood next to their cars. The driveway and the street pavement were wet, but the rain was on hold. They could see lights through the trees from the nearest neighbor's home maybe two hundred yards away. A quiet, secluded area in this affluent town of fewer than 15,000 people.

"You want us to check with the neighbors?" Sergeant Ballan said. "See if anyone has spotted the son around recently?"

Dyer nodded. "Might help. Find out what vehicle he's driving, anybody see a different car here," he said. "Maybe get a line on any friends or acquaintances the neighbors know about."

"We can do that" Ballan said.

"Tell your chief I'll call. It would also help when your regular patrols make a pass by here, keep an eye out for other vehicles, any activity at the house," Dyer added.

Another thirty-seconds of small talk and everyone was back in their cars and leaving Courtney Drive.

In San Diego, Lisa Bryan packed two bags; a carry-on and a larger suitcase that she would check. She had found a 7 o'clock Southwest flight Sunday morning and booked a Business Class seat, paying a premium for last minute booking. The flight had a scheduled stop-over in Chicago and a Providence ETA of 5:30 PM.

After the phone conversation with Detective Dyer, she had decided against telling her sister, Sandi, about the murder of Cliff Torres. As she hadn't told her sister that Cliff was helping her track their nephew's activities, no reason to call her now, at least not until she knew more about the circumstances of Cliff's death. And until she'd had a chance to meet with the lawyer in Woonsocket.

Although Lisa had told Dyer about the boating accident – he acknowledged recalling some news reports during the weeks after the incident a year ago – she wasn't convinced that the detective was prepared to accept her speculation of Nathaniel's possible involvement in the Torres shooting. Recent legal activity, initiated by the surviving sisters, had yet to get any play in the media. That could change soon.

Dyer told her that the police in New Jersey were attempting to locate relatives of Cliff Torres. She regretted not being aware of, or having been interested enough, to know *any* details of Cliff's personal life. He had been a friend of Sophia and her husband. Lisa had seen him only a few times over the years and was grateful for his contact and interest after Sophia's death.

Regret and pangs of guilt were not going to help now. More likely to produce results would be the actions of her attorney and any judge ruling on the merits of the case. The insurance company covering the boat would pursue their own investigation. They had investigators who dealt with wrongful or false claims.

Wheeling the larger suitcase to the kitchen, Lisa had a flashback to her August shouting match with Nathaniel. He had refused to tell her if and how much of a payment he had received from his mother's life insurance. The will had been clear that he was the beneficiary of that policy. But had the company paid?

Other matters related to Sophia's estate, including the family home, were not yet completely resolved. One reason being the surviving sisters' challenge, which could prevent him from receiving any portion of his mother's personal assets, including the one-third share, 8.6 million dollars, from his grandfather's estate.

Lisa found hope in the *possibility* that once she and her attorney brought forth the information about her confrontation with Nathaniel, about Cliff Torres observing his recent activities, and now Cliff's death, that this would help to expedite a quick ruling from the court.

Twenty

It was colder than Nathaniel had expected it to be at the camp. Slushy snow on the ground outside. He'd managed to get a weak fire going in the old wood burning stove inside.

He'd found the breaker panel in the bathroom and turned on the electricity. Lights, a toaster, a microwave oven and a small dorm-style refrigerator. An old clock radio in the bedroom. That was it. Any attempts for cooking would be on the combo two-burner gas stove and grill on the porch. If the weather stayed like this, two or three weeks here might be pushing it. At least he had the new tank of propane.

Chad had told him that there were sheets, pillows and some wool blankets in a closet in the bathroom. There was a standard size bed in the only bedroom, and a fold-out sofa, plus a roll away bed in the living room. It was more one big open room with some furniture; two old worn recliners in the middle of the room, and four plastic chairs with a small, scratched-up dining table. That was where he, Chad and two of their friends had played poker on his only other visit here.

Finishing off a bottle of the IPA, he opened another, took a swig and went to his car to bring in the food and supplies that he'd brought with him. It took two trips. Then he carried the propane tank to the porch and placed it next to the stove. He could hook it up in the morning. Finally, he returned to the car to get the bags with his clothing, cash and the Ruger SR9c semi-automatic pistol.

When he had everything inside the camp, he checked the signal on his iPhone. One bar wavering on and off. Not good. Maybe better back near the general store. Before he left Rhode Island, it had been his thought that once he got to the camp and settled in, he would have to make some day trips into Brattleboro, perhaps over the mountain to Bennington. Move around some was a better idea.

He pulled from his pocket a folded sheet of paper on which he'd written notes from his phone call to Chad. The closest neighbor was a man named Dean Chase, who supposedly lived even farther back in the woods on the opposite side of the dirt road. He would go find him in the morning.

The microwave oven had to be at least thirty years-old, but it worked. He set the clock; 8:22. From a bag of groceries and food items, he pulled out a small frozen pizza and read the instructions for preparing with a microwave. He unwrapped the pizza and placed it directly on the glass platter inside the oven and set the timer for 5:00 minutes on medium.

Removing the Ruger from its black leather holster, he popped out the 10-round magazine, checked the safety, jacked the chamber open and closed, then removed a flashlight attachment from his bag. He snapped the light onto the rail that ran along the bottom of the gun barrel, checked the light, put the magazine back in, set the safety and laid the pistol on the table in the living room.

Vermont is one of fourteen states in the US that has unrestricted 'concealed carry' reciprocity, as are New Hampshire and Maine, unlike Rhode Island, which requires a permit. He was fully aware of this before he had called Chad to inquire about using the camp. In fact, he was fully aware of *all* of the states that allowed either concealed or open carry.

While living in Wyoming, he had obtained a state driver's license, which would remain valid thru 2019, and he had studied the concealed carry regulations before applying for and having received a permit. Now he had an updated Concealed Carry Reciprocity map of the states that honored the Wyoming permit. He also regularly checked various websites to pay attention to what was going on with firearm legislation around the country.

After the incident on Union Street in Providence twenty-four hours ago, Nathaniel was hoping to *avoid* any need to use the Ruger again in the days ahead.

But then, you never know.

Twenty One

On Sunday morning, Becky, Louie and I were back in The Vig having breakfast. Unlike yesterday, the place was packed. Might have been a lot of the people from the book expo going on next door at the convention center.

As soon as we were seated in a booth, Becky patted my hand and asked how I was doing. It was the second time this weekend that she'd done this. She gave me her pleasant, knowing smile.

It had been more than a year since I had experienced a devastating personal loss, the sudden death of a former lover and friend, Bonnie Mackin. The Ragsdales had known Bonnie. Not that long ago we had done a few things together as couples. After Bonnie died, Becky had gone above and beyond in finding ways to check on me. Quick, but sensitive and tactful, offering words of support, and more recently nudging me in the direction of finding new companionship.

Probably the best thing that Becky had accomplished was influencing her smartass husband and getting him to let up a little with the frequent ribbing about my 'love life'.

Louie, somehow, had mustered genuine seriousness in our conversations and in his own way had also been supportive in the months after Bonnie died.

"Have you spent any time with Virginia?" Becky said, referring to my neighbor back in Quechee, Vermont.

"Yeah, some. We've had dinner a few times. Actually, I went with her to a movie two weeks ago. Telluride at Dartmouth," I said. "They bring some of the top films from the Telluride Festival to Hanover every year."

"What was the film?" Louie said, pretending to show interest.

"Right up your alley, Captain. An artsy French film. *Disparaitre*," I said, trying to get close to the French pronunciation.

"Disappear," Becky said. I nodded and gave her a thumbs-up. Louie exaggerated a look of being puzzled.

"Amazing cinematography," I said. "And a very lovely, young, apparently *new* French actress."

"Here we go. What is this 'lovely' young actress's *name*?" Louie said.

"Can't remember."

"Sure. And the film has *sub-titles*, right?" Louie added.

"Of course. It started out fine. But about half-way through, you realize that a guy you *thought* was OK, is behind a major drug trafficking operation, even though he'd formerly run a drug-fighting agency for the French government," I said.

"Great," Louie said. "I'm certain that I woulda' just been crazy about it."

"I thought so. After we left the movie, I told Virginia, 'Ragsdale would love this." I added, "You must know of one or two here in the US who've drifted to the wrong side of the battle, huh?"

"Oh-h, you *don't* wanna know," he said.

Becky turned to her husband. "When you finish up with the task force, maybe you could get a consulting job in France. Nobody will know you. You would *really* be undercover."

"Maybe not," Louie said.

"Fine. Back to Virginia" Becky said, looking at me. "Are you helping her fix up the house and that old barn. And other things?"

"Especially *other* things," Louie said. Becky ignored him.

"Not recently. She had an amazing crop of tomatoes in early September. I helped get those in. She canned a lot and made soup that she freezes," I said.

Louie was trying to get the attention of our server so we could order some breakfast. I knew that Becky was up to her frequent 'emotional maintenance of Michael' bit and appreciated it, even though her husband found it more entertaining to take a different tack.

Some more yuk, yuk among the three of us and ten minutes later, we were enjoying the Hilton's breakfast buffet. When we'd finished eating, Becky wanted to go to the hotel fitness center to burn calories. She was safe with the knowledge that neither her husband nor I would tag along.

The rain seemed to have stopped, for how long was uncertain. I pulled out my phone.

"You're not going to check the weather app again," Louie said.

"Nope. Think I'll call Detective Dyer."

Louie gave me his Category 2 smirk. "You just can't let it go, can you Hanlon? Chase down the story."

"Hey. He *gave* me his card," I said. "That's part of it, who shot your vic Friday night? But I'd like to talk to the old guy who was with him in the tavern."

"Guy in the rain coat?"

"Yeah. Paul, the bartender, told me the guy used to be a college basketball ref," I said.

"So?"

"Now he's a janitor at a church. Gotta be a story there."

Louie rolled his eyes and turned toward the front door in the lobby. "Yeah. And I'm sure he's just been waiting for someone like you to come along and ask him all about it."

I hesitated, then pulled on his elbow. "Someone like you," I said. He looked at me.

"I can hear it in a song. Linda Ronstadt, maybe," I added. He exaggerated taking a deep breath.

"Someone like you... makes it hard to live... without somebody else," Louie said. "Tim Hardin, Reason to

Believe. 1966." He stood at the revolving door. "Bunch of artists covered it," he continued. "The Youngbloods, Scott McKenzie. Rod Stewart had a pretty big hit with it years later. Doubtful that Linda Ronstadt ever recorded it. I'm not remembering that. Maybe on an album."

"Could you look it up for me?" I said, pulling Detective Dyer's card form my billfold.

Louie shook his head and went outside.

Lisa Bryan's plan was to call the police as soon as she arrived in Providence and talk with Detective Phil Dyer. Let him know that she was scheduled to meet with her attorney and that she had the idea of going out to her late sister's home in East Greenwich.

Initially, she couldn't make herself accept the possibility that her nephew had murdered or had *arranged* for the murder of Cliff Torres. But on the first leg of the flight from San Diego to Chicago, she had played over and over in her mind the numerous discussions with her sister, arguments with her nephew, spasms of grief and disbelief from when her father had died three years ago and, more recently, recalling an exchange with her attorney.

All this recycling of events and conversations brought her again to the belief that Nathaniel Crane, II, her late sister's only son, was a sociopath, or a psychopath, or *whatever* label was being applied these days to people who displayed aggressive, violent behavior and had absolutely no conscience.

Before she would go to Sophia's home, she would call her lawyer again. She knew that he was likely to advise against her going there.

Dyer told me that police headquarters was in the Public Safety Building, ten-minutes from the Hilton Providence. Louie and I turned west and crossed Dave Gavitt Way, then headed south.

Reluctantly agreeing to go with me, Ragsdale was quiet for the first two minutes as we walked. Then he piped up with more music trivia.

"Tim Hardin had a short life with a tragic ending. But he was good songwriter. And get this" he said. "He wrote one of Bobby Darin's biggest hits, *If I Were A Carpenter*. And Darin wrote the only chart hit that Hardin recorded, *Simple Song of Freedom*."

"How do you *retain* all of this stuff?" I said.

He flicked his eyebrows and gave me a shrug. "All those nights I played 45s and LPs on the radio, I tried to stay out of the way of the music. No bullshit, no talking between tracks. None of the hotshot DJ stuff. I just played the music. And read. Most of what I read was about recording artists, songwriters, bands. More than one person oughta' know."

The pedestrian walk signal changed and we crossed to Dean Street. Not a lot of traffic on a Sunday morning.

"Back to my question. How do you retain it? Plus, it is *ancient* history, pardner."

Again, the shrug. "Must be like guys who can recite all the stats and which teams somebody played for. Gets embedded on your brain and you'll be mumbling it to someone when they haul you away," he said.

"Guess anything's possible," I said.

As soon as we spotted a parking lot full of patrol cars, I pointed at the back of the building.

"He said to come in through this entrance. There's a buzzer," I said. "His office is on the third floor."

"Gotta hand it to him," Louie said, looking at his watch. "Sunday morning. And he's on the job."

Twenty Two

After a brief exchange with a woman's voice, via exterior wall-mounted speaker next to the rear entrance of the Public Safety Complex, a policeman showed up and buzzed the door open to let us in.

We followed the officer to a chest high counter situated next to an airport style security passage booth. He asked us to sign-in pointing at a clipboard on the counter. We showed him ID and began emptying our pockets for the screening.

"You're good," the cop said, waiving us off from the booth and motioning around the counter. He gave each of us a clip-on visitor's pass.

"Sergeant Dyer told me to send you on up. Elevator's over there," he said, pointing to our left. "He's on three."

It was a quiet ride that lasted all of ten seconds. When the elevator door opened, Dyer was there talking to another man. He put his hand up to acknowledge that he saw us, finished his conversation with the other guy, who then proceeded to walk away from us and went down a long corridor through double doors. Dyer stepped toward

Ragsdale and me, we shook hands and he motioned for us to follow him.

"You want coffee, water, anything?" he said.

"Nah, we're good. Thanks," I said.

We walked past a small room where one man was working with what appeared to be equipment right out of a radio broadcast studio. "Teddy. How's it going?" Dyer said to the man as we went by.

"Hey, Sarge. Good. Trying to catch up on a report we're doing for that Pawtucket homicide."

"Dress sharp if you're going to court," Dyer said over his shoulder. The guy laughed.

When we were seated in a small conference room, Dyer closed the door behind us and pointed back to the corridor. "That is maybe the *best* IT forensics detective in the Northeast," he said. "Makes things go a hell of a lot easier for those of us out on the street."

He sat across the table from Ragsdale and me, shifted to get comfortable in his chair, then arched his eyebrows. "So, what can I help you with?" he said.

I gave up a nervous chuckle and pointed with my thumb at Louie. "Brother Ragsdale here thinks I'm too nosy for my own good. Only reason he stays close is to try to prevent me from being arrested."

"Good to have friends in law enforcement," Dyer said, winking at Louie.

"Naturally, I'm curious about the man who was shot. Like I said on the phone, I'm sure you're busy." I went on,

"But Pauly, the bartender. We were talking last night about the old man who came into the pub with you. Pauly says that you know him pretty well."

"Billy?" Dyer said.

"The guy in the trench coat," I said. "Yeah."

"William 'Quick Whistle' Woodson. He's been around a *long* time. I was a patrolman just starting out when I first encountered Billy," he said, tilting his head up and scratching under his chin. "When he was sober, he worked at a little corner newsstand. Sometimes he put on one of those old canvas shoulder bags and peddled newspapers up near the state capitol."

"Paul says he's doing janitor work at a church and runs errands for people," I said.

"That's correct. I think he hasn't had a drink in maybe eight, nine years now."

"And that he used to be a college basketball ref, then there was an accident that killed his wife and son, that's what put him on the streets?"

Dyer nodded, closing his eyes, then inhaled through his nose. "Yeah. Damn near drank himself to death. Maybe stopped not a day too soon." He scratched his chin again and looked at Ragsdale. Louie remained silent. Maybe he'd taken a vow that he'd forgotten to tell me about.

"Lot of sad situations out there, unfortunately," Dyer added. "Why are you interested in Billy?"

I hesitated. It was my turn to shift in my chair.

"I'd like to talk to him. Hear about his days as a ref. I

had an uncle from down in Pennsylvania who was a ref. He's the one who got me interested in college basketball," I said.

Louie gave a little laugh, leaned forward in his chair and placed a hand on my left shoulder. "You will notice that my friend Hanlon, ahem, is, shall we say, height challenged. That's why he wound up working in radio and *not* playing basketball."

Dyer had a bemused smile, but at least he didn't laugh out loud.

"So, you want to *record* an interview with Billy?" Dyer said.

"Maybe. If he would do it. But I'd at least like to talk to him, perhaps pull together a story, write it up."

Dyer was looking at Louie again. I wondered if there was some silent code that cops have that signal 'is this guy *legit*?' Then he glanced at the digital watch on his left wrist. I got that signal.

"Anyway, Paul's the one who suggested that I speak with you first," I said, rising from my chair.

Dyer stood up, then Louie slowly rose from his chair.

"How long you here?" Dyer said.

"In Providence?" He nodded.

I looked at Ragsdale. "Tomorrow, maybe Tuesday morning. Louie and his wife are travelling separately. You're going to Newport?" I said to Louie. He nodded.

"Why don't you call me tomorrow afternoon?" Dyer said. "See if I can set something up with Billy. Maybe go out and pile some sand bags along the river."

"I haven't looked at the forecast. Still more rain?" I said.

Dyer nodded. "Might stop before Halloween."

"Right. Tomorrow is the official *calendar* observance of Columbus Day. You're working?" I said.

"My entire squad is on this murder. Yeah, I'll be here. But call my cell again."

He escorted us back to the corridor and we shook hands again before heading for the elevator.

"Thanks. I will call," I said.

Walking back to the Hilton, Louie had fallen back into his Marcel Marceau impersonation. I wasn't sure if he fully appreciated that every time he went silent, I went vocal. You never want dead air.

"How many in a squad?" I said.

"Depends," he said. "Dyer is the head of the squad, Detective Sergeant. Probably has another four detectives working with him."

"How many squads with a police department in a city the size of Providence?" We walked another twenty yards before he answered.

"I think the population here is still under two-hundred-thousand. Average of something like… twenty-three cops for every ten-thousand people. So, Providence

PD is probably four hundred plus. Of that, maybe a third doing detective work. More crime than the average hamlet. I'm guessing, just investigative, 24/7, four squads per shift."

"Really? *Twenty-three* cops for every ten thousand people?" I said. He looked at me and we kept walking.

"You think that's a lot? New York, Miami, cities like Chicago and Philly, more like forty policemen for every ten-thousand people. DC probably has fifty plus. Course that includes admin people, some civilian jobs. Not everybody's wearin' a badge," he said.

We were crossing Dave Gavitt's street again and a light rain had resumed. I looked down at the traffic, then back to the street ahead of us. By the time we got to the hotel, not counting the parking lot back at the Public Safety Center, I'd seen only two patrol cars out on a Sunday morning.

Twenty Three

Nathaniel went to find the neighbor across the road and farther up another cut into the woods. There was no sign of anyone around. A set of tire tracks in the melting snow and the smell of wood smoke lingered in the dooryard. It was likely that someone had been there recently.

He looked at his watch; 10:20 on Sunday morning. Could be a church guy.

Sliding back behind the wheel of the Mitsubishi, he turned on the radio and found 92.7 Bratt FM 'We Play Everything' a local station from nearby Brattleboro. Keeping the volume low, he picked up his iPhone to check the signal. Barely a mile away from the camp, it continued showing only one bar, but it was steady.

The neighbor's house hadn't been painted in years. It was twice the size of the Chad's chicken coop, but still small. The front porch was crowded with all kinds of tools and boxes of auto parts. The front steps were old cinder blocks chipped around the edges. There were automotive engine parts and some other equipment scattered around the yard.

Ten minutes. He doesn't show up, I can always come back.

No sooner had he had that thought when a flatbed truck pulled in behind him and blocked his car.

Lisa Bryan changed planes at Midway International Airport in Chicago. She was in the gate area waiting for a boarding announcement and the continuation of the trip on to Providence. Departure was still another forty-five minutes away.

Sipping coffee, she took out her phone. She wanted to let Detective Dyer know that she was coming east *today* and hoped to be able to meet with him tomorrow morning. She was surprised when he answered almost immediately, then remembered that she was calling his cell number.

"Phil Dyer," he said.

"Detective. It's Lisa Bryan from San Diego. We spoke yesterday. About the man who was shot, Cliff Torres."

"Yes," Dyer said.

"I wanted you to know that I'm on my way to Providence and to see if you've been in touch with Cliff's family." Another flare of the guilt that she knew next to nothing about Cliff's personal life.

"Slow going with the police in Jersey," he said. "Had a call this morning and, so far, no indication of relatives. They're going to talk with some of his neighbors. And try to reach management at the company where he worked, see if they can help."

"You know that he recently retired? He left the company in July," she said.

"You told me that when we spoke earlier."

"Sorry. I wasn't sure," she said, now uncertain of what else she'd told Dyer. How much about the pending court action that her lawyer was pursuing? She did remember that she had told him that Nathaniel had been staying at his mother's house as recently as a month ago. "Has anyone been to my sister's home?"

"I went out myself. Last night," Dyer said. "Nobody there, locked up tight. A couple of lamps on, but we presume there are timers. The East Greenwich PD will continue to watch the house, see if anyone returns." After a beat, he added, "Do you know what kind of vehicle your nephew drives?"

Lisa thought about her visit in August. Nathaniel had had some kind of two-door model, comparable in size to her Porsche. She remembered; ECLIPSE across the taillight the entire width of the car.

"He had a Mitsubishi two-door," she said. "A black ECLIPSE."

"Do you know if it's the sporty roadster, or the crossover SUV model?" he said.

"The roadster."

"Has the spoiler across the trunk?" he said.

"Yes. It had a Wyoming license plate in August."

New information. The DMV had been able to locate a Nathan Crane who lived in Westerly, near the Connecticut border. That man owned a Chrysler 300 registered in his name. Turned out that he was the local fire chief.

"So, your nephew was living in Wyoming?" Dyer said.

"Yes. He's made several trips back east. And he spent a lot of time in Rhode Island right before my father had a heart attack and died, in December, 2015."

She continued, "Most of the summer a year ago, when he bought the boat, he was staying with his mother. Then the explosion out in the ocean, when Sophia disappeared." She added, "Nathaniel lived at his mother's house for several months after that. I believe that he's been back and forth ever since."

While she was talking, Dyer pulled up the Wyoming DMV registration page and was looking at a license plate that was, in fact, similar in color to the Rhode Island plates. Except the Wyoming plate had a silhouette of a cowboy bronco and a dark border across the bottom of the plate.

"This helps," he said, not mentioning the phone tip they had received about a car leaving the area close to where the Friday night shooting had occurred. "We'll check registrations out there," he added.

"I have a meeting with my attorney in Woonsocket in

the morning. Would it be appropriate if I have him call you after we've talked?" she said.

"That's fine," Dyer said. "Or, you can call me. We might know more sometime tomorrow."

Twenty Four

The man wore a brown sun bleached Carhartt barn jacket with a hood. The hood was folded down, jacket open at the neck. It appeared he'd been wearing the coat his entire life.

"What can I do for you?" the man said, standing tight to the driver's door of Nathaniel's car.

Tufts of gray hair protruded from beneath a faded orange hunter's cap. Chiseled face, gaunt features, large, gnarly hands. The man leaned forward, resting on an age-darkened hiking staff, or shepherd's crook. It was about the size of a baseball bat, only longer, and came up to his chest. There was a rawhide loop through the end of the staff at the top.

Positioning himself to make it difficult for Nathaniel to open his door, the man waited.

"Are you Dean Chase?" he said, looking up from the window. The man's stare was dead on, the iris of his eyes coal black.

"That's me," he said, momentarily shifting his gaze to check out the interior of the car.

"I'm Nathaniel Crane, a friend of Chad Williams. I'm staying at his camp. Got here last night. Chad suggested that I should let you know."

The man straightened, nodded and without speaking, looked away in the direction of the camp, then turned back to look at Nathaniel.

"You come all the way from *Wyoming*?" he said, eyebrows arched and a nod toward the rear of the car.

Nathaniel shook his head. "No. I've been down in Rhode Island visiting family. Chad and I went to school together. I've been at the camp once before."

The man nodded again, then stepped back enough for the car door to be opened.

Nathaniel stayed put. A dog barked from inside the cab of the truck, still idling a few feet away.

"*Duke*," the man said in a gruff command, holding his right hand up to signal the dog to be quiet. No more barks.

"I'm not sure how long I'm going to be here," Nathaniel said. "Maybe a couple of weeks."

Again, the nod. "I'm here mosta' the time," the man said. He jerked his head again in the direction of the truck, an older model light-blue Dodge three-quarter-ton flatbed.

"I'll move so you can get out," he added. He went to the truck, climbed inside and backed around to allow Nathaniel to move his car.

After the conversation with Dean Chase, he followed the dirt road back to Route 100, then headed north to pick up Route 9 east toward Brattleboro. This would be strictly a reconnaissance run. He needed to get a sense of what the drive was like and the lay of the land around Brattleboro.

According to his lawyer just a week ago, the earliest they could expect any response from the insurance company underwriting the policy on his boat, would be November 1st. The lawyer told him that he believed the company had done all that they planned to do and would now either pay up, offer a reduced settlement, or deny the claim.

Following months of delays, three interviews with the company, two by phone and one in person with an adjuster, a claims manager told his lawyer that they were reviewing the final report from the US Coast Guard. The lawyer told Nathaniel that was bullshit. They'd had the report since March and that they were doing what most insurance companies do; stall.

More pressing to him was the fervor of his two aunts with a threat of going to court again to hold up the settlement of his mother's estate. Lisa had promised him that 'that's exactly' what she planned to do. Then she'd hired this man Cliff Torres, an old friend of his parents, to spy on his activities.

With the information he'd obtained from Lisa's hacked emails, and once he confirmed that Torres was actually in Rhode Island, he'd panicked.

Now there was a police investigation underway in Providence and Nathaniel skipped town. He believed that he could lie low in Vermont long enough for his lawyer to get the insurance check. If he had to fight with his aunts, he could do that from Wyoming.

Twenty Five

Becky Ragsdale had extracted a 'Sure' from her husband that he would go with her to see a memorial to victims of the Armenian genocide of 1915. Louie was telling me this as we sat in my hotel room watching the rain through the window. I had the TV on mute, some Sunday morning show featuring panelists haranguing each other.

"She's been reading about the Armenians and the Turks from a hundred years ago," he said.

"Huh," I said.

"Yeah. There was an evening course she took two years ago at Lyndon State. Apparently, some of the material was connected to Armenians in New England. Mostly Massachusetts and Rhode Island," he said. "The guy teaching the course took part in the dedication of this monument."

"Is it right here in the city?" I said.

He nodded. "Beck says it's not far from the restaurant last night."

I laughed. "You remember that character at the diner on the Cape last summer?"

Louie smiled. "The one making cracks about who gets

more money for their rugs?" he said.

"That's the guy. I'm pretty certain he had Armenian ancestry."

"You think?" Louie said.

"Are you gonna' *walk* to this monument?" I pointed outside.

He got up and went to the window. Twisting his neck to look up at the sky, he bent forward, then straightened and went back to stand next to the chair.

"You know that raindrops start out as snowflakes," he said.

"Yes, I do know that, thank you. And if these had remained snowflakes, we'd be up to our ass about now. Like three feet or something," I said.

"You can come with us," he said.

"Think I'll take a nap." I said, gesturing to the TV. "Maybe watch highlights from the Sox game."

"Don't eat!" he said, jabbing a finger at me in his best Drill Instructor imitation.

"Tonight, it's Italian," he added as he went out the door.

I did not take a nap. Instead, I finished drinking a bottle of water, put my shoes on, used the bathroom, got my rain slicker and went down to the lobby.

Thinking back to the crowd earlier at breakfast, I recalled that the New England Independent Booksellers were encamped next door. Louie and I had seen the signs inside the Convention Center when we'd left the antique radio collector's exhibit.

At the front desk, I spoke with a woman named Celeste. Lovely smile; professional and courteous. She thought that the book expo was continuing all afternoon.

Detective Phil Dyer took a call from the East Greenwich PD. The patrolman reported no sign of activity and no cars in the driveway on two trips past the Crane house.

Dyer told him about the black Mitsubishi Eclipse with Wyoming plates and that they were checking registration to confirm that it belonged to Nathaniel Crane.

"Talk with your guys. See if anybody's seen that car around recently," Dyer said. "Soon as we get a plate number and confirmation, we'll put it out."

Nothing yet from New Jersey. Dyer didn't want to call again, as he'd already phoned twice in the last twelve hours. They find a relative, or get something from a neighbor, they'll call.

He did call his wife and told her that he was coming home for a couple of hours, maybe get some sleep, and that more than likely he would need to return to the station this evening.

Billy Woodson read The Providence Journal front to back, a habit that he followed every Sunday afternoon. Catch up on the news, see what's going on in sports. Other than watching basketball games, college and pro, he did not spend much time watching the small TV in his room.

There was an ad in the paper for some hearing aid company that showed a man wearing a tweed hat. The hat was very much like the one the guy was wearing who got shot on Union Street Friday night. Billy made a mental note to stop at Paul's, see if there was any information that had not made the news. Phil Dyer must still be working this case and might have said something to Pauly.

Billy studied the newspaper ad. Are these real people who have a hearing impairment, or old models just pretending? Is that woman in the ad his wife? Wonder how much they get paid for this?

It was going on three o'clock. The rain had momentarily stopped. Nothing to do at the church until four o'clock, so now was a good time to have a walk. He put his shoes on, got up from the chair, took his trench coat from the back of the door and headed out.

Twenty Six

The East Greenwich patrolman making the pass on Sunday afternoon spotted a man in a driveway next to Sophia Crane's home. He looked to be in his senior years, wearing a faded US Marine Corps cap and dark green rain slicker as he used a garden rake to poke at the end of a culvert.

The officer pulled over to the side of the street, got out and walked back to the man. The man looked up, stopped what he was doing, placed the rake on the wet grass and stepped up onto the pavement.

"Afternoon," the cop said. "Looks like you're making progress there." There was a lot of water flowing through the pipe.

The man removed a pair of work gloves, wiped his hands on the legs of his pants and looked back at the culvert. "Yeah. Couple of months of lawn clippings slowed it down, but it's clear now," he said.

In this section of town, most of the homes were secluded, each one with its own private drive. The officer pointed at the next driveway. "Curious if you've seen

anyone around the Crane residence in the last few days,"
he said.

The man studied the young cop, then looked at the
driveway. "The boy's been here, on and off. Nathaniel," he
said. The man had a tone of disapproval when he said the
name.

The officer nodded. "Seen him recently?"

"Yesterday. I was working in my garage," he said,
pointing back to his house. "I had the door open. Heard a
car start up, so I walked over to the edge of the trees and
I watched him backing out."

"What time was that?" the cop said.

"After lunch," he said, then added, "Between one-
thirty and two. I was listening to the football game on the
radio. Brown just scored, so it was still in the first half."

The cop hesitated, then said, "You didn't see him
come back?"

The man shook his head. "Boy's always been a little
funny. Moved out west after his dad died. Then that boat
accident, his mother drowning." He looked down at his
feet, shook his head again, then eyeballed the cop.

"There's a few people," the man began, pausing, then
resuming with, "*Some* people speculating maybe wasn't an
accident with the boat. Gossip had it that his mother was
in line for a nice inheritance after her father died couple
years ago. Guess she had some sisters somewhere, too."

The cop fumbled in his shirt pocket, came out with a
business card for the East Greenwich PD and handed it to

the man. "Be a big help, if you see the son again, or anyone else, give us a call."

The man studied the card, then tucked it in the side pocket of his lobsterman's rain slicker. He nodded. "I see him, I'll call," he said.

"Thanks," the officer said, turning and going back to the patrol car.

After watching the cop get in the car, ease onto the street and slowly drive away, the man pulled on his gloves, picked up the rake and walked back up his own driveway.

What's that Crane boy up to now?

Neighbors, townsfolk and most others around this section of Rhode Island were not yet up to speed with the ongoing, behind-the-scenes activity surrounding the death of Sophia Crane.

There had been initial news reports a year ago and some follow-up stories in the papers over the winter and spring. But details of insurance haggles and family matters remained under wraps. Rumors, yes. Speculation? No more than the usual amount anytime a body is not found.

Sophia Crane, and when he was alive, her husband, did not carry on 'high profile' social lives in East Greenwich. They were not completely off the radar but avoided participation with civic organizations and churches. An exception to that came after Steven died. Sophia decided to take golf lessons and had played a few times with another woman from town.

There was no local memorial service after the boat accident. The sisters, having buried their father just over a year earlier, had agreed that at some future date they would consider private gathering. Part of their ambivalence about holding a service stemmed from the fact that there was no body, for burial or cremation.

Then, within weeks of the 'accident', the fighting began. Lisa was the first to observe her nephew's questionable behavior. With a lot of time to grieve and to dredge up memories, from days long gone as well as more recent years, Lisa began peppering her sister, Sandi, with suspicions about Nathaniel. And it wasn't long into that series of conversations when Lisa began piecing together still more doubts and questions, now about her father's death.

It had taken a few months, innumerable phone calls and two visits back East, before Lisa was able to persuade Sandi that they should proceed with legal action. Once they had retained an attorney in Rhode Island, Lisa handled all the communications and paying the upfront fees.

The lawyer, Kevin Byrne of Woonsocket, was quick out of the starting block. He had immediately contacted the attorney processing Sophia Crane's estate, then the insurance company listed as the carrier of the policy on Nathaniel Crane's boat. Just a week ago, at the end of September, the attorney drafted a request to a district court judge asking for an order to be issued to open an investigation into the unattended death of Donald Bryan in 2015. Bryan's cause of death had been ruled from natural causes; a heart attack.

Nathaniel Crane was the last person to see his grandfather alive, having visited him earlier in the evening at the old man's home in Cranston.

Unaware that Detective Phil Dyer had identified the car, which would trigger a nationwide 'Be On The Lookout' alert for the vehicle, the East Greenwich patrolman did as he'd been instructed by his chief; he called Dyer with an update and told him about the neighbor having seen Crane's car leave the mother's residence just over twenty-four hours earlier.

Thanking the officer, Dyer told him about the alert for the Mitsubishi Eclipse. He said that he would be in touch, but should the neighbor come up with anything, 'please let me know immediately.' Every police department has its protocol and Dyer wanted the East Greenwich cop to know that he appreciated the direct contact.

Excluding the Rhode Island State Police force, the Providence PD was the largest around. They had a long-standing reputation of being supportive and cooperative with smaller municipalities. And any cop who'd been on duty even a few months, would have a handle on his own department's policies and procedures, particularly *when* to report up the chain first and *whom* to keep in the loop.

It was 1:45 PM. Dyer called Detective Angelo Incerpi to let him know that Nathaniel Crane had been seen at his mother's home as recently as yesterday afternoon. He asked Angelo to check on the report from the Wyoming DMV. They agreed to talk later in the evening, if not sooner.

Lisa Bryan picked out a four-door, white Toyota Camry from the Enterprise rental lot at the T.F. Green Airport. From previous trips, she knew that the drive to downtown was under fifteen minutes, depending on traffic.

After placing her bags in the trunk, she adjusted her iPhone GPS app with the rental car's navigation system. As soon as the dashboard screen acknowledged that the phone was paired, she tapped the 'Search' icon and gave a voice command, "Hilton Providence."

Traffic on I-95 North from the airport in Warwick was light. It was a Sunday evening, not many commuters out and limited commercial activity on the highway, save the occasional tractor trailer blowing by headed for Boston.

Taking Exit 21 toward Broadway, she merged onto the service road and followed the audible GPS instruction, 'In five-hundred feet, turn right onto Atwells Avenue.' She spotted the Hilton straight ahead.

Twenty Seven

An hour or so after checking out the book vendors at the Convention Center, I decided to take advantage of a break in the weather and go for a walk. It was a little after three o'clock. My dinner rendezvous with the Ragsdale's wasn't until six-thirty.

Perhaps a sign of more birthdays than one pays much attention to, but in the past few months I had developed an appreciation for long walks. This seemed to take hold during a week on Cape Cod a year ago. For most of that visit I had a lot of beach time with my new live-in friend, Rocco, a three-year-old Golden Retriever. Presently, he was enjoying 'other' companionship at a kennel back home.

When you live in a rural area, long walks are often taken on wooded trails or unpaved roads. Now, crossing the street, I scanned the high-rise buildings all around and headed east toward the river. We don't have buildings of twenty-plus stories in Vermont.

Earlier, talking with the concierge at the Hilton, I learned that the Rhode Island School of Design and Brown

University were both located on the other side of the Providence River. I resisted looking at my phone app but checked my watch, then determined that I would walk at a brisk pace in one direction for thirty minutes before changing course.

Then again, walking around in the woods does not require stopping every couple of minutes to hit a button, wait for the light to change, and then cross the street.

Dyer and Angelo sat across the table from one another. Even though the rain had stopped, the gray light coming through the window made it feel later than 3:30 in the afternoon.

This was the same table in the same conference room used for daily morning briefings, at which the head of the Investigative Division, Major David Lapan, along with other detectives working other cases, got in synch with what each squad was doing at that moment.

Angelo tapped his phone, scrolled down to read something, then tapped the screen again.

It was also the same third-floor interview room where a Providence police officer was murdered in 2005. A suspect in a stabbing murder of an elderly woman was being questioned by two detectives when one of the officers momentarily left the room. The suspect was able to distract the other cop, grabbed his gun and shot him twice. Detective Sergeant James Allen, a twenty-seven-year veteran of the force and father of two children, was pronounced dead at the hospital.

The suspect escaped by jumping out a window. He was captured within an hour a few blocks from the police station. The man was tried and convicted of the murder of both Detective Sergeant Allen and the elderly woman. In 2006 he was sentenced to life without parole.

"Mitsubishi Eclipse GT," Angelo said. "First registered in Wyoming as a new vehicle, May 2015. Registration most recently renewed in 2016. Same address, in a town called Horse Creek, close to Cheyenne, near the Colorado border."

"Let's find out what the folks in 'Horse Creek' know about Nathanial Crane," Dyer said. "See if they have anything on him out there."

Angelo twitched his nose, scratched it for a second, then began typing into his phone.

"The sister from California is due in pretty quick here," Dyer said, looking at his watch. "Says that she would like to have a chat before she meets with her lawyer tomorrow morning."

Angelo nodded but didn't look up from his phone.

Outside the Public Safety building – somewhere in the distance – was the muffled sound of sirens blaring. Fire trucks, patrol cars, rescue vehicles? Hard to say. Not an uncommon occurrence any time of the day and often into the night.

Dyer got up from the table and walked to the window.

The rain was still on hold.

"You want coffee?" Dyer said.

Angelo held his hand up and shook his head. "I'm good.

"I'm gonna' stay here," Dyer said, going to the door. "Wait for the Bryan woman to call. Let me know when you're headed out."

Taking the College Street pedestrian bridge across the river, I followed the wet red brick walkway along the edge of the water. I stopped to look at a towering World War I memorial in front of the County Court House.

'BY THIS MEMORIAL THE CITY OF PROVIDENCE COMMEMORATES THE LOYAL COURAGE AND FIDELITY OF ALL HER CITIZENS WHO SERVED IN THE WORLD WAR WHOSE HIGH EXAMPLE STILL SUMMONS US TO LOVE AND SERVE OUR COUNTRY.'

That was over a century ago and this monument was dedicated in 1929. Who was *here* for the dedication? What would they think *today*? 'ALL HER CITIZENS WHO SERVED.' I thought about Becky and Louie somewhere else in the city looking at an Armenian memorial and wondered about the ethnic mix of Providence a hundred years ago as compared to today.

Turning back to follow the River Walk, I set out to find RISD, the Rhode Island School of Design. My thoughts jogged along at a faster pace, circling around the subjectivity of 'HIGH EXAMPLE' and 'TO LOVE AND SERVE OUR COUNTRY.'

Today it is common on some cable TV shows, in what often seems like a race to the bottom to be the most partisan on virtually any topic, when more than a few people routinely thump their chests and pontificate about patriotism.

Not really a 'high example' to follow. And some of these same TV yahoos frequently put on blinders to the plight of others who are less fortunate. One might ask about 'to love and serve our country.'

Wonder where all the chest thumpers come from? What's *their* ethnicity? And who were *their* ancestors? But, hey, I'm just a guy out for a walk.

Then it struck me, as though I'd been off on a voyage and just getting the news: tomorrow, Monday, October 8th, would still be Columbus Day to many, but in an increasing number of states and cities around the US, it would be observed as Indigenous Peoples Day. Maybe both were observed in some places.

I had a memory recall from years ago, when on an October afternoon I had been walking in downtown Hanover, New Hampshire. I saw several college students wearing buttons that said, '500 Years of Tourism is Enough. Now Go Home.'

Looking at faces of people out walking today here in Providence, I tried to imagine their ethnicity. It appeared to be a pretty good mix. No way of knowing how accurate

I was in my guesses. But I didn't have to file a report with anyone.

It took another half-an-hour to make it around the main building of RISD and skirt the southwest corner of the Brown University campus. Then I reversed course and started back toward the hotel. I smiled at the memory of a friend who had told me about some Brown alums who wrote and produced a play, '*Buddy Cianci – The Musical*' about the notorious former mayor.

One of the songs was something like *Six Times Elected, Twice Convicted*. Never saw it, never heard it. Still, sounded like it could've been a hit.

Coming back up to Broadway, I thought that perhaps I could bait Ragsdale into inquiring about Indigenous Peoples Day at the Italian restaurant we were going to this evening.

The walk was a good idea. The rain had held off and by the time I was back at the Hilton, I'd been out for more than ninety minutes moving at a pretty good clip. I looked at my watch; eight minutes to five. I still had time for a shower before dinner.

Approaching the revolving door at the hotel entrance, I watched as an attractive woman handed her car keys to one of the attendants. She then wheeled a large suitcase onto the sidewalk, juggling another bag over her shoulder. I stood aside and allowed her to go in front of me.

"Thank you," the woman said.

Lovely smile.

She pushed the suitcase in front of her and stepped toward the door. It was one of those swivel cases and had eight wheels, which caused me to wonder if there was a *sixteen-wheeler* model available.

When the door rotated, I stepped in and followed behind her.

Twenty Eight

Nathaniel tried to remember the last name of a woman he'd met in Wyoming who was originally from Brattleboro. She was pretty hot. Also, pretty damn crazy, at least when he'd known her in a very brief, week-long encounter back in the winter of 2014.

Annie … uh, Annie *Render*? Rennel, maybe. Annie Renner?' Get a phone book, look through the Rs. Spot a name that might help. He'd never seen her on facebook. But then, he wasn't into facebook back then. Really not that much into it now.

Sitting in his car outside a McDonald's on the north end of Brattleboro, he finished eating his fries and watched people going in and out of the place. A few cars moved behind him snaking through the take-out lane and coming out at the other end of the building.

Looking at his phone, he saw the icon for a weather advisory. He tapped the screen and brought up the information from AccuWeather.

'RAIN CONTIUING TONIGHT, HEAVY AT TIMES - SOUTHEASTERN VERMONT, MASSACHUSETTS AND NORTHERN CONNECTICUT BETWEEN THE HOURS OF 8 PM

AND MIDNIGHT. TEMPERATURES WARMING TO UPPER FIFTIES OVERNIGHT. POSSIBLE FLOODING IN LOW-LYING AREAS.'

It'll be dark soon. Better head back to the chicken coop. Explore more tomorrow, come back when the post office is open. Maybe rent a PO box. Find a copy center that has fax machine.

He started the engine, backed out of the parking space, then turned south onto Route 5 to go through the center of town. Directly ahead three teenage boys were walking on the sidewalk in front of a shopping plaza. He swerved to get closer, then hit the gas pedal to spray water from the street.

As he pulled up in front of the camp, Nathaniel realized that the place was only slightly smaller than the one-bedroom house he had rented in Wyoming. Just like here in Vermont, the place in Horse Creek was remote, a half-an-hour from the nearest civilization, Cheyenne, with a population of sixty-thousand or so.

The contrast of rural versus urban only seemed strange when you thought about eliminating buildings, pavement and people. The mountains of the west could make one feel small and insignificant, much like being in a boat out in the Atlantic a few miles off shore. Yet it was that proximity and everyday access one had to the ocean that proved to be a strong pull for him. He traced it back to his youth, first on the Maryland shore and then in Rhode Island.

But something had happened since he'd come back East. In less than two years, he had begun to slip into a mindset that had frightened his mother, or she always *told* him that it frightened her. She frequently prodded him to find other things to do besides sailing. 'Find some friends, go back to school, do *something* that will make you happy as you grow older.'

What had been marginally tolerable during his first weeks back in Rhode Island, had soon grown to be annoying at best. And that was near infuriating if he had to spend longer than a few days at home with his mother. But her carping and whining was a *picnic* compared to the frequent dressing down he faced each time he was around his grandfather. Nothing that Nat said, or proposed doing, could please the old son-of-a-bitch.

Nothing like a 'self-made' son-of-a-bitch.

Nathaniel long ago had convinced himself that the old man was always pissed that he never had sons, just two daughters. Then an adopted third daughter. *They* would not carry on the family name. And being the only male grandson, Nathaniel was a Crane, not a Bryan.

Long hours alone on the boat got him to imagining what life might have been like if his father were still alive. It didn't take much time fantasizing until Nathaniel was choosing sides; he and his father pitted against his mother, her sisters, *and* their domineering father. And he often found himself in imaginary conversations with his long dead father.

But here we are. My father is gone, my grandfather is gone. And now my *mother* is gone.

Now, everything starts with *me*. And it will end with me, no matter what 'Aunt Lisa' tries to pull off. And this led to his recurring thought about Lisa, the adopted daughter: she has no blood connection here.

She's not really my aunt. She has no more right to any inheritance than I do.

To hell with Lisa and her asshole lawyers.

Twenty Nine

The restaurant that Becky had chosen, possibly with input from her husband, was Il Massimo. The break in the rain seemed to be holding, so we decided that we could make the ten-minute walk.

Louie, like me, talks a good game. But when it comes down to cutting through all the hype, Becky gets serious about actually doing the research. Before we came to Providence, it was Becky who did all the reading. Louie and I were focused on the old timer's radio exhibit and maybe a pre-season basketball game or a practice. When the cop, Dyer, had suggested the place Los Andes, Becky already knew about it and knew that it had received lots of positive reviews.

As soon as we arrived we were seated at a table near the large front windows looking out to Atwells Avenue with a steady parade of pedestrians and cars passing by.

Wasting no time, I asked for the wine menu and immediately handed it to Becky.

"You go first," I said. "Pick something you like, we can try it. When we order the food, maybe we can have a bottle of red."

After a minute, she held the menu to our server and pointed to a selection. "The Ferrari-Carrano," she said. "Let's have a glass of the Fume Blanc before we order dinner," she added, giving her husband a look. He simply nodded.

"Three glasses," Becky added. "I think you'll like this, Michael. A friend of mine has it all the time and it is really very nice."

"Fine by me," I said.

We made short work of Bruschetta con Prosciutto and Calamari Fritti, then slowly worked our way through dinner - risotto with shrimp, sun-dried tomatoes and peas; sea bass with lentils, cauliflower and capers with lemon; and house-cured duck confit, with a fig walnut and mascarpone ravioli. Each of us had at least one bite of the entrées and they were all outstanding. I'd played it safe with the wine and we finished off a bottle of Seghesio Zinfandel.

Looking at the dessert menu, I flashed on a phone conversation a week ago with my sister, Laura. More health conscious than the average bear, she'd recently taken to quizzing me not just about my 'love life' but had started chatting up 'sensible dietary choices.'

With a family history of some heart issues from both parents, Laura had then emailed links to articles about Coronary Artery Disease and other cheerful topics. About as much fun as a blister on one of my big toes.

"Maybe just decaf coffee for me," I said, closing the menu. That was a lot of food we'd just consumed.

Ragsdale stared at me. Becky was still reading through the selections.

"You're not feeling well, Brother Hanlon?" Louie said.

Amused by Louie's little dig, 'Brother', I shook my head.

"Feeling fine, thank you. My sister recently convinced me that perhaps I've had more than my share of sweets and rich desserts. Maybe change the pace a little. Ice cream once a month instead of three times a week, eh?"

"How 'bout the oatmeal raisin cookies?" Louie said. "You giving them up, too?"

"We'll see."

"You know, you could reduce the sugar in that recipe," Becky said. "With all the fruit you put in the dough, I would cut it back to just one-third of a cup of light brown sugar."

Now Louie was giving Becky the smirk.

"You said that before, when you made your batch," I said.

Becky nodded. "You have the craisins, the apricots, *two* bananas *and* the raisins. And the orange juice and the maple syrup. It's more like a fruit bar than a cookie."

"I sometimes have one for breakfast," I said.

Louie put his hands over his ears and opened his eyes wider. "While you talk about healthy recipes, I'm ordering the Lemon Ricotta Cheesecake," he said.

"I'll have a bite," Becky said, folding her menu and placing it on the table.

When the dessert and coffee arrived, I also had a bite of the cheesecake. Louie gave his credit card to our server, something that he'd announced ahead of time when we ordered our dinner, as I had picked up the tab for the previous night.

Walking back to the Hilton, the Ragsdales confirmed that they were going to drive down to Newport tomorrow. It was quiet inside the hotel lobby and we stood there talking for another minute. I repeated that Detective Dyer might be able to connect me with the old basketball ref for a story.

"Sounds thrilling. Sorry I can't help," Louie said.

"And if Dyer knows any more about the guy who got shot, I might listen to that for a while, too."

"Right. Maybe even do a stand-up out in front of the pub. Eyewitness radio, huh?"

"Becky," I said, placing a hand on Louie's shoulder, "this man is such a cynic."

"But I love him anyway," she said, patting his cheek.

"Seriously, Hanlon," Louie said, "you going all 'news reporter finds *human-interest* story?' Or, is this one of your 'private eye sniffs around the edges'?"

"We'll see."

Becky and Louie went to the elevator and I turned and walked across the lobby to The Vig. It was a few minutes before nine.

Sitting at the bar was the woman with the eight-wheeler swivel suitcase, i.e. the woman with the lovely smile. She did not have the suitcase with her.

Head forward, sipping a drink through one of those tiny straws, she was focused on her tablet. She swiped a finger across the screen. I could see a couple of rings on each hand, but no wedding band or engagement ring. I eased myself onto the stool next to her. She looked up.

"Hi," I said. "Mind if I take this seat?" She studied me for a couple of seconds.

"Depends," she said. "Where are you planning to take it?" The smile was now one of bemusement.

"Thought if I went next door to the arena, they might let me in for half price if I brought my own seat."

"Not bad," she said. Glancing at her watch, she added, "It's late. Who's playing?"

Maybe late thirties, fit, black hair cut in a smooth, short bob style with bangs. My brain was reading Asian genes, in her face and eyes. Best guess was Korean. The few words I heard her speak clearly had an American accent, with a smidge of playful sarcasm.

"*Sorry*?" I said, adjusting my position on the padded stool and lifting my feet.

"Next door. What *sport*? And who are the teams?"

She was going to see how far I could take this. Before I could think of a witty reply, the bartender, a young guy with a tiny diamond stud in his left ear and longish blonde hair brushed straight back, asked what I would like to drink.

"Johnny Walker Red, ice, no water," I said. Glancing at the woman's drink I added, "No straw."

He reached under the bar, came up with a paper coaster and placed it in front of me, then turned to get my whisky.

"Michael Hanlon," I said, holding my right hand toward the woman.

Logging off the tablet and closing the cover, she placed it on the bar next to her drink.

"Lisa," she said, turning back to shake my hand.

"Nice to meet you. If you're busy, I won't yak at you and be a pest."

There it was again. And this close, the eyes were as good as the smile. She might be forty.

As she took a sip of her drink through the straw, Louie's voice was in my head. "Hanlon, *you're* the one who oughta' be showing ID here. And just how old are you, sir? And, you think they *all* have lovely smiles." His voice was now rising in decibels. Glad that only I could hear it.

She placed her left hand on the cover of her tablet and moved it away to one side.

"It's fine. I spend too much time staring at devices." She shook her head and tapped the cheekbone just below her right eye. "You would think that people who spend most of the day looking at a computer screen," she added, "might break away from it when they have a chance."

The bartender placed my drink in front of me. "Mam," he said, gesturing to her drink.

She shook her head. "No thanks," she said, stirring with the little straw. There didn't seem to be any ice left in her drink.

I first sniffed my whisky, swirled the ice cubes, then took a sip. Lot of guys I know who drink scotch go for the high-end single malts, often drinking it neat, no ice. On the occasions when I drink liquor, I like the blended stuff, preferably Johnny Walker Red.

Pointing at her glass I said, "What is that you're drinking?" It had a pinkish color to it.

"They call it a 'Performance Enhancing drink'." She laughed, then added, "Basically, it's a Margarita with some passion fruit juice. It's good, though."

We spent fifteen minutes or so in casual conversation. I learned that she lived in California but had grown up in Rhode Island; that she ran her own media consulting firm and traveled a lot but was in Providence on a 'family matter'.

She didn't ask as many questions of me as I did of her, but from a reporter's habit I threw in personal tidbits to keep the conversation moving. And I talked for a couple of minutes about my sister, Laura, a school teacher now living in northern California.

Standing from the bar stool, she removed a billfold from her bag, getting ready to pay for her drink. I held up my hand. She tilted her head and looked at me.

"Let me get that," I said. "Please."

"That's very kind of you," she said, but pulled out a twenty-dollar bill and started to place it on the bar.

"No, really," I said. She stared at me and held the twenty in her left hand.

"Like I said, I'm from Vermont. I don't think I've ever bought anyone a Performance Enhancing drink before. My treat, honest."

"Thank you." She put the twenty back in her billfold, picked up the tablet and placed it in the bag, zipped the bag closed, then extended her right arm to shake hands.

"It was nice to meet you," she said. "I hope the weather clears up for the rest of your visit."

"Yeah," I said. "I'm a little reluctant to go out walking in the rain. I was at a place couple of nights ago, guy was leaving and got shot and killed on the street not a half block from the bar."

The woman named Lisa stared at me. Face gone pale and with a look of disbelief, she didn't say a word. Slowly, she placed her hand bag up on the bar, sat down again and took a deep breath.

Thirty

"The man who was murdered Friday night was a close friend of my late sister," she said.

It was my turn to stare. No, we *both* stared at one another. No smile, her head tilted in my direction, dark eyes unflinching.

I didn't know what to say. Ragsdale's voice in my head again, 'So, Hanlon, any *other* wisecracks you care to offer up?'

"I'm sorry. I didn't mean be so flippant," I said.

She took another deep breath and placed her hands together on her lap, her body turned slightly toward me. I felt a little dumb.

"It's one of the reasons that I'm here," she said. Unlike a few minutes earlier, her voice sounded empty, no light heartedness, no bemusement.

"The man was Cliff Torres. He was here to do a favor for my sister and me. The Providence police contacted me after he was shot."

I swallowed once to make sure that my mouth wasn't hanging open at what she was telling me.

"Before I came downstairs to get something to eat and have a drink, I was on the phone with the detective who is in charge of the investigation," she said.

"Dyer," I said.

"Yes. How do you know that?"

"He came back to the pub after the shooting. Talked with the bartender. Then asked me some questions," I said. "And I've talked to him again since then," I added.

We were back to the staring. Stay quiet, Hanlon. Let her talk.

And she did.

At first, slowly, in little bursts of information. Then she seemed to pace the narrative, starting with her father's death three years ago, then the boating accident and her sister's drowning, the suspicions about her nephew, her other sister and the lawyer they'd hired. She went on about Cliff Torres before he was murdered, while shadowing the nephew, and a then tying the whole story together with a recap of her conversations with Detective Sergeant Phil Dyer.

For a moment, she looked as though she might begin to cry. But she held it back.

"I'm not sure why I am telling you all of this," she added.

I remained silent a few seconds longer. Nothing more was coming. I glanced at my watch; nine-twenty-eight.

"Would you like an espresso?" I said. "I have an idea of why you're telling me all of it."

She raised her head again to look directly at me. Dead on stare; faint smile, great eyes.

The bartender brought two cups of espresso. While he was making it, I had excused myself to go to the men's room. Lisa was stirring her small cup when I sat down again.

"I'll try the short version," I began. "It goes back a few years, but I've had a long time to think about it and it makes more sense to me now than it did when I first heard it." I sipped my espresso.

"My former wife, we were only married for eight years, divorced in 2011," I continued, "she regularly tried to keep me from wandering too far into left field." I laughed and shook my head.

"Almost always with humor, never being negative or with a put down. She thought that I should have studied to become a priest. People were always opening-up and *telling* me things." I shrugged. It puzzles me to this day.

"There were times when friends would just voluntarily confide all of this personal stuff that I *really* didn't want to know. When I came home in the evening, my wife would say, 'So, Father Hanlon. What'd you hear about today?" This got the smile from Lisa.

"Just a knack I seemed to have developed when I started working as a reporter. Listen, don't interrupt when somebody is telling you about something. Try to ask questions that keep the story going." I shrugged and added, "Body language, I guess. And, most cases, real empathy for the person who is talking."

She sipped the espresso and, perhaps, was getting back to the neutral state of half-an-hour ago.

"Makes sense," she said. "Did you share it with your wife when she asked?"

"Some of the silly things, yeah. None of my friends' personal stuff."

I shrugged again, held out my hands and laughed. "I'll tell you one other thing," I said. "My former wife, shortly after our divorce, she was giving me a hug at the time and had another piece of advice."

Lisa's eyes conveyed 'And the advice *was*?'

"She said, 'Michael, if you *do* enter the clergy, be damned sure they let you date women!"

This got another smile. Good thing Ragsdale's not here to give his spin on it.

Thirty One

Nathaniel's plan, as it had evolved over the last seventy-two hours, now centered on staying out of sight. His lawyer could do the heavy lifting and get him the money he was entitled to.

As long as he could avoid court appearances and communicate only by phone, the bare-bones camp tucked away in Vermont was possibly a better place to hide than immediately going back to Wyoming. More than a few people knew him out in cowboy country.

The rain and snow had stopped. It was a crisp autumn morning and the little accumulation from the previous day would melt by late afternoon. The foliage was beyond peak in most places, but here in the southern end of the state, there were still splashes of reds and yellows. And still enough canopy that made the camp feel isolated.

With no cell coverage back in the woods, he'd conceived a routine that would require road trips. The first one would be to Wilmington. Not as big as Brattleboro, with a population of ten-thousand plus, Wilmington has only a couple thousand people. But it most likely had some cell towers tucked away that offered a decent signal. And it appeared to be about a fifteen-minute drive from the camp.

It was 8:03 when he pulled off the highway in front of a sign that read Southern Vermont Medical Center, Deerfield Valley Campus. There were three cars parked on the side of the single-story structure and two others parked in front.

He looked at his iPhone, which he'd set to Field Test Mode. He tapped in some numbers, held the power button for five seconds, watched the screen until he saw a reading of -30. Good enough for placing a call.

Ten seconds later he was listening to his lawyer's voice explaining, "I'm not available right now. Please leave a message."

The overpaid, overrated shithead is probably still in bed, he thought. After nearly a year of interaction with this guy, he had thoughts that hiring this particular lawyer was maybe not a good choice.

"It's Nathaniel Crane. I'm on the road. Call me back as soon as you hear this. If I don't answer, tell me when I can call back and when you *will be* available."

Asshole.

Detective Sergeant Phil Dyer was the first to arrive in the conference room. Rarely did anyone else show up before Dyer. He couldn't remember the last time that had happened in more than two years.

Never mind that today was officially a federal holiday. It was Monday morning and the weekly session with the Providence PD Detective Bureau's A Team. By the time the briefing would get underway, there would be nine people in the room. These meetings normally lasted an hour. Before they ended, everyone would have a sense of what everyone else was dealing with.

Waiting for the others to arrive, Dyer studied a weekly, city-wide Crime Comparison Report. It covered all crimes through 10/7/18, Week 40 of the calendar year. Sorted by Violent Crime, Property Crime and Other Crime, the report had three columns; 4 Week Trend, Past 28 Days and Year to Date. Each column listed fifteen individual classifications ranging from Homicide at the top, down to Liquor Law Violations at the bottom of the sheet. Across the bottom of the page were graph charts reflecting six major crime categories with annual totals going back to 2013.

Aggravated Assault, Aggravated Assault with a Firearm, and Robbery were consistently the big hitters in the Violent Crime category. Dyer's focus this morning was on line number one, Homicide. His squad was charged with leading the investigation of a case that was about to add a number to that classification under the Current Week, even though it wouldn't be reflected in the report until the following week.

The head of the Detective Bureau, Major David Lapan, ran the meeting. His office was adjacent to the conference room. Like the Providence Chief of Police and several other high-level officers in the department, Lapan had started his career as patrolman in the Uniform Division and had been promoted up through the ranks.

Dyer thought of Lapan as his mentor, even if he didn't use that term when bitching about the tendency his boss had for succinct declarations when oral reports were completed. Such as, "Today, please." Or, "Before lunch, yes?" And Dyer's favorite, "We're not taking votes on this one. Just get it *right*."

Other detectives were now coming into the room, a total of seven men and one woman. Greetings were exchanged and, predictably, a few snide comments from a couple of the attendees. At one minute before nine, Lapan entered and took a seat at the head of the table nearest his office door.

"Anybody have a flooded basement this morning?" he asked for an opener.

A couple of groans, some shifting in the chairs and one of the younger detectives raised his hands to the ceiling as though he was beseeching the heavens for the rain to stop. "Unbelievable," he said.

"Pretty bad, huh? Lapan said, with a restrained grin.

"When we bought this house," the detective went on, "the inspection report said the basement was clean, dry and *without* cracks. Now, maybe eighty-per cent of the entire lower level has a couple inches of water. And I just installed new laminate flooring this summer."

"The joys of home ownership," another detective quipped.

"You'll get it cleaned up, don't worry," Lapan said. "You have a shop vac?"

"I do now. Bought the biggest model I could find Sunday morning," he said.

Dyer gave him an A-OK sign and said, "Good move. It'll come in handy."

"Phil, you wanna tell us where you are with the homicide from Friday night?" Lapan said.

Opening a folder on the table in front of him, Dyer pulled out a sheet of paper, studied it for a few seconds, then looked at Lapan before he spoke.

"Very little on the victim. We have a driver's license from New Jersey, his cellphone, nothing yet regarding family or next of kin. Metro guys in a town called Parsippany are checking with neighbors and the man's former employer. Might have something later this morning.

"Text messages and a voicemail put us onto a woman in California," Dyer went on. "I've talked to her twice." He paused and looked up. "She's now here in Providence. Flew in late yesterday," he added, information he'd already conveyed to Lapan in a phone call Sunday night.

Turning the sheet of paper over, Dyer ran a finger down half way and stopped.

"Dispatch took a call on Saturday from a woman who saw a car speeding away from the area near where the shooting occurred. I spoke with the woman and got a description. It matches a car registered to a guy we're looking at."

Looking across the table at Detective Dan Cettin, Dyer said, "Dan, that boat incident when the woman went missing off Sakonnet Point. You know one of the fishermen who found the guy on the life raft."

Cettin nodded. "Yeah. August last year," he said.

"Didn't you tell us later there was speculation that it didn't smell right? Coast Guard and insurance company digging into what really happened?" Dyer said.

"It's been in the papers," another detective piped up, the only woman in the room. "The son hired a lawyer. No charges filed, at least the last story I read, maybe a month ago" she added.

Dyer glanced back at the sheet of paper in front of him.

"2015 black Mitsubishi Eclipse, registered in Wyoming to one Nathaniel Crane, recently seen at his mother's home in East Greenwich," Dyer said, then adding, "The same Nathaniel Crane discovered in a raft by two fishermen after his mother disappeared when his boat exploded."

"Good start," Lapan said. "You and Angelo stay on it. Let us know you need any help," he tacked on with quick hand gesture to the others around the table.

"Just one other thing," Dyer added.

"Yes?" Lapan said.

"Teddy's trying to get a track on the guy's mobile.

Might take a while. Don't know who his carrier is yet."

"*Anybody* can find it, Teddy's the man," Lapan said.

What was not shared in the meeting was the fact that the woman just in from California who knew the victim, the woman Dyer had spoken with twice, was also a sister to the woman gone missing in the boating incident.

He had discussed it with Lapan, but Dyer and his partner still needed to work this angle, including the woman's story that the shooting victim had been acting on her behalf. It would either checkout or not. Based on his brief meeting with Lisa Bryan, Dyer's instinct was that the woman was telling the truth.

As soon as she had had her face-to-face with her attorney, Bryan had promised Dyer, she would share information the lawyer might have discovered regarding both the Coast Guard report and pending action from the insurance companies.

Dyer anticipated hearing from Bryan by the end of the day.

Thirty Two

Becky was waiting in the lobby when I stepped off the elevator. Seated in a comfortable looking chair next to a large vase with fresh cut flowers, she had her head down and I could see a book on her lap.

No sign of her husband. We were going to meet for breakfast. There was no one else sitting or standing.

Off to my right, at the front desk, a man was turning in a room key and getting ready to checkout. The woman behind the counter was not one that I'd seen previously. I walked over to Becky and tapped her on the shoulder. She looked up.

"What're you reading?" I said.

Moving a bookmark to the page open, she closed the book and handed it to me. A thin book, maybe a couple hundred pages. I laughed at the title, *Barking to the Choir*.

"Another dog book?" I said. "Your husband trying to steer you away from getting a little yip-yip?"

She shook her head. "Nope."

I looked at the cover. *The Power of Radical Kinship* was the sub-title. Gregory Boyle, Founder of Homeboy Industries was the author. I turned the book over. "I think

145

I saw this guy on some PBS show. He works with gang members in Los Angeles." I said.

"Yep. That's a sequel to his first book, *Tattoos on the Heart*," she said. "Both of them are inspiring, funny, and give you some hope to help offset all the superficial nonsense thrown at us every day."

I looked at her. "Superficial nonsense. Have anything specific in mind?"

She pointed at the book. "Those stories are about *real* people we almost never hear about. Their families. And how they're trying to make it in the world." She stood up, then added, "Not a phony soap opera in the news everyday about a rich, self-absorbed family messing in politics and who don't give two owl turds about what really matters."

"Care to give me some names?" I said.

She took the book back. "You know who I'm talking about."

"Well, now that you mention it..." she cut me off.

"Louie's over there looking at the sports things." She pointed toward the entrance to the hotel restaurant. We headed in that direction.

Along the corridor leading to The Vig, in floor to ceiling wooden cases designed to look like lockers, there was an assortment of old athletic gear on display: boxing gloves, football shoes, several trophies, old baseballs and softballs, fielders' gloves, and a folding courtside chair with PROVIDENCE COLLEGE stamped on the backrest.

Ragsdale was leaning in to read one of the trophies. He saw us and straightened up.

"1946 World Badminton Cup," he said.

"I think I heard the match on radio," I said.

"I'm sure you did," Louie said, turning toward the restaurant. "Right after the Farm Report on Pennsylvania's best local AM station, no doubt."

As we entered the room, I surprised myself by wondering – and looking around to see – if Lisa Bryan was anywhere in sight. Apparently not. No one seated at the breakfast bar and she was not at any of the tables.

When we sat down, I pointed at Becky. "I see that we're now sharing woodchuk profanity at home," I said, giving Louie a look.

"What?" he said, throwing back a puzzled expression.

"Your wife just scolded me by using the term 'two owl turds," I said. "Why do I think that Becky doesn't come by that language in her quilting group?"

"Are you kidding? You should *hear* how they talk," Louie said. "When they all come to our house, I'm *embarrassed* by the language. And the raunchy jokes!" He covered his ears.

Becky was shaking her head. "Not true. He's making it up," she said.

Lisa Bryan was feeling the time difference. It was 4:30 AM back in San Diego. Easing out of bed, she went into the bathroom and turned the shower on. She took a step, stopped, thought for a second, then turned and shut off the water.

Better to use the hotel's fitness room for a few minutes, then shower, before she would drive to Woonsocket to meet with the attorney. Her appointment was scheduled for eleven o'clock. She would come back up to her room and order breakfast to be sent up, then call her sister Sandi.

If today's discussion with the attorney went as anticipated, based on recent phone conversations, he would be prepared to file a motion as early as tomorrow to force her nephew to appear in court. At this point, since Cliff Torres' murder three days earlier, Lisa was convinced more than ever that Nathaniel was a psychopath. And she hoped more than ever that if the police could connect him to the shooting of Friday night, they would find him and put him in jail.

Dressed in shorts and a tee shirt over a sports bra, she pulled on a pair of running shoes, took a bottle of water and a towel, closed the door to her room and headed for the fitness center located on the floor below the lobby.

Thirty Three

Billy Woodson stood outside Paul's Pub waiting for the man to arrive. He looked at his watch; 9:03 AM. Glancing up and down the street, no one coming in his direction.

One minute later, just as Billy was considering putting in his earbuds, turning on the radio and heading back to the church gym, he saw the man with a beard coming up the street. It was the same man from inside Paul's the night the guy got shot out on the street, the night Billy had come to the bar with Detective Phil Dyer.

The man coming up the street waved. Billy kept his hands inside his pockets and waited. What does this guy want? Dyer said the man was a private detective from Vermont, but really wanted to talk to Billy about basketball and officiating. Maybe write up something, Dyer said. 'Write up something' for whom, Dyer did not say. He just told Billy the guy seemed to be on the level and was genuinely curious about Billy's story. And Billy knew that *Dyer* knew his story as well as anybody.

"Mr. Woodson," the man said, extending his right hand. "I'm Michael Hanlon. Thanks for being able to meet." They shook hands.

Billy looked at his watch; 9:05. "Five minutes late. Thought you might've forgotten, I was ready to leave."

"Sorry. You OK to get a cup of coffee?" Hanlon said.

"Nobody calls me Mr. Woodson. It's Billy." Looking across the street, Billy pointed up the street. "We can go to Capalanni's. Couple minutes from here," he added as he began walking. Hanlon fell in next to him.

Not much traffic out, but Billy hit the crosswalk button. They waited in silence until the light changed indicating that it was safe for pedestrians to cross.

"Detective Dyer says you're from Vermont. Which part?"

"I live in little village called Quechee. It's in the town of Hartford, but most people think of it as White River Junction. Right along the Connecticut River, on the border with New Hampshire," he said.

Billy stopped and put a hand on Hanlon's right arm. "Close to Hanover," he said.

Hanlon observed that Billy's expression brightened. "That's right," he said.

"I officiated in a tournament at Dartmouth. Long time ago," Billy said and resumed walking. "Back when they had some decent basketball teams. There was a white farm kid from Nebraska, but he *jumped* like he was Bill Russell. Could shoot, too."

"I didn't realize that you reffed in the Ivy League," Hanlon said.

"Couple of times. Usually when the assignor was

ticked at somebody and couldn't find enough guys to do a game. Most of the games I did were in the New England Conference and a few Mid-West."

"You've been here in Providence for a while, now?" Hanlon said.

"Close to 50 years." Billy stopped at the door of Capalanni's Grill.

"So, you must've known Dave Gavitt."

Billy held the door for Hanlon to go in front of him. "Everybody knew Dave," he said.

"Wasn't he a Dartmouth guy?" Hanlon said.

"Indeed, he was. Played there, coached there, before he came home. One of the best basketball men of his time," Billy said. "You know they named the court after him over at the Dunkin Donuts Center," he added as they entered the restaurant.

By the time we'd almost finished a second cup of coffee, and had spent more than an hour talking, Billy was in a groove. The stories just flowed. I was watching a man who morphed in front of my eyes. One might believe that Billy could pull on his shoes, grab a whistle and be ready to hit the court this afternoon.

"You know, I got a nickname. It was at the end of my career." Frowning, as though reading my thoughts, he added, "Quick whistle."

I laughed. "Probably came from those teams who

were *trailing*, right?" I said.

He shook his head. "No, at that point I was washed up. I'd started to drink a lot. Tried to cover it up, but everyone knew." He became quiet, the earlier enthusiasm draining away. "It was humiliating beyond belief. But that only hit me later. I was trying to fool everybody." He shook his head. "Only fooled myself."

I didn't know what to say, so kept my mouth shut.

Shaking his head again, he inhaled through his nose, leaned back and sat a little straighter.

"I'm one of the lucky ones," Billy said. "A few rough years when I could have died. *Should* have died." He looked me in the eye and held the gaze for a couple of seconds before continuing.

"Some good people looked out for me. Helped me when I didn't realize they were doing it. Detective Dyer's one of them. Could have thrown me in jail more times than you could imagine."

"You've known Dyer for a long time?" I said.

Billy nodded. "Since he was a young cop. A very good cop. I only learned that later." He gave me the dead-on look again, then added, "Only reason I'm here telling you these stories is Phil Dyer."

"I truly appreciate you taking the time. And thanks for letting me make some notes," I said, glad that I had not asked to record the conversation. Unlikely that he would've opened-up so much.

"What is it you want to do with this?" He pointed at

my notebook.

I shrugged. "I'm not sure. I used to be a reporter and still like to chase a story that sounds interesting. After we were in the pub the other night and you came in with Dyer, then I got talking with him later," I held my hands palms up, "I just wanted a chance to visit with you and hear about your career."

Billy smiled. "I have a new 'career' now," he said, making air quotation marks.

"Really?"

Holding the smile, he studied me for a couple of beats.

"Would you like to see what I do now?" Billy said. "Might help tie-up this story you decided to chase."

"Sure. I *would* like to see what you're doing now," I said.

He looked at his watch, then looked back to me. "You up for a walk?" he said.

I held up my umbrella with my left hand and pointed at my shoes with my right. "Not exactly court shoes, but they're comfortable. I had a good walk yesterday, down by the river."

Billy stood and started to place money on the table for our coffee.

"No, no. This is on me," I said, placing a ten-dollar bill and three ones next to my coffee mug.

"Thank you," he said, and we headed back out to Dean Street.

Fortunately, we were at one of the in between slots of the lingering showers. The heaviest rain, according to a report I'd watched on TV back at the hotel, was now behind us. The man on the weather report had made a wavering hand gesture when he said that 'most of the state would experience on and off rain' for the next few hours.

"This way," Billy said, turning left and setting the pace.

From two steps behind, I watched him and thought that he could be one of those marathon walkers. Earlier, based on some of the stories he told, I'd calculated his age as somewhere in his mid-seventies. I knew men half that age who would have had to hustle to stay with him.

Thirty Four

On the third floor of the Providence Public Safety Complex, squirreled away in a small tech lab behind all the other offices, Detective Ted Nichols was working his way through cellphone carrier data. He could read the material in the same way a stenographer could read shorthand.

The data he was working on was for the police department in Pawtucket, where Nichols would testify as an expert witness in a case of an armed robbery at a convenience store. A clerk had been shot and killed, the cops arrested a suspect and they had his cellphone. Nichols' work, based on the cellphone activity before and just after the robbery, would show that the phone had been in the immediate area at the time of the robbery.

Reviewing the data alternated from flipping through pages of a printout, to frequent glances at his computer screen. Nichols had been at it for more than an hour when Phil Dyer knocked on his open door and poked his head in.

"Teddy. How's it goin'?"

Nichols glanced back at Dyer, held up his hand, then

marked a spot in the printout with red paper clip.

"Going OK. How 'bout you," Nichols said, closing the binder on the desk in front of him.

"Can I talk to you some more about this shooting Friday night?" Dyer said.

Nathaniel's conversation with his lawyer was frustrating. After a missed return call, then another voicemail, they connected live while he was at the Pettee Memorial Library in Wilmington, Vermont.

He'd gone' outside with the phone and was sitting in his car with the driver's door open. It was close to one o'clock, a mostly sunny and warm October afternoon.

"Nothing more than what I told you last week," the lawyer was telling him, in a tone that indicated a trace of exasperation. "Just as soon as the judge sets a date, could be in a couple of days, I will have to appear in chambers to answer questions about our response to their filing.

If the judge *accepts* what I have to say, we'll be looking at a court date mid-to-late November. It'll either happen before Thanksgiving, or the week after. Maybe not until December."

Nathaniel held his annoyance in check. He wasn't going to tell the lawyer where he was, wasn't going to tell him that he was even more anxious than he had been a week ago. If he had an inkling that something was happening in the investigation of the Friday night shooting, something that could be connected to him, he certainly was not going to consult with his attorney. At least not *this* attorney.

"I still can't believe that my aunts would do this," Nathaniel said, a lie that he was starting to believe. Feigning 'poor victim' to the lawyer, he went on. "It's Lisa. And all just because she was adopted, then became this overachiever, always needing to show my mother and my aunt Sandi, how smart she was."

"Yes, you've expressed that once or twice before," the lawyer said.

Nathaniel wanted to tell the asshole to shut up, just do his job and get the settlement. But he didn't say that.

"Apparently, right after Lisa graduated from college and went to California, she spent some time trying to find her real parents. When that didn't work out, she sucked up to my grandfather and spent years posturing as his 'best' daughter," Nathaniel said.

"Nathaniel, let me tell you something, if I may. If it comes to that, you will have a chance to make a case before a judge. You are *rightfully* entitled to your mother's share of your grandfather's life insurance and his estate. If part of the story that you have to tell is about how your Aunt Lisa *manipulated* the man who adopted her, and gave her a good home with two sisters, then we will certainly make that case."

After a pause, the lawyer went on. "Anything you can offer to support that, especially if we can show that Lisa has been weaving this whole story since your mother's death, and that your Aunt Sandi was dragged into being part of the action to deny you the share that would have gone to your mother, that can be a very strong case."

"And will that get some attention when you go to the judge's chambers to answer questions?" Nathaniel said.

"No, it would be too soon. If the court, that is, the judge, grants our request for a hearing, that's when we will make the case. It sure as hell would have helped if your mother had updated her will after your father died," he added.

The lawyer knew that, in fact, it was a large chunk of the father's insurance payout that had enabled Nathaniel to hang out in Wyoming while not making any serious effort toward gainful employment. Most of that money was now gone.

"So, a minute ago, when you said, 'if the judge accepts what you have to say' about the filing, what *is it* that you plan to say?"

The lawyer sighed. He was too old for this. And this client was either too spoiled, or too dense, to grasp even the basics of civil litigation.

"Let's not plow that ground again," he said. "Let me *meet* with the judge, answer the questions, and get us a date for a hearing. Then we will have ample time to build a case from the day you were born to the horrible day when your mother drowned. Can we do that?"

That answer was not sufficient to talk Nathaniel down

from the ledge. Of course, there was a lot of information and a considerable amount of fear that he had and that the lawyer didn't have. But further conversation was not going to change that at this moment.

"I'm visiting a friend in Vermont," he said. "Phone coverage is spotty. Gonna' be here for probably a few days. Call or text me after you meet with the judge."

"That is exactly what I plan to do," the lawyer said. "Take care of yourself. We'll get beyond this. Bye for now." And he was gone.

Nathaniel turned off his phone, got out of the car and went back into the library. Easier to check online news stories there than on his tablet at a remote camp with no service.

Thirty Five

Lisa Bryan's attorney, Kevin Byrne, had a reputation of being one of the best lawyers in Rhode Island. And his fees reflected that. At $500 an hour, with an upfront retainer of $10,000, his work to date had moved them into the twenty-thousand-dollar range and they had yet to have a hearing date set for the probate suit filed against her nephew.

Following the weekend phone calls and her trip across the country to meet with this man, she knew that Byrne was not convinced of the likelihood of her nephew's involvement with a shooting of a man on the street in downtown Providence.

It was her intention to make that case to him now.

Escorting Bryan into his office and closing the door, Byrne gestured to a leather club chair. He started to sit right next to her in a Regency caned library chair, then hesitated.

"Would you like some coffee? Or tea?" he said.

"Thank you, no. I had some on the drive from the hotel," she said.

Byrne sat, pulled on the creases of both pant legs, clasped his hands together, leaning slightly forward, and rested his arms on his legs. Taller than six feet, this maneuver placed them at eye level.

"Why don't we start with what the Providence detective told you?" Byrne said.

For the next ten minutes, Lisa Bryan recounted all that she could from the two phone conversations and one in person meeting with Detective Sergeant Phil Dyer. Byrne didn't interrupt once. Twice while she was talking, he made a note on a yellow pad.

When she had finished, Byrne stood, walked behind his desk, put the pad down and loosened his necktie. He sat, facing Lisa. Placing both of his hands flat, thumbs hooked under the lip of the desk, he looked directly at her. Simultaneously, at first flapping the fingers of both hands in sync, he then began tapping the desk in an alternating rhythm, as though he were sending Morse code, left hand doing the dots while the right was doing the dashes.

"The Providence Police Department is one of the best in the country," Byrne said, abruptly rising from behind the desk, both hands now supporting his frame as he leaned forward and maintained eye contact with Lisa.

"I don't know Dyer, but I know his boss. In a city of more than 180,000 people, a lot goin' on. They have their hands full, no question. *But*, apprehending perpetrators of violent crimes is something they do as well as, if not better than, any comparable city police force anywhere."

Lisa said nothing. She watched Byrne move from behind the desk and return to where he'd been previously, lowering his frame into the chair next to hers. He tugged at the creases in his slacks again, then crossed his legs.

"Let me talk to Dyer. See where he thinks this is going, if they know anything about your nephew."

"Cliff was doing this as a favor to me," Lisa said. "He wouldn't accept anything for coming up here. He said that if he stayed for more than a couple of days, I could reimburse him for his hotel.

And now he's dead."

Byrne put a hand on her shoulder. "You can't beat on yourself for that. It's another tragic example of where our society is; innocent people get shot just walking down the street."

"But, he was walking down *that* street because he was helping *me*."

Now Byrne remained silent. Lisa took a breath, shook her head, put both hands to her mouth and kept them there.

"First things first," Byrne said. "I will follow up with the court, see if we can expect a date soon. Then I'll talk to Detective Dyer."

He stood again, Lisa followed his move and rose from her chair.

"Thank you," she said.

"How long are you planning to be here?" Byrne said.

"A couple of days. I'm going to Taunton to see Sandi."

"You said on the phone that your sister doesn't know about Mister Torres' murder."

"No. I didn't want to tell her on the phone. And I want to explain to her in person *why* I asked Cliff to see if he could watch what Nathaniel was up to." She shook her head again, then added, "I don't think Sandi would have gone along with that plan if I told her before-hand."

Police in Parsippany, New Jersey had little more information today than they had after the first phone call from the Providence police regarding the murder of Clifton Torres.

One of Torres' neighbors, a woman in her twenties, thought that he might have originally moved to New Jersey from Virginia. But he had lived in the condo development long before she and her husband had arrived. She told the police that while Torres had always been polite and friendly, they had never had a substantive conversation. He was considerably older, old enough to have been her grandfather.

Thermoform International had not been much better with details on Cliff Torres while he was employed by the company. The Director of Human Resources was on vacation and the Jersey cops were growing impatient, to the point of dispatching two of their own detectives to interview the company president.

In Providence, Dyer had already initiated contact with the Social Security Administration's office in Maryland.

Find out where Torres was born, where he'd lived prior to New Jersey, and anything else that might shed a little light on his early life. And *maybe* find out why someone would want his life to end.

Without undue speculation, both the Providence PD and their counterparts in New Jersey, accepted the possibility that Torres' murder might not have been premediated. It could have been the result of some random street thug being sufficiently pissed off at life in general, angry at the world and ready to shoot a stranger walking down the street. Wouldn't be the first time. Not to mention somebody zoned out on drugs, or mentally disturbed, perhaps hallucinating, and having perceived Clifton Torres as an enemy invader from God knows where.

Cops see it all. Especially in urban areas, where guns of all variety can be obtained illegally.

Not yet commonly known to the public, however, is a shift in violent assault crimes with a weapon. In the state of Rhode Island, anyway, the shift has been fewer firearms to more knives being used in assaults.

If an adult is convicted of first degree murder in Rhode Island and used a *firearm*, the result is mandatory consecutive life sentences. That same conviction when the assailant used a knife, is only a life sentence with a chance of parole after 20 years.

Who was the first person to say, 'Go figure?'

Thirty Six

The gymnasium was empty and quiet. Billy stood at the center of the court, turning slowly, both arms stretched wide in a welcoming gesture. I was standing two feet away, close enough to block a shot if we had been playing pick-up.

"This is where I work most of the time," he said. "Don't get a lot of fans cheering here."

As I looked up at one of several two-by-three-foot skylights staggered around the roof, the overcast sky outside couldn't match the brightness of the enclosed fluorescent light fixtures. Spaced in among the ceiling tile, the lights were covered with some variation of chicken-wire, or a light mesh metal screen. The tile was old and stained in spots and a few of the bulbs were burned out.

Billy looked at his watch. "Kids will be coming in about an hour," he said. "With all this the rain, might have more than usual today."

"What ages?" I said.

"Mornings, mostly the little ones. Gym rats. Later in the day, might have a few of the twelve and thirteen-year-olds."

"Ever get any of the high school kids, the ones who don't make the team to play JV or varsity?"

"More in the winter. Some of the other churches put teams together, come here to play," he said. He walked to the side of the court and pulled out a couple of plastic folding chairs, handing one to me. We unfolded the chairs and sat down.

"The world has changed since I was a kid." He studied me for a second, then added, "Even since *you* were a kid. Too many other things for young people to do these days. Playing basketball, almost any sport, not as important as it once was."

"Eh-h, I'm not sure," I said. "Some places around the country, a kid gets into a sport, they might play just that one sport nearly year 'round. Go off to a summer camp to get better and play even more."

"Rich kids," Billy said. "Not the kids I see."

In my head I heard Louie; 'It's all relative, Hanlon,' one of his short-circuits to my generalizations about the rich and the not so rich.

As he had earlier when we were having coffee, Billy pivoted to a recollection of some long-ago game in another gymnasium, this memory involving high school players attending a basketball clinic that he worked forty years ago. I kept my mouth shut and let him run with the story, hoping that I would be able to reconstruct enough to write notes when I got back to the hotel.

Some forty-five minutes later, only when we could

hear someone coming through the door where we had entered, did Billy pause. He had been weaving one tale after another as though he were preparing an introduction to *Basketball Refs 101*.

Glancing again at his watch, Billy wiped a hand across his mouth, wet his lips and then swallowed. I suspected that after all the talking, he almost certainly needed a drink of water.

I looked at my watch; eight minutes to twelve.

Billy stood and started to fold his chair. "Better get some basketballs out and get ready for the kids," he said. On cue, the person we heard coming through the door appeared. He looked to be about nine-years old, a skinny dark-skinned boy just under five-feet tall.

"You can stick around, if you like," Billy said.

"Thanks," I said. "Since the rain's stopped, I'm going to drive around and visit some of the sights. It's my first time visiting Rhode Island."

He held his hand out to shake mine and gave me what I thought was a wistful look.

"I would love a chance to talk with you some more," I said. "Your stories reminded me of some players that I'd like to ask you about."

This brought a smile. "Old refs never die. They just smell that way," Billy said, giving me a wink.

I gave him an exaggerated groan and shook my head. "ESPN is *not* likely to invite you on with gems like that. *But*," I pointed at him, then added, "if you sit down with me again, I'll bring along my little digital machine and when we finish, I'll send a recording off to the Basketball Hall of Fame."

"Sure. Tell 'em I knew Gavitt and *never* gave him a Technical. And you know that he raised a boat load of money for that place," he said.

No, I didn't know that. But hearing Billy offer still another piece of basketball trivia, it was clear that all he needed was an audience of one. I took a business card from my minimalist-style wallet and handed it to him.

"I will come find you," I said. "But that has my phone number."

He studied the card, then looked at me. "Private Investigation. You down here working with the police?" he said.

"No. I just happened to be coming in out of the rain the other night when that guy went out and got shot. You saw me. I was there in Paul's Pub when you came in with Dyer."

He nodded and shook my hand again. "Good enough. Yes, I would be happy to talk about old players. And a few coaches, too."

"I will be back. Thank you," I said and walked out past two more kids coming through the side door.

Thirty Seven

When I got back to the hotel, the Ragsdales had checked out and gone off to Newport. They planned to see the mansions. We'd agreed at breakfast that we would talk later and meet for dinner somewhere.

Billy's question about 'working with police' gave me a momentary reportorial twitch. Over the past few years, nearly from the day we met in rural Maine while working on the same case, Louie rarely missed an opportunity to chide me about 'letting go' of what he referred to as my 'Radio Rick' tendencies.

'There are lots of stories out there,' was part of one of his mantras, ending with, '*you* don't have to cover all of them.'

Easier said than done. He had been a municipal policeman for many years, who then became a much-in-demand undercover drug cop, and despite near endless lip service, Louie was having a really hard time trying to retire from law enforcement and do something else. Besides fishing.

We'd spent a lot of time together and, with effort, I had learned to check myself when I noticed that my opinions being offered at any given moment, sounded like preaching. Didn't seem to bother him. And I could never tell if my advice really carried much weight with him anyway.

So, what the hell? I pulled out my phone and called Detective Dyer. He answered on the second ring.

"Phil Dyer."

"Detective. It's Michael Hanlon. This a good time to talk?"

"You get to connect with Billy this morning?" he said, causing me to assume that it was an OK time.

"Yes, Thanks for setting that up. The man has a ton of stories."

"I've heard most of them. Maybe more interesting since he's been sober for a while now."

Billy had said that Dyer, and other cops, could have put him in jail many times. It didn't take a Pulitzer Prize winner to know that over the years they likely heard much of Billy's soundtrack.

"When I left him at the gym a few minutes ago, I gave him my card. He asked if I was doing private investigation down here working with you?"

Silence.

"I told him no," I said. "But, full disclosure, as they say, kind of a fluky coincidence occurred last night."

"You met a woman in a bar," he said.

So much for worries about *me* sharing information without consent, huh? Then I remembered that Lisa Bryan had, in fact, told me that she was going to be speaking with Dyer this morning before going to meet her lawyer.

"Yes. Guess she told you all about it."

"She didn't tell me what you had to drink," Dyer said.

"Scotch. With a teaspoon of maple syrup. Helps me sleep better."

"So, what can I help you with?" he said.

"I'm sorry. It is *really* difficult for me not to snoop around some when a thing like this happens," I said. "Besides, as you know, I was there in the pub and spoke with the man a few minutes before he was shot."

Silence.

"Anything more on the man who was killed? You said the name was Torres," I said.

"Not much. Yet. I believe that I told you and your friend that the victim was from New Jersey. And didn't Ms. Bryan fill you in last night? Torres was here in Rhode Island on her behalf."

Guess Lisa Bryan gave Dyer the full account of our conversation.

"It was my impression that Torres *volunteered* to come here," I said. "Wasn't he an old friend of the family? And, yes, Ms. Bryan told me about her sister and the boating incident last year. Said that she has had these strong suspicions all along that her nephew was behind it."

Dyer cleared his throat. "I believe there's more to it than that. But, I'm not in a position to share information about a case that is not in our purview," he said. "We have a man shot and killed on a street in our city. That is my focus. If we find a connection to the nephew and all these other family issues, we will focus on that connection."

"I'm guessing the boat story and the missing woman got a lot of media coverage," I said. "Am I correct that it happened August last year?"

"Sounds right. And, yes, the press was all over it."

"Think my best bet is to go online and find some old stories."

"I'd start with the Journal," he said.

"Thanks, I will. And thank you again for getting Billy to meet with me. I really think there's a story there that I'd like to write about."

"He survived." Dyer then added, "More than can be said for a lot of other people in similar circumstances."

"OK. Maybe we can talk another time."

"Stay dry," Dyer said, then clicked off.

Thirty Eight

In just over a year since the boating accident, when his mother's body was *not* found, Nathaniel Crane had learned about frugality in ways that he had not previously known.

Not long after his father died, he'd received a payout from a term life insurance policy, a measly one-hundred-thousand-dollars. He knew that a much larger insurance benefit had gone to his mother. When he'd piddled through most of his hundred-grand, it took less than three years, he had begun to cajole his mother for more 'family funds'.

At first, his mother sent him monthly checks for twenty-five-hundred dollars. Later, when attempting to persuade her that he had a real business opportunity in Wyoming and that he could *really* use a hundred-thousand on short notice, she balked. It led to a very unpleasant argument that played out during several phone calls, and no additional funds from mom.

She told him to visit his grandfather and, she was sure, that if he could convince her father that it was a promising investment, he might see his way to write a check. His mother even suggested that her father might join Nathaniel as an investor.

That was in the fall of 2015. He had fumed for days. His mother was clearly beginning to pull back from her willingness to 'send more money.' Yes, the investment idea, to join a friend in Colorado who was ramping up an operation to grow, market and distribute cannabis, was an unlikely fit for someone his mother's age.

So, after sulking for a week, he convinced himself that his grandfather, a successful, self-made residential construction magnate, would see the merits of the opportunity and front Nathaniel some cash.

Nope. Years earlier, when the old codger had turned 80, he had become greedy and suspicious. He laughed at the cannabis start-up idea and went into this lengthy harangue about what a privileged life Nathaniel had had to date and that it was long past time for him to 'shape up'.

'Put that education to work and make something of yourself,' the old man had taunted. Then he trotted out still more of his boring, who gives a shit stories, about men he'd known who came from nothing and built small empires that would sustain their families long after they were gone.

Later, during a visit with his grandfather a week before Christmas, Nathaniel began yelling and flailing his arms, provoking a heated exchange that ended with the old man telling him that it was 'time to leave.' The words went back and forth for another five minutes before the grandfather rose from his chair, took Nathaniel by the arm and started walking him to the front door.

While Nathaniel kept up the verbal assaults, the old man, highly agitated, jaw clenched and red in the face, firmly moved him toward the door with both his hands against Nathaniel's back.

Nathaniel lost it. He whirled around, threw off his grandfather's hands, then called him a 'selfish old blue-collar bigot asshole.' He shoved the old man just enough to make him fall backward and lose his balance.

When his grandfather fell, he struck the back of his head. It was a minor blow, only a brush against the edge of a banister newel.

As the old man lay there, still conscious, he rolled to one side. Nathaniel stood over him, doing nothing. Then his grandfather, struggling to breathe, made a gasping sound and pulled both hands to his chest.

Nathaniel watched. Pretty obvious that he was having a heart attack. Too bad.

After twenty minutes, enough time to work out a story in his head, he dialed 9-1-1. It took the paramedics only three minutes to arrive. Too late.

Later that evening, from the ER waiting area at the hospital, Nathaniel phoned his mother to expand on what had happened. The crux of the lie was that when he had arrived at his grandfather's house, he found him collapsed and not breathing. Subsequently, he faced the usual questions that come with 'an unattended death,' but he was able to maintain his story sufficiently enough that no charges were made at the time.

In the week following his grandfather's death, when Nathaniel's mother and her two sisters sat for the reading of the will, all three women were stunned at the amount they were to receive as equal beneficiaries to the estate, an estimated $8.6 million each, mostly in cash, with some stocks and bonds.

Fast forward six months, Nathaniel's family contortions began in earnest, mostly with his mother, but with both aunts, as well. Nothing he did, however, seemed to make a difference.

His mother had not completely shut him down, but she was stingy in the amount of money she gave her only child. Near the end of the following summer after his grandfather died, she sent Nathaniel a check for twenty-five-thousand dollars. The amount was just enough to fuel his rage. And it seeded the idea that ultimately led to planning her 'disappearance.'

Now, more than a year after his mother was gone, legal maneuverings on the part of her sisters, especially Lisa, were depriving Nathaniel of his mother's share of the old man's estate.

Going to Vermont, hiding out from *anyone* who knew him, and especially distancing himself from police investigations in Rhode Island, he was facing a squeeze on his resources. He would not fritter away money eating at restaurants, or any non-essentials.

Parking for a second time in two days outside the

Jacksonville General Store, compiling a short mental list of additional food items that would see him through another week, he could feel himself becoming more anxious by the hour. The creeping paranoia that was gaining ground had caused him to stop using credit cards. As of this very minute, it would be all cash for everything.

Maybe one meal a day should be the new plan. There was no freezer in the old refrigerator at the camp, just a little compartment for two ice trays. As unappealing as the thought was, perhaps he should buy only canned food and packaged items that required minimal preparation, things that had long shelf-life.

He climbed out of the car and walked to the front steps of the store.

Thirty Nine

The age difference among the three sisters was unusual. Sophia would have turned sixty-seven in February; Sandi, ten years younger, had observed her fifty-sixth birthday in July; and then came Lisa, adopted as a toddler, now about to observe her fortieth birthday in three weeks.

Growing up, Sandi was more a mother to Lisa than older sister. She had been completing the first year of college when her parents shocked the two older girls by informing them of their intention to adopt an orphan. Apparently, the process had been underway for months when they broke the news. First to Sophia, recently married at 29, then to Sandi, who was 19. They would meet their new sister the following week, Easter of 1981, when the parents returned with her from California.

Mi-Cha was her birth name. She had spent two years at the Children's Home Society of California, in a facility in Oakland. It was during a time when the organization was shifting focus from orphans and adoption, to a variety of other services for children in need.

The adoption idea had come from the girls' father. He knew about the work of CHS of California from the months he spent in the Bay Area while serving in the US Navy. The sister of one of his closest pals was on the staff and through her, Donald Bryan learned of the work with child welfare, especially the services to children coming from stressful environments.

A longtime supporting donor, Bryan and his wife, Katherine, met some of the children in residence at CHS during a two-week California trip celebrating their wedding anniversary. They were captivated by Mi-Cha. With a lot of effort, and two subsequent trips in the following months, they were able to pull it off.

Three years after the adoption, Katherine Bryan died of complications from breast cancer. Mi-Cha was in the first grade. Older sister Sandi was about to graduate from college. At her insistence, she stepped in to help care for the little girl. Sophia had moved to Maryland with her new husband. It was a challenging run for everyone involved: Sandi, her father, and two different nannies employed over ten years.

Mi-Cha became 'Lisa', as the result of a boy in her kindergarten class. Instead of calling her by her birth name, for whatever reason, the boy couldn't get it right. It always came out sounding similar, but wrong.

She told her mother that she liked the new name. She asked everyone to call her Lisa. Within the family, the two names became interchangeable. At the age of nine, she made up a story and told friends that her name really was

Mi-Cha Lisa, that her mother took it from Mona Lisa.

Only when she reached high school did she consider going back to Mi-Cha. She settled for using that name with her closest friends. Even then, it became too confusing, so most kids still called her Lisa.

Thirty-seven years after they first laid eyes on each other, having shared happy and sad times, occasional heartache, a long awkward stretch during the younger sister's adolescence and, more recently, tragedy, Lisa was about to inform Sandi of the latest development in what was beginning to feel like a family curse.

Seated at a dining room table in Sandi's small home in Taunton, Lisa used a tissue to dab at the corner of each eye, sniffled and then wiped her nose.

"You remember Sophia's friend, Cliff Torres?" Lisa said.

"He worked for Steven a long time ago. And came to his funeral," Sandi said.

"Yes. And he visited Sophia after Steven died."

"I didn't know that."

Lisa nodded. "Not long before…" she hesitated, took a deep breath and sat forward on her chair. "It was a few weeks before she disappeared. Cliff was vacationing on Cape Cod and he made a point of coming to see Sophia."

"That was thoughtful," Sandi said.

Lisa leaned toward Sandi, reaching to take Sandi's left

hand in both of hers. Another deep breath.

"I need to tell you something."

Sandi titled her head slightly but didn't reply. Lisa continued to hold her sister's hand.

"Cliff was murdered."

"Good Lord," Sandi said, moving her free hand to her mouth. She leaned back, pulling away from Lisa and held both hands to her lips. Swallowing whatever she was about to say, Sandi inhaled through her nose, closed her eyes and shook her head from side to side.

After a few seconds, lowering her hands and clasping them together between her knees, she closed her eyes again. "Oh-h-h," Sandi groaned, "That is horrible," still shaking her head in disbelief. "*How*? And when did this happen?" she added.

"He was shot. Friday night. In Providence."

Sandi twisted her head as though she needed to hear better, eyes signaling confusion.

"In Providence? I didn't know that he lived in Rhode Island."

"Sandi," Lisa said, again reaching for her sister's hand. "Cliff was in Providence because of me. He was there following Nathaniel."

"What are you *talking* about?"

"He wanted to help. Cliff called me on the anniversary of the boat accident. We talked about Sophia. I told him that we didn't believe that it was an accident. And I told him about dad's heart attack, that Nathaniel was there when it happened.

"I don't know what I was thinking," Lisa added. "First, he asked if we had hired anyone to watch Nathaniel, what he was doing now. The next thing I knew, we were discussing him, *Cliff*, to do just that. Apparently, he had a lot of time his hands. He'd just retired."

Sandi stared at her sister. She began rolling one hand over the other, then clasped the hands again between her knees and squeezed tightly. She rocked her upper body for several seconds, which caused her head to move back and forth. She patted her feet on the carpet each time her body came forward.

"Lisa. *Why* didn't you tell me this?"

"You wouldn't have agreed. We would have had another argument. I just didn't want to upset you," Lisa said. "You know that you were uncertain about hiring the lawyer, to fight what Nathaniel is trying to do."

Sandi's rocking stopped, but she kept up with the foot patting, more slowly, but louder each time the soles of her shoes came down in unison.

"Sandi, he *did* kill his mother. *Our* sister. I know that you still are not convinced. But the police will prove it. Even if the Coast Guard – and the insurance investigators – haven't been able to. I know that he did it. And we *both* know that he did something, or said something, that upset dad enough to cause his heart attack."

"Please," Lisa went on, "try to understand that Cliff really wanted to do this. I was frustrated. Nothing was happening. It was easy to agree with Cliff's idea." Lisa was on the verge of crying, an unusual emotional response that Sandi had rarely seen from her little sister.

"What are you going to tell the police?" Sandi said.

"I've already spoken with them. They found my number on Cliff's phone and they called me. That's why I decided to come immediately. I didn't just come here to meet with our lawyer."

"Are you going to be in any trouble over this? What did you tell them?" The foot tapping stopped, Sandi's body language appeared to have softened. Lisa shook her head.

"I went to the Providence Police Headquarters as soon as I got here," Lisa said. "I told them everything. The detective knew the story about the boat exploding and Sophia's body never being found."

"Has anyone there spoken with Natty since Cliff was murdered?"

"Not as of this morning. At least as far as I know. The Providence detective was in touch with police in East Greenwich. They're trying to locate him" Lisa said.

"Do they know if he's still in Rhode Island? He may have gone back to Wyoming," Sandi said.

"One of Sophia's neighbors told police that Nathaniel had been at the house off and on for at least the last month."

"All right," Sandi said, blowing out a breath. "Now what? Do they have a suspect in Cliff's murder?"

"Not yet."

"You said that you met with Kevin Byrne this morning. Does he know about a court date?"

Lisa proceeded to explain what she had learned in the meeting with the attorney, and added a few inferences based on all the phone conversations she'd had with Byrne. Sandi had never met the lawyer in person, having only spoken with him on the phone. This had all been Lisa's undertaking, Sandi somewhat skeptical from the start. Perhaps less so now.

When she finished talking, Lisa was back to her 'take charge' persona. She stood and held her hands out in a gesture to pull Sandi from her chair. Sandi took her sister's hands but didn't immediately get up.

"Could we go for a walk?" Lisa said. "Remember how you always took me for a walk and talked to me when I was upset about something? I always felt better."

Sandi looked up, put her hands on her knees and stood slowly.

"Yes. A walk probably is a good idea."

Forty

Police in at least two jurisdictions were actively on the lookout for a black 2015 Mitsubishi Eclipse. No results in either Rhode Island or Wyoming over the past thirty-six hours. Dyer was ready to re-submit the vehicle on a nationwide BOLO alert with additional information about the Wyoming registration.

Detective Angelo Incerpi would handle the update. It would take all of five minutes for every PD in the country to receive the description, plate number and last known sighting of the car, allegedly October 5th, the night of the shooting in downtown Providence.

On any given day, there are hundreds of vehicles listed with law enforcement all over the US actively 'on the lookout'. Some are located within hours, or even minutes, and some are never found. When a state police car is parked in the grass median on an interstate highway, the officer is not just watching for drivers exceeding the speed limit. And when the state issuing the registration is known, if not the actual plate number, the chance of spotting the car is much greater.

If Nathaniel Crane's Mitsubishi with Wyoming plate

number 22-12850, was out there on some state highway or one of the interstates, especially during daylight hours, the driver could be in for a real 'anxious moment' when flashing blue lights appeared.

Dean Chase was a throwback to the 1970s. He preferred *good* country music - Marty Robbins, Buck Owens, Merle Haggard, Loretta Lynn and the like – not the new country artists and songs that might show up on some TV awards show but got no votes from him.

Like a lot of people living in rural areas forty years ago, Dean also had both a Citizens band radio *and* a police scanner in his truck, mounted right below the dashboard radio. He rarely listened to the CB but transferred it to this latest rig which he bought used. On the other hand, he frequently listened to the police scanner, usually when he was parked in his driveway.

Most of the chatter on the police scanner came from dispatchers and local cops, or volunteer firemen. Dean knew many of these people. On occasion, when he ran into one of them at a convenience store or in front of the post office, he might ask about something he'd heard them chattering about. Depending on who it was, and what they thought of Dean, sometimes he got more information than the snippets which eventually made their way onto the southern Vermont grapevine.

Slowly scratching between the ears of his German Shepard, Dean arched an eyebrow and cocked his head toward the scanner when he heard a vehicle description and the reference to the 'Wyoming license plate 22-12850.' Dean stopped scratching his dog's head.

"Well smack me with cow shit and call me a Meadow Muffin," he whispered to Duke.

The dog didn't respond.

Forty One

Nathaniel was back at the camp. The weather was better, he opened two windows to allow fresh air to circulate and left the front door open as well.

The level of agitation that he'd he felt earlier in the day when he talked with his lawyer was climbing once again. For the same reason; it was the money.

These circular, inner conversations that he had were reaching a point of feeling like one continuous monologue. Much of the talking to himself happened while he was driving. Most of the time, but not always, the words stayed inside his head. Only when the anxiety peaked did he blurt out fragments of sentences or accusations. And almost always, they were aimed at his youngest aunt, Lisa. And his anger about not getting his mother's share of the inheritance.

Attempting to calm himself, he got a beer from the old camp refrigerator. Opening the bottle, he went out to sit on the steps next to where he'd parked the car at the side of the camp. Lowering himself, shifting into position with his back against the porch railing, he took a long pull of the beer.

Nathaniel knew that psychologists use the term 'inner speech'. He'd once read an article in a *Scientific American* about studies of *how*, *when* and *why* people talk to themselves, from infancy all the way through old age. The article had caught his attention because he came across the magazine after the incident with his grandfather's heart attack and resulting death. Nat didn't need a study. He traced this new awareness of his own conversations to that particular evening.

"Greedy old bastard," he said aloud, recalling the night. He took another swig of beer.

The money. Lisa and Sandi were in line to get all of it now, if he was unable to prevail on a judge to release his mother's portion. And his lawyer had indicated that he was going to need access to funds from somewhere – sooner rather than later – to continue moving the case through the court.

It came to him in a flash. "I wasn't there," he said out loud, resting the beer bottle on his knee.

Then he whispered, "I was right here. In Vermont."

Now the voice went internal again. He began working on how he could use the excuse that he'd been staying at a friend's camp and was *not* in Rhode Island when a guy on a street got shot in the rain. Never mind that there could be a chance that it was something he might never have to deal with, that somehow, some other suspect could deflect suspicion away from him. Better to have a solid alibi and get it down pat before he had to improvise on the spot.

The voice went quiet. Or was subdued by thoughts on how to create a believable story. He would then go back to Rhode Island, go see his lawyer in person, push for the hearing date, get the money.

Going back to a gray, rainy afternoon from his youth, Nathaniel conjured up a memory of a teacher from seventh grade; Miss Wade. The woman was amazing in the way she could command the attention of every student in the room, even the slackers.

He could see her now, standing with her back against a tall bookshelf at the side of the class room, auburn hair and a magnificent bosom restrained under her white blouse. She was reading aloud from a literary anthology.

What he now realized was the way she nearly hypnotized her students and brought the stories to life as she was reading; it was with her pacing, with pauses and using different voices, through her inflection and breathing. She would find the absolute right spot in the story to *stop*, softly close the book, gaze around at her students and then seductively offer up just the slightest of a smile.

Nathaniel wasn't sure if other students found the smile seductive, but he did. Then and now. The effect those readings had on him, she always read aloud when she was introducing a new work from the anthology, was to make Nathaniel *want* to read the rest of the story. And he always did.

Until the following year, eighth grade. That's when he began to think that most of the teachers were boring and predictable. From that year onward, he'd trudged his way to becoming an unmotivated, mediocre student who did enough only not to fail his courses.

The inner voices, *they* could help make his story believable.

Empty beer bottle in his left hand, Nathaniel opened his eyes and looked around. A thinning canopy of green, yellow, orange and red leaves glistened through the surrounding trees. Perhaps more soaked leaves on the ground than still on the branches.

He focused on just one voice. The slow, deliberate, confident cadence that could have been his mother. But in his head, it was a man's voice.

"It's a lie," Nathaniel said out loud. "She... is... lying," he enunciated, then added, "My mother *wanted* me to have this money."

Another voice whispered to Nathaniel, "Prove it."

Forty Two

Texting as though we were playing ping pong, or perhaps a digital game of tag, Louie and I settled on a place in Cranston called Marchetti's, another Italian restaurant that had been around for a long time and gotten great reviews, at least according to Becky.

The Ragsdales would get off the highway on their way back north from Newport and I would make the fifteen-minute drive south. We agreed to meet at seven, so I had a couple of hours to do whatever. Walking across the lobby of the Hilton Providence, I thought how overused that word has become, *whatever*! I could hear a reverb-enhanced male voice on a Vermont FM radio station that regularly proclaimed that the station played, 'Whatever, whenever.' Okay.

I took the elevator down one level to the hotel's business center, a small room with three computers and one printer. Nobody else was there. I logged on and began a search for 'retired NCAA basketball officials/referees.'

Overwhelming. *Seventeen* pages of links to related stories.

'Candid Coaches: who is the best referee in college

basketball? Ref considering retirement after controversial call in UNC game. First Female NBA Ref Retires. Your List of the *Worst* College Basketball Referees.'

Enough stories, opinions and video clips to make you want to go play croquet. Nothing in anything that I bothered to read showed any indication that I was likely to find the name Billy Woodson.

Next, I went to the website for The Providence Journal, clicked on 'All Access' and scrolled to FAQs. If I subscribe, what can I get? It took all of two minutes to discover that the site archive tools would only take me back to 2013. Come on. This paper's been around since the administration of Andrew Jackson. So where are your archives from forty years ago?

After reading an update story on the Rhode Island gubernatorial race – incumbent Gina Raimondo versus Cranston Mayor Allan Fung, the election less than a month away – I logged off, stood up, stretched and left the room.

Stepping off the elevator directly in front of me was the woman I'd met at the hotel bar, Lisa Bryan. We'd exchanged business cards before she went to her room last night.

Now, she was wearing a bathing suit and carrying a large white towel. She looked at me, gave the slightest of smiles and offered a distracted greeting.

"Hey," she said.

"Hi."

She appeared to be lost in concentration when she

saw me. Or maybe upset about the murdered friend and her meeting with Detective Dyer. The demeanor was certainly different from last night.

"Coming or going?" I said, gesturing to the door of the pool behind me.

Cute, Hanlon. She's getting *off* the elevator. You're getting on. The towel would appear to be dry. Any other greeting you'd like to try?

She nodded toward the pool, her smile up a notch.

"I need to do some laps," she said. "It's been a difficult day."

My mind scrambling to get back to some spot other than 'not so cool', I heard my voice saying, "Have any plans for dinner?"

At six-forty-five, we met in the lobby. I had been there for ten minutes when Lisa came down. She wore black slacks, a magenta colored, sleeveless silk top and was carrying a sweater, maybe it was a shawl, sort of ivory or beige. She had a small black handbag on a strap over her left shoulder. I tried not to look at her shoes as she now appeared to be an inch taller than me.

But the smile was back.

"Are you sure this is a good idea?" she said.

"What?"

"Your friends. They don't know that you are bringing someone to dinner. Am I correct?"

I hesitated, not positive that I'd should say my first

thought. Nonetheless, I had at it.

"Becky will be happy that I invited you. Her husband, Louie," I shook my head, "has probably been *wagering* with her since we arrived in Providence three days ago as to just how soon I was going to have a date. He has this penchant for, uh… an ongoing, let's call it a 'crystal ball analysis' regarding my personal life. Louie smugly likes to predict, then *confirm*, much of what I do. Especially when it comes to women."

"So, this is a date?"

"We're going to dinner, aren't we?"

The parking lot at Marchetti's was crowded. I found a spot near the far end and we walked back to the front of the building. Small trees in planters along a terrace wall and a couple of white, wooden benches on either side of the entrance.

The last text I'd sent to Louie, an hour earlier, said 'Get a table for 4'. I didn't bother to expand on it and deliberately had not bothered to look at his reply. As soon as we got inside, his smirk stood out from all the other faces, people waiting to be seated. Becky had her back turned and didn't see us come in.

"Thought that you might have some pull here," I said by way of greeting. "How long's the wait?"

Becky turned to face us. Unlike her husband's grin, Becky's smile was warm and welcoming.

I made introductions. Could've been my imagination,

but the polite 'hello' that Lisa gave to both Becky and Louie, was not in the bemused, laid-back manner I had observed when we met last night. She seemed to have gone to a 'shy and reserved' setting.

After a couple minutes of small talk about their visit to Newport, a young woman showed us to a booth. Framed photos of celebrities and other people all along the walls, as well as behind the bar, and two flat screen TVs above the liquor bottles. Every seat at the bar was occupied.

Lisa quietly observed the banter between Louie and me, with Becky slipping in a comment or question to keep us in check. If not on his 'best' behavior, Ragsdale was doing okay. One might think that all our conversations were like this. We stayed clear of wisecracks, or smartass critiques of other patrons. Louie did give me a quick head nod and eye roll at one man seated at the bar. He looked to be about six-five and three-hundred pounds, the kind of guy you would want on your side no matter what you were doing.

We shared fried calamari and stuffed mushroom caps to start. Becky ordered Fettuccini Alfredo, Lisa went for Tortellini Carbonara, Louie asked for the Broiled Seafood Platter and I had to try their homemade Lasagna. We agreed on a carafe of the house red wine, a Chianti.

All through dinner, Lisa responded to questions from Becky or me, but never initiated any of the conversation. Her answers were short. She was clearly somewhere else. Maybe this wasn't such a good idea. And in thirty-minutes of eating, Louie offered up maybe a total of five words. But the food was delicious.

After splitting an order of Tiramisu and a grapenut pudding, we paid the bill and were out of the restaurant by eight-thirty. The air was a little cool, but the dampness of the past couple of days was gone.

"You driving all the way home tonight?" I said to Louie. He shook his head.

"We're staying at my brother's," Becky said. "It's less than two hours from here."

"John. He lives out by Greenfield, yes?" I said.

"Orange. Right along Route 2. We'll go through the backroads in the morning and get on 91 in Northfield," Louie added. "Make it home by noon."

"It was so nice to meet you," Becky said, shaking hands with Lisa.

"Yes, the same, thank you. And *thank you* for dinner," Lisa said, turning to shake hands with Louie.

"You're welcome. Make Hanlon drive carefully. He's not used to traffic," Louie said.

"Hey. They see the Vermont plates, they'll know. Stay clear! This guy's liable to wander anywhere."

"You'd think he was following a hillbilly goat trail the way he drives," Louie went on. He gave me the shoulder punch and added, "Be careful."

Forty Three

As Lisa fastened her seatbelt, I was thinking that I had not told Ragsdale anything, nothing at all, about her connection to the man who had been shot on the street. Had he or Becky known that, it might have helped to explain her reticence throughout dinner.

"Becky and Louie were with me on Friday night," I began. "We were in the pub right after your friend was killed."

Lisa looked at me. "Oh. So, they know?"

"Yeah. Actually, I'm surprised that Louie didn't bring it up."

She took a deep breath.

"I didn't tell you this before," I went on, "but Louie is an undercover cop. Works all over New England, mostly with drug enforcement squads, state and local police. And a few feds scattered here and there."

"Is that what you do working with him?" she said. I shook my head.

"No. Anything that I do is really outside official law enforcement agencies. I work for companies and private citizens." I laughed, then added, "Louie likes to say that it's somewhere between Magnum PI and Morning Joe."

"There must be tens of thousands of people who do that in California. Men and women," she said.

"Private Eyes? I'll bet. I suspect, however, that they get *paid* a lot more than I do."

"Don't be so sure. You would be surprised how many people work at two, or three different jobs at the same time," she said.

"But, it never rains in southern California, right?" I said.

"I know that song."

"Still hear it occasionally. Can't remember the artist," I said. "Louie would know. And the year."

I turned the radio on and hit the SEEK button for FM stations. We sat for a minute. After it had looped through multiple three-second sound bites and started the cycle again, I tapped the button to stop at 88.3 as they were playing Fleetwood Mac's *Rhiannon*.

"You okay with this?" I said.

"Sure," Lisa said.

Adjusting the volume lower, I slipped the car in gear and slowly pulled out of the parking lot. Louie's bullshit about my driving notwithstanding, I carefully signaled the turn out onto the street. Only a few cars in either direction. We would be on the highway and back in Providence by nine o'clock.

I was not going to ramble on at Lisa just to get a conversation going. If she wanted to say something, I'm sure she would. Hanlon: never miss an opportunity to keep your mouth shut.

As I was observing the speed limit on I-95, signaling for the exit to downtown, Lisa pointed at the radio.

"Hear that?" she said. "My school." The guy on a show called '*Rock of Ages*' had just done a station ID – WQRI, Bristol, Rhode Island.

I looked over at her. From the glow of the dashboard, I could see that a smile was back.

"Really?"

"Roger Williams University. Class of 2001."

Quick math. That would make her probably 39, maybe 40.

"Huh. Afraid I know nothing about the school. I *do* remember who Roger Williams was," I said. "Must be a small school. What's the enrollment?"

"Probably close to five-thousand now. It was less when I was there."

"Bristol. That's on the water, right?" I said.

"Water all around. The school is on a peninsula. Narragansett Bay is on one side, Mount Hope Bay on the other."

"What was your major?"

"Management."

I glanced at her again. She pursed her lips and nodded in the affirmative. "Yep. I thought that I would go to grad school and get an MBA."

"And you did. Or didn't?"

"Did not."

Silence. Except for the radio, which I turned off. We were approaching the Hilton Providence. I turned into the spot in front of the hotel where I'd first seen Lisa arriving with her rolling suitcase. Moving up the ramp to the parking deck, I hit the button and took a self-park ticket.

We walked back to the revolving front door and went inside.

"Care for a drink?" I said. The smile.

"Sure. Why not?"

It appeared that she was coming back to maybe a 'neutral' zone from wherever she'd been most of the evening. Again, could've been my imagination, but I thought that I detected a somewhat more at ease in her body language, as well. And her tone sounded much like the previous night, when she'd toyed with me about 'taking my seat' to the Dunkin Donuts Center.

We walked into The Vig and sat at one of the tables.

Phil Dyer had finished thirty sit-ups and ended his exercise routine with three, two-minute planks. He did this every-other-night, working out for just shy of half-an-hour. He would then stand in the hottest shower he could take for five minutes, abruptly changing to ten seconds of cold spray down over his head, shoulders and back. When he'd finished, before toweling off, he would stand completely relaxed, as though he was a model for a Rodin sculpture.

Exercise and shower over, before going to bed, he would sit at his kitchen table, in his gym shorts, slowly drinking an eight-ounce glass of orange juice. Only his wife knew about this rather odd regimen. Everyone at work presumed that his fitness schedule revolved around a couple of early mornings a week in the weight room, and the occasional pick-up basketball game where most of the players were considerably older than Phil.

But it was this late in the evening drill that both strengthened his core and leveled him at the same time. Sitting at the table, even after he'd finished drinking the juice, allowed him to process everything that had occurred that day. Though the workouts were spaced for alternate nights, the kitchen table routine with the orange juice was a nightly habit.

It was going on ten o'clock. Phil's wife, a teacher, was already in bed. She'd had the holiday off but spent most of the evening preparing for a new week with fifth-grade students at the George J. West Elementary School in Providence.

Part of the post exercise 'processing' gave him time to think clearly. First about his wife, then his parents and his extended family. Once that compartment was intellectually and emotionally locked-down for another day, he would shift focus to whatever happened to be the most pressing issue or case within the department. In twenty-three years on the force, the Providence PD, particularly the Detective Bureau, never lacked for pressing challenges.

Tomorrow morning he would dig deeper into the 2017 boating incident involving Nathaniel Crane and the disappearance of Crane's mother. Pull and read everything he could get his hands on; Coast Guard account, Massachusetts State Police summary when Crane was questioned after the two fishermen brought him ashore, and any newspaper accounts of the story. Angelo could contact the insurance carrier that had a policy for the boat.

Others would either find, or *not find*, the Mitsubishi Eclipse. If and when that happened, and *where*, obviously it could expedite the chances of finding Crane.

Flesh out the motive. How did Crane know that Clifton Torres' was in Rhode Island? Where was Crane on the night of the shooting? Does the man own a 9-millimeter gun, like the one that fired the bullets that killed Torres?

Will took the glass to the sink, rinsed it and placed it in the top rack of the dishwasher. Turning out the kitchen light, he quietly walked down the hall to the bedroom, whispering to himself, "Where are you tonight, Nathaniel Crane?"

Forty Four

My suggestion for a night cap was Bailey's Irish Cream. "A good finish to the grapenut pudding," I said. Lisa agreed. The woman working the bar was back with the drinks while we sat in silence watching a playoff baseball game on one of the overhead TVs. The sound was on mute and the Red Sox were ahead.

Stirring my drink with its little red straw, I had a marketing flash.

"Whatd'ya think of the idea of some pub serving these with a tiny, plastic Leprechaun hat on the end of the stirrer?" I said.

"They're probably already doing that somewhere in Ireland," she said, holding her glass to me for a toast. "Go Sox," she added.

We each took a sip. Mine was pretty good. Sorry that I didn't have more of the pudding to go with it. I put the glass on the table, then dabbed my mouth with a paper napkin in case any cream might be in my beard.

"So, tell me about Roger Williams University," I said. "Why did you go there?"

"Friends were going to enroll there. I wasn't exactly

sure what I was going to do," she said. "My dad liked the idea of me being close to home. My sister wasn't crazy about it, though. It's not in the Top 25 or anything, but it's a good school."

"You lived at home?"

She shook her head. "No. I lived on campus. Had a roommate the first two years. Then three of us shared a suite later."

"You said that you got your degree in Management?"

A nod. She was having another sip of the Irish Cream. She put her glass down.

"Would you mind if we talked about something else?" she said.

There you go, Hanlon. Wanna' ask her if she played soccer? Maybe inquire about boyfriends?

"Not at all," I said. "It's just that I had never heard of the school." I shrugged.

"No, that's perfectly OK. I don't mind," she added. "I just would like to tell you about a long conversation I had this afternoon, with my sister, Sandi."

"Sure."

"And maybe ask for some advice about something," she said.

"I'm listening," I said, and reached for my drink.

For a stretch of what seemed like a solid half-an-hour, Lisa methodically recounted not just the tense, start-and-stop discussions earlier in the day with her sister, but backtracked through family events covering much of her adult life, interspersed with a few stories from childhood and adolescence. Her tone was steady, only slightly louder than a whisper, and the pacing was that of someone wanting to make sure that the listener was getting all the details.

She did pause briefly when the bartender asked if we wanted another drink. We declined but asked instead for water. She brought two glasses and then left us alone. Lisa picked up the saga pretty much in the same neighborhood of the things she had told me the night before. Specifically, coming around to talk about Cliff Torres, expanding on why she was here now and what she hoped to accomplish.

Taking a drink of water, moving slightly forward on the high stool, straightening her shoulders and looking directly into my eyes, she waited a beat. I didn't say a word.

"So, the lawyer I told you about? He's a little more understanding of why I agreed to have Cliff see what he could find out on Nathaniel. He *did* say that it might have been better to have discussed it with him first, since he knows and works with a number of private investigators," she said.

I nodded. "I'm sure."

Again, a pause, but she maintained the eye contact. Pursing her lips, inhaling through her nose, which swelled her shoulders and chest, she wagged a finger at me as though I was about to be scolded.

"Now-w," she exaggerated, "*here* is what I would like some advice on."

"Okay, shoot." I regretted using the word about a millisecond after my brain let it out. It didn't seem to bother Lisa.

"When I talk to Kevin Byrne tomorrow, he's our lawyer, and I tell him all about the long talk with Sandi, do I tell him to go ahead with hiring someone to find out about Nathaniel's activities?"

My turn to wait a beat. I took a sip of water.

"Well, I think that would depend," I said.

"On what?"

"If you have told all of this to Detective Dyer, which I believe you said earlier that you had, they're going to be all over it. For all we know, they may *already* know where he is," I said, then added, "They could have him scheduled for a little interview as we speak."

Giving her my two-handed, open palms 'correct' gesture, I waited for a response. Zip. She wanted more.

"No matter what, though, you have to tell the lawyer. He may have information on your nephew that he's tucked away in the file waiting until you get to court."

"I know he does," she said. "He assured me that we would review all of that before we appear in front of a judge."

"So, back to 'finding out about Nathaniel'. I'm not sure what to tell you there. I mean, it's a bit *late* if, in fact, he really killed Torres. The cops are going to run that down, pretty quickly, I would imagine. And if Nathaniel has gone back to Wyoming, or some other place, I'm not sure that a local gumshoe is going to make much progress. Gotta take 'em a while just to get up to speed."

Lisa's smile had returned. Then she laughed. "Did you really say *gumshoe*?"

"Ahem. I think the term came into existence when shoes had soft soles and one could sneak around quietly," I said, hoping to save face. Not a chance. She laughed again.

"Do you watch a lot of old movies?"

"Never," I said.

"I think that you are not being completely truthful with me."

"Once in a while, maybe. When nothing else is on," I said.

"And *you* are not a gumshoe?"

"Nope."

Forty Five

"Reckon you know cops are lookin' for ya? Anyways, lookin' for a car like that one," Dean Chase said, motioning with his head and right shoulder toward Nathaniel Crane's black, two door Mitsubishi parked next to the camp.

Chase was standing on the porch looking at Crane, who now held the door open and was momentarily startled to hear a knock at 10 o'clock at night. Crane held the pistol behind his back.

"Looking for *me*? Why do you think that?" Crane said, attempting to feign surprise.

Chase gave him the 'crusty old Vermonter' stare, just a trace of knowing smile that conveyed 'don't horseshit me, fancy boy'. Chase nodded.

"Wyoming license plate sounds just like that one," Chase said. Again, the head jerk in the direction of the car. "Pretty sure what I heard was 22-1285-zero," he added.

Crane said nothing, but looked down at his feet, trying to come up with a reply that would sound plausible. He moved his left arm behind his back and pulled his shoulders back at the same time in a stretching motion. He shoved the gun into the back of his waist band, then stretched both arms over his head and yawned.

"Excuse me," he said, faking another yawn. "I'd just fallen asleep in the chair," he lied. But then he had his reply. Crane stepped forward onto the porch, forcing Chase to move back a step.

"Damn parking tickets," Crane said. "I must have a dozen over the summer. All in Providence."

Only light from the kitchen falling onto the porch, so Crane might not have registered that Dean Chase was not buying it.

"Sounds like I better haul my ass back and take care of them before they impound my car. And *fine* me three times what the tickets are," Crane said.

Somewhere out in the woods, close to the camp, an owl gave a high-pitched call. Nathaniel Crane turned his head in the direction of the sound. Neither man spoke. The owl called again.

"What *is* that?" Crane said.

"Barn owl," Chase said. "First time you heard it?"

"Yeah."

"He's around 'bout every night. Time of the fall when they're lookin' for more food," Chase said.

More silence, then the owl. It sounded like a squeaky screen door closing, a rather long k-r-r-rick.

"How'd you find out they're looking for my car?" Crane said.

"Scanner," Chase said, jerking a thumb in the

direction of his truck. "I keep it on when I'm out doing errands."

"State police?"

"Dispatcher for county sheriff," Chase said. "Suspect if he's got it, state police had it first."

"Sounds like I better go see somebody before I get arrested," Crane said.

"Sheriff's office is in Newfane. On Jail Street, off Route 30. There's a sign tells you where to turn."

"Thanks. I'll go over first thing in the morning," Crane said.

Back in the cab of his truck, Dean Chase patted Duke on the neck. He was sitting straight, ears up, eyes locking off into the darkness. And he certainly heard the owl.

"Parking tickets my pecker," Chase said, scratching Duke's left ear. The dog's eyes stayed focused on the windshield. Turning the key in the ignition, Chase turned his lights on and began backing out onto the dirt track that led back down to the road.

It had been around Labor Day when Chase had told a man in Newfane that he would come take a look at his barn, talk about removing an old milking shed so they could jack the barn up to pour a new concrete floor.

"Well, tomorrow's good a day as any, I s'pose," he said to himself. "Quick stop at the sheriffs on the way back through town," he continued advising himself, at the same time keeping his right hand on Duke's neck while he eased along out onto the road and turned in the other direction.

"Might be not a half-bad idea, ya think?"

Forty Six

We stood just inside the door of my hotel room, fourteenth floor of the Hilton Providence. Daybreak, now twenty minutes along, was coming through the large window behind us. Perhaps the rain had finally moved up the coast.

Lisa held both of my hands, gently, playfully pulling as though she was trying to get me to move off the spot. We were standing approximately seven inches apart, not quite touching. Clothes back on, she *was* a half-inch taller than me. In her shoes. I was still barefoot.

"I really don't know what to say," she managed, in a soft whisper. My thought was that she'd been rather vocal about an hour ago. And the smile, at this moment, could only be classified as a tease, as in, 'I probably *could* say quite a bit if only I put my mind to it.'

Pulling my left hand free, I placed it on her neck, leaned in and kissed her right ear. Her hair tickled my nose.

We studied each other's face for a few seconds.

"You... don't... have to say... anything," I said. And meant it.

She raised her right arm and gently took hold of the back of my neck, pulling me toward her. It was a light, soft kiss, unlike much of the energy-filled, mouth-to-mouth, tongue exploring contact that we'd experienced over the past few hours.

"Do you know what time it is?" she asked, looking over my shoulder at the draperies I'd left open.

I shrugged. My watch was on the night stand next to the bed.

"Must be close to seven o'clock," I said. "I think the sun is up out there somewhere."

She had both of my hands again, swung them out to the side, then back together so our wrists were touching. She took in a deep breath.

"I *do* know what to say," she said.

"Okay."

She kissed me again. "Thank you."

"Pretty amazing," I said, giving her my best smile, which most likely would be classified as somewhat understated.

Releasing my right hand, she picked up her purse from the floor and put the strap over her shoulder. She turned to open the door. After poking her head out into the corridor, she turned back to face me. I laughed.

"You're down on ten," I said. "You remember where the elevator is, just over there to the right."

She nodded, started through the door, her fingers slowly releasing my hand.

"If you still have my card," I said, "my cell number's on it. Maybe give me a call later in the day?"

"I think I lost it," she said.

"Bummer."

Just another ounce of tease for good measure. She patted her purse. "Right here."

The smile, then she added, "*Yes*, I will call you."

"Great."

After a shower and getting dressed, I took the elevator to the lobby, went outside and around the corner to a Dunkin Donuts shop. It was small, shoehorned into a street level space which was part of the Hilton. And it was right next door to... the *Dunkin Donuts Center*.

Two guys who looked to be college age were seated at a table, travel bags on the floor next to them. They struck me as being jocks of some type. In line in front of me was a man, maybe sixty, who asked the younger men if they wanted anything to eat. Both declined. He had three cups of coffee in a carton and sat down across from them.

There was no trace of facial or physical resemblance among the three. The younger men were considerably taller. I decided that maybe the older guy was their coach. Or, maybe an agent.

I ordered a large dark roast coffee and a veggie egg white omelet on a croissant. The guy behind the counter brought me the coffee. The sandwich would be ready in two minutes., he said, handing me a receipt showing date, time and order number. It had a pink DD sticker inviting me to download the on-the-go mobile ordering app. Maybe not.

Taking the coffee to a table next to the other men, I put the cup down and placed my phone on the table next to it. Looking around, no newspapers anywhere in sight. Should've taken a copy of USA Today from the lobby. Guess we'll have to get the news online this morning. I swiped the screen on my phone and brought up Google News. It took all of fifteen seconds and four different headlines to persuade me there was nothing I urgently needed to read.

As I was typing in providencejournal.com, the man at the counter called my number. I put the phone down and walked back to fetch the breakfast sandwich

Eating, sipping coffee and half listening to the men at the next table, I was slowly scrolling through local stories when my phone vibrated. The screen showed an incoming call; a 401 area code, so I knew that it was a Rhode Island number.

"Michael Hanlon," I said.

"Morning. It's Phil Dyer."

"Detective. How are you doing?"

"I'm good. Have some news thought you may want to

know about," he said. His voice was clipped and to the point. My quick assumption was that there had been a new development on the Friday night murder. But he wouldn't call about that.

"What's up?" I said.

"Billy Woodson was taken to the ER earlier this morning. Looks like he had a stroke."

"Oh, no. I'm sorry to hear that. Do they think he's going to be okay?" I said.

"Don't know yet. Father Mike says might have been an aneurysm. They have him stabilized, he was sleeping ten minutes ago."

The men at the next table were getting up to leave, laughing about something and it was difficult to hear what Dyer was saying.

"Hang on just a minute," I said, placing my hand over the phone and waiting for the guys to clear out. When they were at the door, I got back on the phone.

"Sorry. Too much background noise. It's okay now."

"Billy asked about you," Dyer said.

"What?"

"Yeah. Asked the priest if the 'radio guy' was coming to interview him."

I didn't know what to make of that.

"Might be confused," Dyer said. "They've got him on something, maybe he was hallucinating."

"No, I did tell him that I would like to come back some time and talk a little more."

"Well, thought you'd like to know," Dyer added. "Let me give you a number for Father Mike. If you want to see Billy, probably oughta call first."

He gave me a phone number and was about to hang up.

"Can I ask," I said, "anything new on the Friday night shooting?"

"Not really. Maybe end of the day."

"Thank you for letting me know about Billy. I would like to go see him."

"Call first."

"Got it. Thanks."

The plan had been to check out of the hotel this morning, take my time driving west out through Connecticut, then north along the New York border and double back into Vermont at Glens Falls. After all the rain, I wanted to see what the foliage was like in southern New England. I wasn't due to get Rocco from the kennel until Thursday.

But that plan was before last night, prior to Lisa Bryan making it clear that she wanted, perhaps needed, a little intimacy. And it was *before* I had responded to her company, the way she had responded to me, and before either of us got very little sleep.

Yep, pretty amazing.

Now, a man that I'd barely known for three days,

possibly hanging on to his life, was asking if I was coming to see him.

I threw my napkin and sandwich wrapper into the trash, took the coffee and headed back around the corner to the hotel.

Forty Seven

Nathaniel Crane had all his personal belongings back in the car and had the camp closed-up by 7:45 on Tuesday morning. There was no doubt in his mind that Dean Chase was not a man who would just let this slide. He would tell someone.

'That old bumpkin is way too sly for his own good,' the inner voice said. 'Fuck him. I will be long gone before he shows up again.'

Exactly *where* he would be 'long gone' to, was still uncertain. He'd spent most of the night wide awake, exploring, dismissing, and then formulating new options. Shortly after five-thirty, it was still dark out, he was closer to a diversion that he thought made the most sense; go back to his mother's house in East Greenwich and take her car.

He would avoid using the interstates and the main highways. East through the backroads across rural New Hampshire, then south down through the smaller towns in Massachusetts and slip into Rhode Island somewhere near Woonsocket. Nat was familiar with plenty of the lesser traveled routes that could get him in the back way. The drive could take four hours, but he needed to be really careful.

After his brief exchange on the porch last night with Dean Chase, one thing he'd decided quickly was that he would, in fact, place a call to the Windham County Sheriff's office. Tell them who he was, that he'd just learned that his car and registration was being circulated among law enforcement agencies and that he was on his way home to Wyoming.

He would continue with the lie about parking violations in Providence, which he planned to settle up as soon as he got home. If he got any shit from the sheriff's office, he would say that it was critical that he get back to Wyoming to help a friend who was coping with emotional and psychological issues.

The real trip, to East Greenwich, would allow time to settle on the plan he believed could work. All the back-and-forth he'd gone through over the past several hours, quick bursts of ideas, followed by equally quick retreats, there were three constants: the money, his lawyer and his two aunts.

Lisa Bryan felt more at peace this morning than she had since getting the news of Cliff Torres' murder four says earlier.

A jumble of anxious thoughts, feelings of guilt, a long plane trip across the country, a marginally productive outcome in the meeting with her attorney. Then a very difficult conversation with her sister Sandi, highlighted by an after-the-fact explanation of why she had agreed to let Cliff become involved. All of this brought on a body/mind tension that was almost unbearable. She had nearly shut down completely, not a thing she would normally do.

After dinner with this Michael Hanlon and his friends, during which Lisa was polite, but distant, she found herself desperately wanting to talk to someone, get another perspective on what seemed like *way too much* unresolved grief and anger. She was very aware of having bottled-up much of how she felt for the past year. Some relief came by way of visits to a therapist in California, as well as establishing a weekly exercise routine at a fitness facility not far from her office.

Then, last night, it all just flowed. First, the near full confessional she'd delivered to Hanlon, followed by the quiet assent in the elevator. But when the door opened on ten, she'd looked at Hanlon and said, "Could we talk a while longer?"

Now, eight hours later, Lisa was certain that she and Hanlon had both known before he opened the door to his room that 'conversation' was not at the top of the agenda. This was borne out by the fact that few words had been exchanged between midnight and daybreak.

Stretched out in a chair now, wrapped in a towel with her hair still wet from the shower, she sipped hotel room coffee. She entertained one new thought, really, a question.

'Now what?'

Dyer and Angelo stood in the parking lot next to the Dean Street entrance of the Public Safety Building. They were talking about the Red Sox and the recent news of the team's Triple A affiliate in Pawtucket and plans to move that team to Worcester, Massachusetts.

The sky was overcast, but it hadn't rained for nearly 12 hours. Uniformed officers were exiting the building and heading for patrol cars. A few waves from some of the cops and then Dyer turned back to face Angelo.

"Even if he brings it up," Dyer said, "*don't* respond. If you let him get started, we'll be taking up a collection to pay legal fees to help keep the team here."

Angelo laughed. "Hey, he has season tickets. I've gone with him to three games this year."

"Stay away from it, I'm tellin' ya. You'll get the Major involved, the Journal will run a story, then the shit will hit... the... fan. You'd be better off going public on *who* you support for governor."

"Okay. I'll keep my mouth shut," Angelo said.

"Speaking of the Major," Dyer said, pointing toward the building, "let's see what's coming down today."

At 7:52 AM, Dyer and Angelo came off the elevator and down the hall in tandem. They greeted Leonor Santos, the chief Administrative Assistant to Lapan. She was also perceived by some as the Detective Bureau's unofficial den mother.

"Good morning to *you*," Leonor said. "Angelo. Captain O'Halleran is looking to have a word with you."

Dyer stopped abruptly, turned to face Angelo, placed a finger to his lips and shook his head.

Forty Eight

At 8:03 AM, the Windham County Sheriff's Office in Newfane, Vermont received a call from a man who identified himself as Nathaniel Crane. The call lasted less than thirty seconds and it was recorded.

"My name is Nathaniel Crane. I just found out that police in Rhode Island are looking for my car, a Mitsubishi Eclipse. Wyoming registration 22-12850. This is the first I'm hearing about this. It's all about some parking tickets."

A woman's voice, speaking for the sheriff's office interjected, "Just a second, please."

But Crane went on. "Doesn't matter. I'm on my way west, going back to help a friend. I'll deal with the tickets as soon as I get back to Wyoming."

He disconnected the call. A minute later, Crane was back on the highway, Vermont's lightly traveled Route 112, only ten minutes from the Massachusetts border. He would take his time.

The dispatcher played the recorded phone call for the Sheriff, who then placed a call to the Providence PD with news of Crane's contact from minutes earlier.

At 8:42, Phil Dyer's phone vibrated. He looked at the screen and recognized the number as being that of the Desk Sergeant, two floors below his office.

Dyer raised his right hand enough to catch Major Lapan's eye, pointed at this phone, then to the door and quietly excused himself from the department's morning update meeting.

"This is Dyer. Someone called me," he said, stepping away from the conference room door.

"Just heard from a sheriff in Vermont," a man's voice said. "They took a call this morning on the Wyoming car you're looking for." Dyer didn't recognize the man's voice bringing him this news.

"Who's this?" he said.

"Sergeant Mendez"

"Hey, Sergeant Mendez," Dyer said. "Tell me about the call."

"The sheriff's name is Kenneth Clarkson. Called it in himself. Said their dispatcher spoke with a man who identified himself as Nathaniel Crane. Claimed he didn't know anyone was looking for him. Said it was about unpaid parking tickets and he would take care of it he got back to Wyoming."

"Did the sheriff say what time they got the call?" Dyer said.

"Maybe twenty minutes ago."

"He leave his number?"

"He did. Ready?"

"Go ahead," Dyer said, pulling a ballpoint pen from an inside pocket of his jacket and wrote the number on the palm of his left hand, trying not to drop the phone.

"Thanks," he said. As soon as he ended the call, Dyer tapped in the Vermont number to connect with the sheriff.

Nathaniel Crane's attorney was ready to file with the Probate Court in East Greenwich, asking for an expedited hearing on his client's request that the judge order release of funds from the estate of Sophia Crane. The basis for the request was to allow his client to pay legal fees and associated costs in preparing to defend himself in a civil action brought by the two sisters of Sophia Crane.

The attorney, Jeffrey Egan, had, so far, managed to keep Nathaniel Crane from diminishing the case by speaking to the media. That had not been an easy task. Crane had badgered his lawyer to let him go public. Other than a short statement to a local newspaper reporter immediately following his August, 2017 rescue at sea by two fishermen, Crane had followed the attorney-imposed gag order.

Throughout the media stories and speculation of more than a year, Attorney Egan's unwavering, concisely worded response to queries from the press had been, "My client will have his day in court. I am confident that Mr. Crane will be able to show that what he reported to the US Coast Guard, is, in fact, what actually occurred in the tragedy that took the life of his mother."

Egan, just like all the reporters he declined to speak with, was unaware of a potentially explosive new development that would connect Nathaniel Crane to a recent murder in downtown Providence.

The Columbus Day weekend storm that dumped nearly 12 inches of rain on Rhode Island, was now moving across the maritime provinces of eastern Canada. The weather in southern New England was beginning to return to normal, as in clearing skies and warmer, October temperatures.

Driving through the rural towns of Massachusetts, observing the speed limit and coming to a full stop at every STOP sign, Nathaniel Crane opened the moon roof on his car. The sun felt good, the air smelled clean and fresh.

It was 9:48, still two-plus hours from his mother's home in East Greenwich.

Forty Nine

Lisa Bryan's phone played a series of repeating chimes. It continued to play the same ringtone through five cycles before the call went to voicemail.

"Lisa. It's Nathaniel. I'm on my way to Wyoming, but I would like to talk to you. *Without* the lawyers," he said. "I'm driving in upstate New York, not great cell phone reception. Please call me. If you don't get me, tell me the best time to call back."

Lisa heard the message when she returned from the hotel swimming pool. The voicemail showed that the call had come in at 9:53 AM, thirty minutes ago.

She tapped the screen on her phone and replayed the message. When it finished a second time, she placed the phone back on the desk next to the television. She went into the bathroom, turned the shower on, removed the wet bathing suit, wrung it out and hung it over a towel rack. She stepped into the shower.

Ten minutes later, standing in front of a steamed-up mirror and brushing her wet hair, Lisa played Nathaniel's message back in her head. 'I would like to talk to you.

Without the lawyers.'

The first thought was to call her sister Sandi. Better that Sandi be the one to speak with Nathaniel. Lisa didn't think that she could trust herself even over the phone. Following the conversation with Sandi when she tried to explain *why* she had excluded Sandi in the decision about Cliff Torres, perhaps this could help mend things.

Accepting the unlikely possibility that she could be wrong about Nathaniel's involvement with the shooting, if he had anything of substance to say, she thought this might lead to a resolution in the fight over his mother's estate. Sandi would be the better one to hear from him directly.

Walking across the hotel lot to my car, I felt a quick *zzt, zzt* signal from my phone that there was an incoming call. I stopped and looked at the screen but didn't recognize the number. Thought that it might be Father Mike calling back after I'd left him a message a few minutes earlier.

"Michael Hanlon."

"Hi. It's Lisa," she said. I was surprised. And pleased to hear from her barely three hours after she told me that 'she really didn't know what to say.'

"You beat me to it. I was going to call you," I said. "Let me guess. You thought of something else to say."

"Yes, while I was swimming. I thought of a lot of things to say. But that' not why I'm calling," she said.

"Bummer."

"You know the things I told you about my nephew. And the lawyers."

"Last night? Or do you mean the first night we talked in the bar?"

"All of it," she said, then added, "from three years ago when my father died, the explosion on the boat, my sister's body never found. Our fighting over her estate. And now, my suspicion that he could be connected to the shooting of Cliff Torres."

"Yeah. You covered it pretty thoroughly," I said. My memory was that she actually had dissected a series of events in great detail the first night we met. But I didn't say that.

"Nathaniel called me this morning."

"Really?"

"Yes, I was in the shower. He left a message saying that he would like to talk," she said.

"You might want to speak to your lawyer first. If this court case is 'on the verge of moving forward,' I think you said, your lawyer may caution you about what to say."

"I am *not* going to call Nathaniel. After the things he said the last time we spoke in person, anything that I have to convey to him, will come from our attorney. Or, perhaps from my sister." Her tone left no doubt about this point.

"That's good," I said.

"I would like to ask a favor," she said. My mind did a couple of quick, ten-yard sprints before I replied.

"Okay."

"I'm going to ask Sandi to come meet with our attorney. I would like you to talk to her too."

"*Why* would you want me to do that?" I said.

"The story that you told me the other evening, about the friend who kept it together and didn't allow emotions to interfere with a family crisis, and what you described as a prolonged legal battle."

I had, in fact, told Lisa about that very thing, a friend in Pennsylvania who managed to navigate a long slog with siblings, his late father's business partner, and God knows who else, in coming to terms and resolving numerous complicated issues after the sudden death of his father.

"Yeah, that was an impressive accomplishment," I said. "Doubt that I have to tell you much about different family dynamics, eh?"

"It's a good story. You know the people and a lot of what occurred then. That example, coming from someone objective, like *you*, it might help Sandi. And me."

I didn't respond. This seemed like a stretch. Yes, Lisa and I certainly had 'good chemistry', but acting as a buffer with her older sister, maybe leave that to professionals.

"Father Hanlon, you can do this," she teased.

"Listen to this. You know the old basketball ref I told you about?"

"Yes, Billy fast whistle. Or something?"

"Quick whistle," I said. "That's right, Billy Woodson.

Poor guy had a stroke."

"Oh, I'm sorry."

"Yeah. I'm going to the hospital to see him in a few minutes. And Billy's priest is... *Father Mike.*"

"It's a sign."

"Lisa," I exaggerated a sigh, "like my *sister*, you have been in California *too* long. It is not a sign. It just happens to be a common name, especially in my generation."

Her reply had the relaxed voice. "Can I tell you one other thing?"

"I'm all ears."

A short laugh, then she said, "Not many people still use the term 'bummer'.

Fifty

Dyer thanked the Vermont sheriff for the repeat confirmation of Nathaniel Crane's phone call. He slipped his phone back into a coat pocket, returned to the meeting and settled into his chair.

The lead detective on a case from back in the summer was describing conflicting stories from two suspects. He stated that charges were likely by the end of the day. Dyer paid minimal attention to what the detective was reporting. He'd already discussed his own case, now he was looking to the head of the table. He gave a slight shake of the head to Major Lapan.

Other than the lead on Crane, nothing of substance had been produced in the Torres case. The cops in Jersey, so far, had not been able to find anything that might offer a connection to the shooting. Dyer was frustrated. He looked at his watch. The meeting would end momentarily. Dyer would find Angelo, tell him about Crane's phone call to the sheriff, and then he would call Lisa Bryan. See if her lawyer had heard anything from the attorney representing her nephew.

Dean Chase shuffled into the sheriff's office reception area like he was looking for a lost pair of reading glasses. He walked slowly, looked at one side of the hallway, then the other, paused to gaze at some notices on the bulletin board, and finally came to a stop in front of the window separating the offices from the front entrance.

"Mornin', Bunny," he said.

The woman behind the desk looked up. Brenda Wilson was called 'Bunny' by very few people these days and when it did occur, she was quick to convey disapproval, usually with an icy stare. But when she saw that it was Dean Chase, an old friend of her grandfather that she'd known nearly all her forty-seven years, she just chuckled.

"Ken around?" Dean said.

"The sheriff had to go to Brattleboro. You just missed him," she said.

"Deputy Whistler in this mornin?"

Brenda shook her head. "On vacation."

"Hmmph. Guess that puts you in charge, huh?"

She knew that he knew there were at least three other deputies on duty. His sarcasm didn't fly.

"What can we do for you, Mr. Chase?"

Removing the stained old orange cap, he scratched one of his bushy eyebrows with the same hand, then put the cap back on.

"Listenin' to the scanner last night. Heard mention 'bout a car with a Wyomin' license plate."

Brenda clicked the computer mouse on her desk,

looked at the monitor in front of her, then stood from her chair.

"Let me see if you can speak to Sergeant Gallo," she said.

Traffic was stopped ahead, three cars and a UPS truck were in front of him and Nathaniel Crane experienced a momentary flash of panic.

Tilting his head, he could see a flagman in the road holding a traffic control sign. The man was dressed in the usual bright yellow top and pants with orange reflective tape. No sign of a police car anywhere.

After two minutes of waiting, Nathaniel looked at his phone and considered another call to his Aunt Lisa. He picked up the phone, looked at the cars in front of him and could see that the flagman was stepping back from the center of the road and about to swivel his sign to let the traffic move forward.

Placing the phone back on the seat, putting the car into gear and edging forward, he then thought of trying another call, to his Aunt Sandi, instead. He would find a spot to pull over.

'She's not a bitch like Lisa,' the inner voice said.

He drove another ten miles listening to the voice. He was now on Massachusetts Route 62 and had just passed through the town of Clinton, driving along the eastern edge of the Wachusett Reservoir. Up ahead was a boat access area. He slowed and pulled off the road next to three empty boat trailers in a gravel parking area.

Shutting off the engine and lowering the windows on both sides, he picked up his phone. Swiping through the contacts list, he found his Aunt Sandi and stared at the number.

'Call her,' the voice said.

Fifty One

I met Father Mike in one of the side visitor areas of the front entrance at the Rhode Island Hospital. Thin, just under six feet tall, dark hair graying at the temples and at the back of his neck. He wore a clerical shirt with neckband, dark slacks and a lightweight forest green parka that doubled as a rain coat.

"Mr. Hanlon," he said, extending his right hand.

"Michael," I said. "Just like you."

He smiled, released my hand and motioned to some chairs away from the entrance.

"Let's sit over here," he said. The smile was warm and engaging. I followed him.

As soon as we were settled, watching this man of maybe sixty, I thought, 'Wow. He really is at peace with the world.' Quickly checking that, my next thought was, 'How could one possibly *know* that about someone else?'

"From the Book of Daniel," he said, holding the smile.

"Sorry?"

"Michael. From the Hebrew mīkhā'ē'l" he said, "he who is like God." He chuckled and added, "Of course, *we* know him as Saint Michael the Archangel."

I was embarrassed by my ignorance of anything pertaining to The Bible. The best I could offer was something I'd been told by a friend, a minister in Vermont. At a small birthday gathering for me a few years ago, he'd read a passage from The Book of Revelation.

"The one who led God's armies against Satan, the war in heaven," I said.

"That he did," Father Mike said. "Helped kick the out the bad angels."

Shifting his body, leaning back in the chair and clasping his hands together, he switched topics. "So how is that you know Billy?" he said, then quickly adding, "By the way, he's resting. They have him on the fifth floor in the Stroke Center. We can go up in a few minutes."

"I really just met him. Yesterday, in fact. We had coffee and he took me by the gym next to your church. I wanted to talk about some old ball players and referees that he knew."

"You're a sports writer?"

I shook my head. "No, I was a radio news reporter. One of the things I do now is to collect stories from people who I think have had interesting lives. I wanted to visit with Billy again. And record the conversation."

Father Mike nodded. "That explains what he was talking about. It didn't make any sense. When I first saw him after his stroke, he repeated a couple of times that he needed to 'make a recording."

"We hadn't set a time yet, but when I told him that I

would like to do it, he seemed ready," I said.

"You're in for a treat. Once you get him started, the stories just go up and down the floor like both teams running a fast break," Father Mike said.

"Yeah, I got a little preview when we were at the gym, before the kids started coming in. That's when I wished that I had my recorder with me. And I only made a few notes. So, I asked if I could come back."

"The neurologist is concerned about another stroke. They haven't decided on surgery," he said, then added, "she has a consultation later this morning. We may know what the plan is by this afternoon. Unless there's an emergency, it wouldn't happen before tomorrow."

"How do you think he's responding?"

"They got an IV started as soon as they brought him in. We don't know how long he'd been on the floor when I found him. His speech is very slow. The doc said that he can talk *at all* is a positive sign," he said.

"It's about the blood flow to the brain," I said.

He nodded. "The drug through the IV drip is to help dissolve the clot. If it's working, the surgery might not be necessary. At least for the moment."

Father Mike was one of those people who made you feel as though you'd know him forever; easy manner, nothing urgent in his tone or cadence. Almost instantly instilling a vibe that I could confide *anything* to him, this caused me to wonder about the Roman Catholic sacrament of penance through confession, something I had only read about or seen in movies.

Hospital staff and other visitors continually moved through the area, a few out patients going home assisted by a family member or friend, others coming in and stopping first at the reception desk.

Over the next ten minutes, I listened as this priest recounted how he first met Billy, alluding to 'on and off the wagon' episodes that he'd witnessed; Billy eventually getting a grip on his life; and the more recent joy of watching the old man encourage, coach and lovingly discipline many of the children who came through the church's youth programs.

Leaning forward in his chair, removing his parka and folding it twice, Father Mike looked around the hospital entrance as though he were expecting someone. Then he turned back to face me and again gave the little chuckle.

"Last week, Billy decided he would instruct two of our most energetic and restless boys on how to officiate a game," he said.

"How'd *that* go?" I said. He shook his head and laughed.

"He'd put one boy at a time out on the floor, surrounded with a brood of eight-year-olds. Gave the boy a whistle and then snapped instructions from courtside."

Bright eyes and a wide-open smile, Father Mike added, "Comical in one sense, but let me tell you, that kid with the whistle? Complete change. You could see *immediately* how serious he was taking this lesson. And how much he wanted to show Billy that he could do it."

He stood up, held the folded parka in his right hand and motioned to me with his left.

"Let's go up and see if he's awake," he said.

Billy Woodson was dreaming. It was a high school game in the early days of his officiating career. Just out of college, newly married and selling life insurance policies to men about his own age, he took as many games as he could get, eager to become a good referee.

In the bleachers at this game, circa 1964, one of the older men who ran the insurance agency Billy worked for, was yelling about a call Billy had just made against the home team. A player on the team was the man's son. The kid was frantically arguing that he had not fouled a player on the visiting team.

Then the boy had used excessive profanity. Partially restrained by his coach, who was also yelling at Billy, the player jabbed Billy's chest with a finger. His officiating partner came running across the court as Billy ejected the player and proceeded to call a Technical on the coach. Everyone in the gymnasium was on their feet.

Attempting to de-escalate the ruckus in front of the home team's bench, Billy turned his back and calmly walked away, heading for the scorer's table. Something struck him on the left side of his head. Billy went face down on the floor. The crowd noise became distant.

"Billy. What happened?"

He knew the voice, but when he tried to answer, his tongue felt like it was glued to the bottom of his mouth. It wouldn't move. And his head hurt. Had someone thrown something at him?

"Billy You'll be okay. An ambulance is on the way. Don't try to talk."

The next thing he heard was an announcement over the public address system. It was woman's voice. That was new. He didn't recall women introducing the team players.

Billy's wife was talking to him, asking him why he didn't get assigned to cover women's basketball.

His son was there, too. The boy wasn't saying anything, but Billy could see his shy expression, innocent brown eyes and the angelic smile of a young boy.

"Billy, how are ya doing, friend?"

Somebody was holding his hand. The voice was not his wife. Not one of his ref partners.

"Someone here to see you, Billy."

Fifty Two

They had Billy in a room large enough to accommodate six patients. The privacy curtains were drawn so I was not sure how many others were actually in the room at this moment.

Father Mike was speaking softly and had taken Billy's left hand. The intravenous fluid bag hung near the head of the bed connected to a line in his right arm. Another line providing oxygen was clipped to a clear plastic mask that covered his mouth and nose. Billy's head moved ever so slightly when he heard Father Mike talking. It appeared as though he was trying to open his eyes.

Gesturing with his head toward Billy while still holding his hand, Father Mike nodded to me.

"Billy," I said. "Didn't think that I was going to have to come see you *here* for our interview."

Very slowly his eyes opened for a second, then closed. I waited.

"It's Michael Hanlon, Billy. You took me to the gym yesterday. We were talking about some of the games you did a long time ago, some of the old players. And all those pesky coaches."

Again, the eyes opened slowly.

It took him a few seconds, but he was able to focus, first on Father Mike, then very slowly, he shifted his eyes to take me in. A few more seconds passed. Billy swallowed, then parted his lips. I didn't think that he was attempting to speak. He closed his eyes again.

"Would you like a drink of water, Billy?" Father Mike said.

He released his hand and looked around. There was a carafe of water and a plastic cup with a straw in a paper wrapper on the table to one side of the bed. Father Mike poured water into the cup, tore the paper from one end of the straw, placed it in the water and then removed the rest of the wrapper. He lifted the oxygen mask and held the straw close to Billy's lips.

Sandi Bryan was ladling tortellini and sausage soup from a twelve-quart cooking pot into small plastic containers for the freezer when the phone rang.

She stepped toward the counter behind her where the phone was located just as the simulated voice announced, "Call from... Wireless Caller."

The screen showed as much when the phone rang again. The answering device voice offered an encore of the 'just the facts, no inflection message'.

"Call from... Wireless Caller."

Wiping her hands on the front of her apron, Sandi picked up the handset.

"Hello."

Silence at the other end. Damn telemarketing, she thought.

"Hello," Sandi said a second time before preparing to put the handset back.

"Sandi. It's Nathaniel."

Sandi thought back to when then teenaged 'Natty' had insisted that everyone address him as Nathaniel, triggered by something that happened with him while he was away at school.

It was obvious that he was using a cellphone. The call was breaking up.

"Are you still there?" he said. "Can you hear me?"

"Yes, I can hear you, Nathaniel. I'm only *surprised* that you are calling me," she said. "We haven't spoken in over three months. The parking lot at your mother's attorney's office, remember?"

"I know. I'm sorry," he said.

Sandi didn't respond. The clock on the microwave above the stove showed 11:03. She pulled a stool away from the counter and sat. If there was going to be a conversation here, he would be the one to get it started.

Nathanial Crane watched a huge man lifting propane gas containers from a rack on the side of an *AmeriGas* truck and loading them into a metal cage in front of convenience store. The man could have been a pro football player; he was huge.

He'd stopped at this spot and parked at an angle at the side of the building, hoping to avoid having anyone spot his license plates. Now he was blocked by the truck. On the phone with his Aunt Sandi, the call wasn't going as badly as he feared that it might. She wasn't talking, but she also had not hung up.

"I'm on my way back to Wyoming," he said into the phone. "I have a friend who's having personal problems and needs some help. But, as you know, I have to come back to Rhode Island when the court date is set. My lawyer said that it could be before the end of the month."

No response from Sandi. They both seemed to be willing to wait it out. Finally, Sandi spoke.

"Lisa's handling the legal matters, Nathaniel. You know that. So why are you calling me?"

Although Lisa had not informed her before-hand of the arrangement with Cliff Torres, she had told Sandi all about the face-to-face shouting match with Nathaniel that had occurred back in August at Sophia's home. It was two days after that heated exchange, when Lisa had returned to California, that she was able to persuade Sandi to go along with more aggressive action from their attorney.

"I left a message for Lisa," he said. "This morning. She hasn't returned my call."

"There is nothing I can do about that. She will either call you or she won't."

"But you can talk to her. This can be worked out. Do we really have to go to court *again*? he said.

Sandi thought about her long conversation with Lisa from the previous afternoon. Once she'd moved beyond her disbelief, surprise and momentary anger with her sister, she had decided that she was more on board than not. By the time Lisa was ready to leave, Sandi had conveyed her willingness to allow the legal action to move ahead. She was not convinced, however, that the murder of Cliff Torres had any connection to her nephew.

"Nathaniel," she said. "Do you remember your parents' friend, Cliff Torres?"

Fifty Three

Detective Phil Dyer leaned on the door frame of Teddy Nichols office/lab. He listened to an explanation of what Detective Nichols would need to do to track the 'pings' on Nathaniel Crane's cellphone.

"Not a big deal," Teddy said. "We get the calls coming in to the Vermont sheriff during that period and, unless the caller was using a burner, we can trace it back to the cellphone carrier and go from there." He swiveled in his chair and tapped keys on his computer.

"Where is the sheriff located?" Teddy added, pulling up a map on the screen.

"Newfane. Maybe 20 miles from the Mass border. Near Brattleboro," Dyer said.

Teddy expanded the map enough to show western Massachusetts and southern Vermont. He zoomed in, slowly moving the cursor up from the bottom of the screen going right to left. Stopping on Newfane he clicked again, which produced the outline of the town's boundaries just east of the Green Mountain National Forest.

"Pretty rural," Teddy said, circling with the cursor around the area on the map. "Doubt there are many cell sites out there."

Dyer handed a slip of paper to Teddy. "The number for the sheriff. See what you can do, okay?"

Angelo was showing Leonor Santos a photo on his phone, a cat that he and his wife had adopted from the Providence Animal Rescue League.

"Big feet, really silky fur. And look at that bushy tail. We think he's a Maine Coon Cat. See those *ears*," Angelo said.

"What's his name?"

"They said at the Rescue League that his name was Matisse. But I call him Honky Cat."

Santos gave him a puzzled look.

"I'm always shooing him away from things that he gets into. 'Get back, Honky Cat.' You know, Elton John."

Santos shrugged. She didn't know.

"Anyway, he's full of it. Karen loves him. We might call him Mookie," Angelo said.

"Here comes your partner," Santos said. "Cute cat. Good luck."

Angelo turned to see Phil coming down the corridor. He slipped the phone back into his pocket and moved toward Dyer.

"Teddy's going to work on the call. Check in with him later, will ya? I'm going to talk with the Bryan woman again," Dyer said.

"He told me that he had to go back to Wyoming," Sandi said. "I said that if he wanted to avoid appearing in front of a judge again, it was up to the attorneys. And that he should talk to you."

"He left a message on my phone," Lisa said. The call now from her sister was a surprise. After leaving Sandi's home Monday evening, Lisa presumed that they both would step back a little, process all that they had discussed, maybe not talk again until a court date was set.

"I can't talk to him, Sandi. He's lying. He *killed* Sophia. They'll prove that sooner or later. I don't care that we will never find her body. He *planned* it, then concocted the whole story. You know that he is pathological."

"Lisa, you have never liked Natty since he was young," Sandi said. "Sophia once asked me why I thought you hated him so much?"

There had been a clearly apparent mutual dislike exhibited between the two. She had perceived him as a devious, selfish teenager. And he showed no affection for her. The recent events dating back to 2015 and her father's death, had only reinforced Lisa's belief that Nathaniel was truly an evil person. She believed that he had tormented and aggravated his grandfather to the point of causing the heart attack that killed him. Then he had gone about planning his own mother's demise to get at the family inheritance.

"Sandi, I love you. We have gone over all of this before. From the day you called to tell me about the boat accident and that Sophia was missing, I knew, *that very minute*, I knew Nathaniel was lying," Lisa said. "I said it again yesterday when we were out walking. And I believe that he killed, or *arranged* for the murder of, Cliff Torres."

Silence on the phone. She could hear her sister take a breath before speaking again.

"I asked him if he remembered Cliff," Sandi said.

"And...?"

"At first he didn't say anything. Then he thought that maybe he recalled who Cliff was. He said his parents had a lot of friends and that he couldn't place all the names."

"You *see*, that's another lie. There is no way to prove it now, but Cliff told me that he had visited Sophia and Steven on several occasions, when they lived in Maryland and after they moved back to Rhode Island when Nathaniel was young," Lisa said.

"Some of that time Natty would have been away at school," Sandi said.

"It makes no difference. He's lying."

"I can tell you this," Sandi said. "When I told him about Cliff having been shot and killed on the street, his reaction sounded... not completely sincere."

"What did he say?"

'Oh, that's *awful*. Providence is such a dangerous city.' Then he said that, 'he had to go' and he was going to call you again. That was fifteen minutes ago," Sandi said.

"I'm going to call the police. And I won't answer if he calls."

"You should call the lawyer," Sandi said. "Tell him about this."

"He already knows. I told him when we met yesterday."

"I mean about Natty wanting his lawyer to negotiate something," Sandi said.

"He killed his mother, *our* sister. They will find enough to arrest him on that. And if he is connected to the murder of Cliff, he will spend the rest of his life where he belongs, *in prison*," Lisa said, adding, "There is nothing to negotiate."

Fifty Four

Billy's eyes remained open, but he looked very, very tired. Or maybe at a drift with the drugs they were giving him.

At first, his head moved back and forth slowly, looking at Father Mike, then in my direction. Now the gaze was focused on me. His expression appeared to hold a weak smile. He opened and closed his lips a couple of times, then began speaking, voice a hoarse whisper.

"You know," he paused, "in Buffalo, one summer" the words coming in short clips, "it once rained so much," now he was clearly smiling, "a thirteen-inch-long… herring," a longer pause, "fell smack… in the middle… of Main Street."

Father Mike laughed. "Billy, who *told* you that?" he said.

Billy just nodded, but his eyes appeared to be 60 watts brighter.

"Michael, if you record this character, be careful of the yarns he will try to put over on you," the priest said.

"I got a sample," I said. "He was telling me yesterday about two brothers playing for a team and switching jerseys at half-time. One was in foul trouble and wanted to wear his brother's number to finish the game."

Billy moved his left arm so that it was closer to the stationary right arm. He held his hands apart and rested them on the sheet that was pulled up to his chest.

"A thirteen-inch herring," he said, emphasis on thirteen.

"Did you hear that on the radio?" Father Mike said. "When did this 'fish from the sky' come down?"

Billy shook his head. "It was… in the paper," he said. Another pause. "Weather trivia. True."

A nurse came into the room, gave Billy a cheerful greeting, said hello to us, then said that she was checking to be sure that 'Mister Woodson hadn't tried convince anyone that he was going home today.'

"Wouldn't dare," he whispered.

The nurse patted his right shoulder, checked the IV drip, then stood closer to the monitor above the bed. I suspected that it tracked his breathing, blood pressure, heart rate and who knew what else. As soon as the nurse left the room, Father Mike gave me a little nod.

"Hey, Billy," I said, "think it would be OK for me to bring my recorder? We could talk some more tomorrow, later in the day. Maybe after your supper."

He reached up with his left hand and removed the oxygen mask, pulling it below his chin and holding it. "Might be… easier…if I don't wear this," he said.

"We'll ask the nurse. Maybe they'll let you take it off for a few minutes when we talk."

Father Mike took his hand again. "Would you like me to bring Abeo over to visit?" he said.

Billy replaced the oxygen mask, closed his eyes and shook his head.

Father Mike looked at me. "Abeo is one of the best coaches at the gym," he said. "Billy's been teaching him the game." Just as the nurse had done earlier, the priest patted Billy's shoulder, then added, "I'll meet him after school and be sure that he has everything."

"He is… a good young man," Billy said. He tapped his arm where the IV was inserted, rolled his eyes back and motioned with his left hand to the monitor that he knew was above the bed.

"When I'm better," he said. "Don't want to scare him."

Fifty Five

Passing through the town of Douglas, Massachusetts, Nathaniel knew that he was only minutes away from the state line. So far, so good.

The police vehicles he'd observed over the past three hours on his slow drive through rural towns had not given any notice to him. That could change in the blink of any eye. As soon as he crossed into Rhode Island, he knew the level of risk would be greater.

Nathaniel began to tense up. And he began driving even more slowly.

Sandi telling him on the phone about the murder of Cliff Torres had tripped the first alarm, nearly causing him to panic and head west. He'd thought about doing that when he'd been near I-90, the Mass Pike. But able to talk himself down, he was staying with the plan; get to his mother's house and change cars. If he could stay there for only a few hours, he could wait until nightfall before taking the Subaru and heading out.

Heading out *where*, that was still fluid.

For the moment, his objective was to get to East Greenwich. The route he'd planned before leaving Vermont was now changing to direct him south, nearly hugging the Connecticut border to the west, down around the Big River Management Area and then turn northeast. All this to avoid getting too close to Providence.

'Don't blow it now,' the voice said.

The inner conversation went on for several minutes, until he spotted a sign indicating that he was about to intersect with Rhode Island state route 102. From there it would be less than an hour, the most critical leg of the trip. If the East Greenwich cops spotted his car and attempted to pull him over, he hadn't decided yet how he would handle that situation.

'*How* did they connect the car? How did they connect the *car*?' the voice repeated.

It was possibly the twentieth time the question came up since he'd first learned from Dean Chase about the description on the police scanner.

But now the answer was obvious. After the call to Sandi, he was certain that Lisa had told the police everything, including that she got Cliff Torres to come to Rhode Island in the first place. Once she'd told them about the pending court action, no doubt they had done a vehicle search and found his registration from Wyoming.

'You already knew that' the voice said.

Yes, Nathaniel must have known it at some level. Otherwise, he wouldn't have been so quick to come up with the ruse he tried to sell to the Vermont sheriff on the phone. And *that*, because he desperately needed to believe it, would focus the search for his car on routes *west* of Vermont.

Reflecting on his last, brief chat with Dean Chase, the voice told him that the old codger could not be trusted, that he was certain to talk to the sheriff. Nathaniel thought that he'd been convincing in his own call to the sheriff about needing to get back to help a friend in Wyoming. And *maybe* he would be lucky now.

'Maybe no local cops,' the voice said.

Detective Teddy Nichols ran his finger slowly across the screen to show Angelo the different pings from cell sites indicated on a map.

"There's one, west of Brattleboro," Teddy said, holding a finger on the spot. "8:03 this morning." He moved his finger and added, "Then here's another one, right here," he pointed at a spot on the map near Gardner, Massachusetts. "Almost two hours later, just before ten o'clock."

Angelo was looking at the computer over Teddy's shoulder. He leaned in closer.

"That's it," Teddy said.

"You can go back before today, right?" Angelo said.

Teddy nodded, typed a command on his keyboard and brought up another page on the screen.

Dyer waited only five minutes for Lisa Bryan to return his call. She told him that she was still in Providence but planning to drive back to Taunton in the afternoon to see her sister again.

"Your nephew called a county sheriff in Vermont this morning," Dyer said. "Someone told him that police are looking for his car."

No response from Bryan.

"He claimed that he was on his way to Wyoming," Dyer said.

"Nathaniel called me, too," Bryan said.

"You *spoke* with him?"

"No. He left a message. I didn't call him back. And do not plan to do so."

"What'd he say in the message?" Dyer said.

"That he was on his way back to Wyoming. That he wanted to talk to me, without our lawyers being involved," she said. "He said the cellphone coverage was spotty but asked me to call him back."

"What time did he leave this message?"

"It was a few minutes before ten. I had just come back to my room from the hotel swimming pool."

Dyer looked at his watch; 11:18.

"What time were you planning to go to your sister's?" Dyer said.

"Later this afternoon, around 2 o'clock," she said. "A friend is going with me," she added. "I'm waiting to hear from him." She decided not to mention Hanlon's name.

"I need to speak with our phone tech," Dyer said. "You saved the message from your nephew?"

"Yes," she said.

"Please look at the time stamp when the call came in. Could you do that and text me?"

"I will do it right now."

"Thank you. I'm going to call you again. Maybe half-an-hour," Dyer said. "But go ahead and text me as soon as we hang up."

Twenty seconds passed before she sent the text. '*9:53 AM. Caller number 307.295.3093.*'

Driving back to the hotel, I was thinking about how frail Billy was. When we'd been seated face to face in the gym yesterday, yeah, he had looked old. The loose-fitting and worn clothing certainly hadn't helped his appearance. But considering the life he told me about, although he was thin, he appeared to be surprisingly fit for a man his age.

Now, the pallor of his skin, the tired eyes, hooked-up to the IV with the medical clip on his finger, plus the oxygen mask, made him appear to be pretty fragile.

Yet he'd managed the silly joke. A fish falling out of the sky in a rainstorm. Where had that come from?

Father Mike told me that a couple of women from the parish would visit Billy, and that he would go back as well. Asking him to let me know if and when they decided about surgery, I said that if Billy remained stable or showed improvement, that I would plan a return visit tomorrow evening.

Now parked in the same spot at the Hilton Providence where my car had been overnight, I made a call to Lisa Bryan. How difficult could it really be to meet her sister?

"Michael," she said, answering on the second ring.

"You know, something just occurred to me. I was at the hospital visiting Billy. I shoulda' asked him for a striped shirt and his whistle if I'm going with you to Taunton."

"Absolutely not necessary. Sandi and I can talk," she said. "It's just that it's such a difficult time and I would like you come with me. It's what I said this morning; you're objective in this. It can't hurt."

"What time you thinking about leaving?" I said.

"Could we go around two?"

I looked at my watch; twenty-five after twelve.

"That'll work. You can drive, yes? You know where we're going."

"I do," she said. "My car's downstairs in the hotel lot."

"What make is your rental car? What color?" I said, scanning all the other cars.

"It's a Toyota Camry. White. Why?"

"No reason. I just came back from the hospital. I'm sitting in my car, downstairs, in the hotel lot."

Fifty Six

Sandi Bryan, not for the first time, was second-guessing her decision of a year ago *not* to hire her own lawyer. When she had first learned that she had been named by her late sister, Sophia, to be the executor of her estate, the thought of needing personal representation had gone through her mind.

Initially, taking guidance from the lawyer who had represented Sophia and her late husband, and before Lisa had persuaded her that something was amiss with Nathaniel's story about the boat accident, Sandi had been content to follow what she assumed to be 'standard procedures' through the probate court process. The shock and grief of losing her sister was still influencing all that she did.

Only days after the meeting with the lawyer and the reading of Sophia's will, Lisa had begun to make what at times seemed to be an incessant case that Natty was lying. It grew more intense when Lisa mixed in the theory that Natty had 'hounded' their father, causing the old man's fatal heart attack.

Sandi had acquiesced, accepting the reasoning about Sophia's presumed death. She had agreed that they should retain the attorney to represent them as surviving beneficiaries of their father's estate. That step, and subsequent court filings, brought them to today. Now, learning of Cliff Torres' murder and Lisa's explanations about his involvement, her ambivalence had resurfaced.

Then, the phone call this morning from Natty. That, plus Lisa was coming back this afternoon to see her again.

And bringing a friend.

Five minutes from the hotel – Lisa's hands gripped at 10 and 2 o'clock on the steering wheel, as though she were instructing a Driver's Ed student – I couldn't resist an attempt to lighten things up before we got to her sister's.

"Look at that," I said, pointing to one of several billboards just off the highway.

"What?" she said, with a quick glance.

"Right there. On the right. See what it says?"

She looked long enough to read it, then glanced at me. Not exactly smiling, she gave me a quick head shake.

The billboard stated in large letters, 'Speak with an attorney.' Below was a phone number and other advice that I couldn't read as it was now behind us.

"You know what that is?" I said.

"What is it?"

"*That*... is a sign."

A straight drive east on US 44 and we were coming into Taunton at ten of three. Earlier Lisa had told me that her sister's house was only five minutes from the highway.

The house was a two-storey colonial with a single-door garage at the end of a cul-de-sac, a large yard around to the back, and a split-rail fence in front of a suburban wooded area. Lisa turned off the engine, looked at me and smiled.

"Thank you for coming with me," she said, lightly touching my left hand.

We had agreed during the drive that Lisa would be up front about why she had asked me to come along and, if appropriate, have me repeat the story for Sandi about my friend in Pennsylvania who had navigated his siblings through a difficult time.

Before we got to the front door, it opened. I guessed the woman standing inside to be mid-fifties. She was about five-foot-seven, brown hair with streaks of gray, no make-up that I could detect, and she wore a navy turtle neck over tan, calf-length slacks and canvas espadrilles.

Lisa hugged her. They held the embrace for a few seconds.

"Hi," she said to Lisa as they stepped back.

"Sandi, this is Michael Hanlon," Lisa said.

"Hello," she said, extending her hand. "I'm Sandra Bryan. It's nice to meet you."

"And nice to meet you," I said.

Turning back to Lisa, she said, "Let's go into the den."

When she'd taken a couple of steps away from the foyer, she stopped and asked, "Would you like a cup of coffee?" now looking at me.

"Not me, thanks. Maybe a glass of water."

"Lisa?"

"No, thanks, San," Lisa said.

"Go on in. I'll be right there. Let me get your water," Sandi said, turning in the other direction.

Lisa led me to a room that appeared to be a combo den/home office. There was a desk in the far right corner and most of one wall was lined with bookshelves. Only a third of the shelves held real books, the remaining shelves were nearly filled with binders, loose manila folders and spiral bound notebooks, plus a few small framed photos along a middle shelf.

I moved toward the shelves, first making a quick scan of the book titles she had, then got closer to look at the photos just as Sandi came into the room.

"I didn't ask if you wanted ice," she said, handing me a tall glass. "I put some in out of habit. Is that OK?"

"Fine, thanks." I took a drink of the water.

"Please, sit here," she said, gesturing toward an upholstered wing chair.

I moved to the chair, Lisa sat in a contemporary leather recliner, Sandi settled into an old wicker rocking chair with well-worn cushions.

"Michael is a private investigator," Lisa began. "In Vermont."

Sandi's expression hinted at mild surprise, but she didn't say anything.

"I've told him everything. Dad, Sophia, and now Cliff," Lisa continued.

Sandi studied her sister for a couple of seconds, then slowly turned her gaze back at me but said nothing.

"I've told him about Nathaniel's phone calls. And that you spoke with him. Because the suit is about to have a hearing date, and the probate court with Sophia's estate is really separate, at least at this point," Lisa continued, "Michael is suggesting that we talk to our lawyer before any direct communication with Nathaniel." Now Lisa looked at me. I gave her a single nod.

Sandi had been perfectly still and attentive listening to this. Now she reclined half-way in the rocker, resting her arms and tilting her head back so that she was looking upward. Her lips were pinched shut and I could see her eyes slowly exploring the ceiling. She patted her hands softly on the armrests and stayed like that for perhaps five seconds, then brought the recliner forward.

"Lisa, what if Natty is telling the *truth*? We know dad had heart issues *before* he died. We don't know what they talked about *before* Natty went to see him. And what if the explosion on the boat happened just as he said it did?" Other than emphasizing certain words, her tone was matter-of-fact, no trace of emotion.

"Sophia *loved* Natty. Yes, they had problems when he was younger, but that's not unusual," Sandi went on. "If she were alive today and somehow all of this was... *turned around*, what do you think that she would do? If one of us had a son, or a daughter..."

Lisa interrupted. "We don't. Neither of us have children, San," she said.

Maybe my imagination, but I thought that I detected a flash of something in the look Sandi gave Lisa in response to this.

"He... is... lying! You *know* that," Lisa said.

A phone rang. It was coming from another room. Sandi stood and went to the desk. I could see a handset in a cradle, its light blinking, but no sound or ringtone. She picked up the phone and looked at the caller ID.

"Natty," she said, holding up the phone but not answering the call. "It's the same number from this morning."

Fifty Seven

The phone number the Bryan woman texted to Phil Dyer matched the number that called the Vermont sheriff's office, the man identifying himself as Crane saying that he was going to Wyoming.

One problem; the later call to Bryan pinged off a site along state route 68 in Gardner, Massachusetts. That cell site was located out near Mount Wachusett Community College, 60 miles *southeast* of the earlier call. Not the most direct route to Wyoming.

The hunch Dyer had that Crane was trying a feint with his line about 'on my way west' had just quickly gone from hunch to a probability. The man lied to the sheriff and lied to his aunt. But why would he be heading back in the direction of Rhode Island? The call to Bryan's phone had come a little before 10 o'clock, over three hours ago.

Studying the map, Dyer knew that Crane knew the police would continue looking for his car. Rather than any highway heading west, if he was still travelling on route 68, he would have by-passed US Route 2. He could be making a circuitous run on secondary roads to enter the state somewhere along the Connecticut border.

Dyer called Angelo.

"So, Lisa Bryan got back to me," Dyer began, "the number used by her nephew when he called her this morning, same phone. And the call was placed from Massachusetts, just west of Leominster. He's *not* going west."

"Okay," Angelo said.

"Go talk with Teddy again. See if he can map cell sites along Mass Route 68 running south, from the city of Gardner down to the Connecticut line," Dyer said.

"I'll do it right now."

"If he can do that," Dyer went on, "ask him to email the map to me. Or, get him to print it for you."

"Get back to you as soon as I have it," Angelo said.

Nathaniel had committed a minor mistake. In his haste to leave after the phone call to the Vermont sheriff, preoccupied with thoughts about both of his aunts and the lawyers, he forgot to gas up his car.

The orange warning light came on. Unlikely that he had enough to get him to his mother's house. He had to make a quick decision about where to stop for gas.

Looking for a place to pull over he wanted re-think the best route for the balance of the trip. After another two miles, he spotted a sign indicating a side road ahead on the right. He slowed and took the turn, drove a short distance, stopped and backed his car in next to a fence along a field.

He shut off the engine and sat. Impulsively, he decided to make another call to Sandi. If he pleaded with her again, maybe she would let him come see her. They could talk about a way to get through this and *not* proceed to a court order. But he would only go to her house once he had his mother's car.

Before she answered, Nathaniel abruptly ended the call.

Bringing up Google Maps on the phone he looked at his options. Continuing south he could either drop down past a busy interchange with I-95, cross over and then head north to East Greenwich. Or take a shorter route through the Big River Management Area, which would get him to his mother's house in maybe forty minutes.

He decided on the more direct route, hoping that he could make the gas stop fast enough to avoid local cops.

'You're smart enough to do this,' the voice said. 'Don't get rattled.'

Fifty Eight

The phone stopped ringing. Sandi stared at the handset and watched the number on the caller ID being replaced by the time and date: 3:09 PM Oct. 9.

She looked at Lisa for a second, then back to the phone. Neither of them said anything. Sandi placed the phone back in its cradle and moved across the carpet to again take her seat in the rocking chair. Save for the distant sound of someone operating a leaf blower a few houses away, the den itself remained silent.

Leaning back, making the chair go back as well, Sandi folded her arms across her chest and tilted her head back so that her eyes were gazing at the ceiling. Knees bent at 90 degrees and feet flat on the floor, she was able to hold the rockers on the chair steady.

"Just what is it, Lisa, that you propose that we do *now*?" Sandi said, maintaining the position in the chair.

Lisa looked at me, shaking her head ever so slightly, then making a shrug with her shoulders. I had the good sense to say absolutely nothing.

"San," Lisa began, "I'm not trying to torment you with

all of this. I know how close you were to Sophia. Then out of nowhere, I showed up. And you took care of *me* after mom... died. And I know that you adored Nathaniel when he was a baby."

Sandi made a barely perceptible noise with her throat, as though she'd swallowed something. I saw her chest give a little heave. Lisa had her hands folded and was looking down at the floor. I doubted that she had noticed.

"Please," Lisa said, "let's not be adversaries here. I *know* that you didn't want to hire a lawyer. And like I said when we went for the walk yesterday, I *know* that it's different for me, being so far away and... *demanding* that Nathaniel be made accountable for the horrible things that he's done."

Uncrossing her arms, Sandi let her hands settle on the armrests. The chair came forward, but she kept her head tilted back.

Both women were silent. I stole a glance at my watch; seventeen after three.

"Michael," Lisa said softly, "do you mind telling Sandi about your friend in Pennsylvania?"

Her look was pleading if I ever saw one.

I didn't respond immediately. But my thought was, 'Great! Just rattle on about people Sandi doesn't know and a family situation considerably different than what I'm seeing here.'

"Is that all right with you, Sandi?" I said, aware of her

own work with their father's construction firm in the years before his death.

She titled her head forward enough so that her neck was straight while her shoulders remained pressed against the back of the chair. She looked directly at me and gave a nod.

"Please," she said, her tone nearly as soft as the one Lisa had been using.

I held my arm out to look at my watch, then looked at Lisa.

"Okay." I shifted, leaned forward, clasped my hands together and took in a deep cleansing breath through my nose, held it a couple of seconds, then exhaled through my mouth.

"This was, uh, about ten, maybe eleven years ago," I began. "I'd gone back to the town where I grew up for a memorial service, the father of a close friend."

For the next ten minutes, I recounted, as succinctly as possible, some things I had learned and had observed, during a very unpleasant family confrontation at a funeral home. By accident, simply because I was with my friend in a side gathering room, I witnessed much of the shouting, name calling and flat-out raw emotion that had just exploded among siblings and some of their spouses.

It had turned really personal and really nasty. When I started to leave the room, my friend pulled on my arm and shook his head. 'Stay, Michael,' he'd said. 'I might need you here.'

Turned out that he didn't need me. When the uproar began to simmer down, there was still a lot of sobbing and siblings glaring at one another. My friend Richard stood up and in a matter of seconds, took control of the whole scene.

With sort of a mixture of 'thoughtful teacher/group therapist', in a no nonsense, firm voice, he was able to get consensus on what the family was going to do in moving forward on contentious issues.

"What has really stayed with me," I said, checking to see if Sandi was still listening, "is how Richard was able to bring it down to a level that actually made everyone *step back* and consider what he was asking of them."

"And what was he asking?" Sandi said.

I let out a nervous laugh, caught myself and gave a quick glance at Lisa.

"Two of Richard's older sisters, and their husbands, apparently are pretty religious," I said. "Richard is not. But, without being offensive or patronizing, he seemed to focus on those two couples in trying to make peace and work things out.

"His closing, if you will, ultimately brought everyone around. He told them, 'I know that some of you have the mantra, What Would Jesus Do? It's probably good that you think that way. I imagine it helps the rest of us.'

'But, let me ask that we try *this*. All of these things that you're fighting about, they didn't happen overnight. It took *years* for some of these things to fester. It is going to take some time to sort it out. And if we *truly* want to resolve this mess, here is the question I have for you: What would our father do? I mean our real father, *your* dad.'

When I'd finished, Sandi was still watching me.

I took another glance at my watch and was glad to see that I hadn't gone on as long as it seemed. Sandi slowly rose from the rocker.

"I'm going to fix some tea. Lisa, would you like a cup?" she said.

"Yes," Lisa said, "please."

"Michael? Would you like some tea?"

"Sure. Thanks."

Fifty Nine

The pumps were located in front of a convenience store. Nathaniel went inside, paid the clerk and put ten dollars of gas into his car. Pulling away from the pump to the side of the building, he sat with the engine idling. After a minute watching traffic in both directions, he pulled onto the road.

Underway again, he was hyper alert for local police cars. The voice was also back.

'What are you going to do *now*?'

Of all the different inner voices Nathaniel had listened to throughout his life, there was one that was dominant. He couldn't recall the first time he'd heard it, but the tone always brought him up short, at times physically jerking his body to attention. That's what he did now, shuddering while he brought the car up to a cautious speed of 45 miles per hour.

"I am not going to panic," he said aloud to himself. "In thirty minutes, get the Subaru and go."

The basic part of *that* plan really hadn't changed since he left Vermont; get his mother's car, leave the Mitsubishi in the garage. What had changed, after he'd spoken with

Sandi and learned that she knew about Cliff Torres murder, was the 'go' part.

For two hours now, the destination kept changing. Nathaniel was unable to concentrate on any preferable geographic location. Wyoming, maybe. Back to the camp in Vermont, no. Stay at his mother's house, not a chance.

California, a possibility. Connect with another friend.

'Go to Sandi's' the voice said.

Then it clicked. Nathaniel realized this voice sounded like his grandfather.

Was it possible that long before he'd become conscious of the voices, at some point early in his infancy, his grandfather's voice had become so embedded in his brain that it controlled the later voices? Or, was it only since his death that he'd noticed the tone becoming more assertive?

"I have no money," he said to himself. "Sandi, if I have to be in court to prove that I am innocent, I have to pay my lawyer," he continued, rehearsing the plea that he would use with her.

A mile farther along, he added, "You control mom's estate. And the trust." A man on a motorcycle whipped past, causing him to swerve to the right nearly going off the road.

With a quick anxious glance at the rearview mirror, then scanning left and right on the road in front, Nathaniel crept back to a safe speed and resumed the conversation.

"I didn't kill Grampa Bryan. And I didn't cause the explosion on my boat."

Silence. Then a voice asked a question. Actually, it was *two* voices, simultaneously; Sandi and Lisa.

"What about Cliff Torres?"

Sixty

"He made another call," Teddy said. "He's in Rhode Island. Got a hit from a site along route 102 in Coventry."

"When?" Dyer said, using his speaker phone mode.

"Fifteen minutes ago. The ping registered at 3:08?"

"Calling the Bryan woman again?"

"No. A number he called earlier, though" Teddy said. "The second call from this morning, after he called Bryan."

"I'm driving. Angelo has the printout. What's the location of that number?"

"508 area code, 821 prefix. That's in Taunton."

"Text it to me," Dyer said. "Lisa Bryan's sister lives in Taunton."

As soon as he disconnected, Dyer considered the proximity of Coventry to East Greenwich. Land mass, Coventry is the largest town in the state, nearly 60 square miles and bordering with the state of Connecticut to the west. But, it also borders with East Greenwich.

"Taunton?" Dyer said to himself.

Located northeast of Coventry, beyond Providence, Dyer guessed the distance between the two close to 40 miles. Depending on traffic and the route, you might drive it in under an hour.

The clock on his dash read 3:24 Dyer tapped his speed dial to call Angelo.

"All set with travel plans, Mr. Dyer. You and your lovely wife will have a stateroom suite on this fabulous cruise," Angelo offered.

"Aren't we just *too cute* for a lowly paid, aspiring detective?" Dyer said.

"Aspirations are good for the soul."

"Teddy got another hit on the Crane phone," Dyer said. "He made a third call about 15 minutes ago from somewhere in Coventry. He's back in the state."

"Okay."

"He's calling someone in Taunton. I think it's the other aunt, the older sister. I'm going to call Lisa Bryan. Go see Teddy and run it down."

"You coming back here?" Angelo said.

"Yeah, that's the plan. But wait 'til I talk with Bryan. I'll let you know."

"Got it."

Dyer had been on his way to Rhode Island Hospital to check on Billy Woodson. He thought that he could be in and out in 20 minutes.

First, he would call Lisa Bryan. He drove past the Eddy Street Lot at the hospital to find short-term, non-public parking next to the Security Building. He saw a spot and pulled in. Looking down at his phone, he'd received a text from Teddy with the Taunton phone number. Using part of a flap from an envelope above the sun visor, Dyer copied the number. He would check it with Bryan.

The call to Lisa Bryan went to voicemail. "It's Phil Dyer. Need to check a Taunton phone number with you. We think it's your sister's. Important. Please call me as soon as you hear this."

Closing the car door, he reached back to the front seat and retrieved a copy of the Providence Journal. He doubted Billy was in any condition to read a newspaper, but there was a lengthy preview article on the Providence College basketball team. Billy could at least see the photos and the headline. Might boost his spirits.

Sixty One

"**It is the official tea of the Boston Red Sox,**" Sandi said, a hint of sarcasm in her voice.

"Really?" I said.

Surprised at how much I enjoyed the tea, I'd just told her, "I'm normally not a tea drinker, but this is pretty good." Hence the information on all those tea drinkers at Fenway Park.

Lisa had come back to the den after having gone to the bathroom. Hearing Sandi and me talking baseball, she asked how the Sox were doing in the playoffs.

"They got out of New York, by half-a-step. Not sure how they'll do with Houston," Sandi said.

My sense was that both women, at least for the moment, were trying to avoid diving back into the discussion of their nephew and lawyers. So we drank tea, talked superficially about sports teams, and watched a scattering of wet leaves falling outside.

After an awkward silence, Sandi guided us around to why we were talking in the first place.

"Natty never liked sports of any kind," she said. "I believe that was a big issue between him and dad.

Certainly, when Steven was alive. Every time I heard dad and Steven talking sports, if Natty was there, he would leave the room."

"Steven was your brother-in-law?" I said.

"Yes," Lisa interjected. "He and my father kidded one another about loyalty to different teams."

"*Especially* the Red Sox and Yankees," Sandi said. "The two of them were always ribbing and frequently wagering on games between Boston and New York."

"Let me guess," I said. "Your father was the Sox fan."

Sandi nearly choked on her tea. Lisa laughed.

"Just the opposite," Sandi said, placing her cup on a glass table next to the chair. "He *loved* Mickey Mantle, Roger Maris, Yogi Berra, you name a Yankees player from sixty years ago, he could tell you just about anything."

"Steven was not nearly as crazy about it as dad was," Lisa said.

"No, he wasn't," Sandi said. She looked at Lisa, then to me and added, "When Steven died, one of the things our father did, was to make a donation of twenty-five-thousand dollars to The Jimmy Fund in Steven's memory."

Listening to the two of them, I wondered about past flare-ups or specific incidents involving their father and their nephew, that had so convinced Lisa that Nathaniel had really provoked the heart attack that killed his grandfather. It was difficult for me *not* to ask questions about it. But I didn't.

In the years of my friendship with Ragsdale and time

spent working on or talking about cases, one thing that I was trying to emulate that Louie did so well, was to 'check my focus'. Louie has a professional self-discipline that is guided by a simple two-part question: *why* am I here and *what* should I be doing?

So, I continued holding back. No other questions about the family, no offering suggestions. Should either Lisa, or Sandi, ask me something, that would be another matter.

Not yet tested, however, was the possibility that my brand new, very personal involvement with Lisa could influence advice or opinions coming from me.

The nursing assistant had fluffed the pillow for Billy to make sure that he was comfortable. Then she asked if he needed anything. He motioned for her to come closer. Apparently he had something to tell her. She leaned in.

"This rain," he said. "Fifty years ago... up in British Columbia." He paused for a few of seconds.

"What happened fifty years ago?" she said.

"Twenty inches of rain... in 24 hours."

"*That* is a lot of rain. They must of have had serious flooding."

"Don't know," Billy said.

"Hey," a voice said. The nurse's assistant turned to see a man standing behind her.

"Hi. I'm an old friend of Billy's," the man said. Dyer

didn't feel any need to identify himself as a Providence PD detective.

"Billy was telling me about a place in Canada that had *20 inches of rain* fifty years ago," she said.

"Before… you were born," Billy whispered. The nursing assistant excused herself to attend to other patients.

"How're we doing here, ref" Dyer said. "Calling any fouls? Thought you might be out in the halls, get all these people in shape."

"Maybe tomorrow," Billy said.

"I brought you the paper. Big spread on the Friars." Opened to the sports section, Dyer held the newspaper up for Billy to see. "Good column by Reynolds."

"Thanks," Billy said.

"Bunch of speculation, projections about Big East teams. Some good photos," Dyer said, flipping a page. He refolded the paper and placed it on a table next to the bed. "You can read it later."

"Did the radio guy come see you?" Dyer added.

Billy nodded. "Coming back," he said. "Went with Father Mike."

"Be sure to tell him how you used to talk with Gavitt." Dyer patted Billy's shoulder. "Not everybody knows how much he respected you."

Billy eyes were closed, but Dyer thought that he could detect a weak smile.

The whole room setting, the oxygen mask, digital

monitor, curtains between other beds, all of it reinforced the seriousness of his condition.

"I just wanted to come by for a minute, Billy. I'll check back on you later."

Waiting for the elevator, Dyer looked at his phone. No new texts or voice messages. Nothing from Lisa Bryan. He would call Angelo when he got back outside.

Going across the lobby, Dyer saw a man in a wheelchair. The woman pushing the chair looked old enough to be the man's mother. He recognized the guy as a character he'd once arrested for some petty crime. He couldn't remember what the incident had been, but he was sure that it was the same guy.

Outside, Dyer had the phone to his ear, waiting.

"Nothing, yet," Angelo answered. "Teddy's been with the Major on another case."

"Okay. I'm headed back. See you in a few minutes."

Sixty Two

Momentarily side stepping further talk about how they would proceed with their lawyer, Lisa switched topics to Cliff Torres. She said that she needed to find out about any relatives.

"I can't just hope that someone shows up and talks to the police down there," Lisa said. "And that his burial will be handled in a proper manner."

"There are still things in Sophia's desk," Sandi said. "She may have had letters from Cliff. I don't remember seeing any."

"Didn't they have an old desktop computer? Could there be something from Cliff on it?"

"Probably not," Sandi said.

"She was never comfortable using a computer. That was mostly Steven. After she had an email account, I don't think I received more than two messages from her in five years."

"Detective Dyer said the police in New Jersey were talking with someone at the company where Cliff used to work," Lisa said. "There must be something in his personnel file. Or an insurance policy."

Sandi had drained the last of her tea. She clearly was more at ease than she had been when we arrived. The tension, the rigid body language during the earlier exchange with Lisa, was gone now. She appeared to be marginally relaxed.

"San, when was the last time you were at Sophia's?" Lisa said.

"In June. Just before Natty came back. I talked with him on the phone while he was still in Wyoming. He was going to go through personal family items before meeting with a real estate agent. That was *before* you were there and had the big argument."

Here we go, I thought. Are these two gonna' find any middle ground on the nephew?

"You can still legally go *in* the house?" Lisa said.

Sandi nodded. "Yes."

Nathaniel Crane followed Division Road past several side streets. He came to an All Way Stop that he knew well and took a right to follow connecting streets through secluded residential neighborhoods. It would bring him out one street away from Courtney Drive and his family home.

Luck had been with him for 200 plus miles. The meandering route had taken him hours at an intentionally *very* slow pace. But no police stops, no close encounters. The next few minutes would be crucial. Rather than taking a chance of being seen by cops who could be watching the house, he would drive to a partially cleared lot, out of sight from the road, where a new house was about to be built. When he'd left a few days earlier, there was no sign of any construction starting and he hoped that was still the case.

At 3:45, he turned into the new house lot two hundred yards through the woods from his mother's home. Shutting off the engine, he planned to walk close enough to observe the house. If nothing unusual was going on, he would move to a spot to watch for police vehicles.

He didn't have to wait long.

An East Greenwich patrol car cruised by his mother's driveway. It stayed on Courtney Drive, not turning in, and gradually accelerated farther along.

Coincidence? Not a chance.

Slipping between trees back to the car, he got in, sat for a minute, then began rhythmically rocking his upper body back and forth.

'Stay here,' the voice said.

He was not clearly visible from Courtney Drive, at least that's what Nathaniel wanted to think. But just in case, he maneuvered the car around to back deeper into the trees. There was a pile of brush that had been cleared and a load of gravel. He parked behind the gravel hoping that it might provide a bunker to shield the car.

If his luck held and nothing happened before dusk, he would wait it out. Abandon the car, get to the house and take his mother's Subaru. Daylight wouldn't dim for at least two hours. He wasn't sure he could wait that long.

Yet going back out on the street was almost a certainty the cops would spot his car.

Leaving on foot *now*, taking the risk of being seen by a neighbor, how dangerous was that compared to waiting?

'Stay here' the voice repeated.

Sixty Three

Detective Phil Dyer looked at the face of Nathaniel Crane, a newspaper photo with the story from August, 2017 about the boating accident. The reporter summarized events about the sinking of Crane's boat and his rescue by two fishermen. It was the second time that Dyer had read the story.

"Wyoming, huh? What the hell were you doing *here* when your boat exploded?" Dyer said aloud.

Dyer knew, or thought he knew, what Crane had been doing. Just because he'd decided to go out west for an undetermined stay, if he'd been like many privileged kids growing up near the shore, Crane would've spent some time on the water. The fact that he had *purchased* a boat, however, did not make him a good sailor.

The story from Lisa Bryan was convincing, at least regarding the motive Crane had to get at the inheritance. The whole thing with the grandfather and the heart attack, how you gonna' prove that?

Angelo came back into the room and looked over Dyer's shoulder at the news story.

"Whatd'ya think?" Dyer said. "This guy look like a shooter?"

"How can you tell from a photo like that?"

Dyer watched Angelo for a few seconds. He was expecting more commentary, but his partner apparently had nothing to add.

"All those photos you take with your phone, family, friends, people at ball games, you ever go back and study their faces?" Dyer said.

"Phil, when I show you photos on my phone, do you recall *anyone* who looked like 'a shooter'?"

"Okay. I'm just circling around here. Until we find Crane and his car, pretty much doing push-ups on a water bed."

"What?" Angelo said.

Dyer stood up, stretched and kept his arms raised with his hands clasped together. He then leaned backward at an angle and held the position for five seconds. Leaning forward, he bent at the waist to reach down and touch the tips of his shoes and held that position for another five seconds before resuming a normal posture.

"I'm gonna' go see Teddy," he said. "Maybe Crane made another call."

Angleo picked up his phone. He began scrolling through photos from a family gathering held at his wife's parents' home over Labor Day.

The late Sophia Crane's nearest neighbor, a retired Verizon/New England Telephone engineer, was fastidious about the maintenance of his home and the land around it. He spent a lot of time outdoors. A few days of rain didn't slow him down.

Pruning shrubbery and small trees at the edge of his property, the man thought that he saw a vehicle through the woods. It was at the lot being prepared for construction of a new house. He only saw a turning motion and couldn't tell if it was a truck or a car. No one had been there for weeks. The last activity had been clearing and leveling of the lot and delivery of two truck-loads of gravel.

Dragging bundles of tree branches and leaf debris to the corner of his land, the neighbor threw them on top of dead grass recently cleared from his driveway culvert. He would have all of it hauled away when he finished.

The effort required multiple trips through the back yard. Each time he returned for another load, he glanced at the building lot, expecting to see activity. Nothing. Maybe the vehicle had come and gone while he worked.

He would ask his wife later what she'd heard from neighbors about the house to be erected. Better yet, maybe when he finished for the afternoon, walk over and have a look before going inside for dinner. See if there were grade stakes or trenching for utilities.

If it was going to happen this fall, you might think they would be after it soon.

Sixty Four

Lisa and Sandi were still discussing the possibility that they might find information about Cliff Torres at their sister's home. I was listening, not talking, and occupied myself by more thoroughly perusing the titles on Sandi's bookshelves.

"There is one drawer in a desk in Sophia's bedroom that has personal correspondence," Sandi said. "Letters, cards, not sure what else is there. I never read through any of it once I realized what it was."

"That was in June?" Lisa said.

"No. I went over then to clear out most of Sophia's wardrobe. Natty didn't want to do it and was happy for me to take care of it. I didn't finish. We took most of the clothing to the Salvation Army store in North Kingston."

"Natty helped you?"

Sandi shook her head. "My friend Judy. She went with me. She's the same size as Sophia. I thought she might want some of the blouses and dresses," she said, adding, "I kept a couple of the hand-knitted sweaters. One for you."

"She had beautiful clothes," Lisa said.

"Yes, she did. Judy thought some of the things could have gone to a consignment store. But I like the work the Salvation Army does and wanted them to get the proceeds."

"Back to the personal correspondence in the desk. When did you see it?" Lisa said.

"Sorry. That was…" Sandi paused, then went on, "after Natty had gone back out to Wyoming. Just after Christmas."

"None of that had to go to Sophia's lawyer?"

"No. We sorted through the banking statements and investment correspondence last fall. He made copies of what he needed," Sandi said. "The letters and cards, most were hand written. You could tell they were of a personal nature. I put rubber bands around them and put them back in the drawer."

I noticed a prolonged break in the conversation. Turning around to look at the two women, Sandi was holding a hand to her mouth, choking back emotion. Lisa had a hand on Sandi's knee. I heard Sandi swallow, then sniffle, and she turned her head away. After a couple of seconds, she reached down and patted Lisa's hand.

Lisa looked over at me. The smile was still lovely, just a little sadder.

"San," Lisa said, "I think that we should consider going to Sophia's house."

Sandi turned to face her. She dropped the hand away from her mouth, took a tissue from a pocket and dabbed at her eyes.

"Now?" she said, her voice softer.

"Yes. I'm here *now*. I hope we can find something more about Cliff. I'm sorry, you shouldn't have to do this on your own. I want to go with you."

They stared at one another, then Sandi looked over at me.

"Michael. You've been listening here," Sandi said. "Since my little sister has brought you along as an arbiter, care to offer some guidance?" Her voice was back to the lighter tone of 'the official tea of the Boston Red Sox.'

I waited before replying. Both women watched me.

"You won't know if you don't look," I said.

Sandi stood, left hand lingering at her side and barely touching Lisa's hand.

"Then let's go for a drive."

"How far is it?" I said, clueless as to which direction we might be heading.

"Half-an-hour, maybe a little longer. Depends on traffic," Sandi said.

"We can take my car," Lisa said. "I'll drive."

"Better take mine. I know the way," Sandi said, walking in the direction of the kitchen. "I don't mind driving. Maybe stop for dinner on the way back."

The sun had dropped almost to the horizon when we came out of Sandi's house. Just the fact that we could see the sun was a mild surprise, as the clouds and overcast had remained dominant when we'd arrived two hours ago.

Sandi backed her car out of the garage. Lisa put a hand on the car door, then stopped.

"Wait a second," she said. "Are we sure this is what we want to do?"

"Hey. If you're having some second thoughts about…" I began, but Lisa cut me off.

"No. I mean do *all three* of us want to go in the same car? Then drive all the way back here, get my car, and drive back to Providence tonight?"

Sandi lowered the passenger window to see what we were discussing.

"Michael, you ride with Sandi." She leaned toward the car window for Sandi's benefit, then added, "There's no sense coming back here later to get my car. I'll follow you."

"Sounds good," Sandi said.

I climbed in next to her and fastened my seat belt.

A minute later, we were back on Route 44 going west, Lisa right behind us. Sandi quickly got her speed up to just over 60 and set the cruise control. Traffic was heavier going in the opposite direction, which I assumed was mostly people commuting back to Taunton.

"Did Lisa tell you that she was the 'princess' for our dad?" Sandi said.

Considering what I'd been listening to for most of the afternoon, the question surprised me. I looked at Sandi. She was smiling.

"I don't think she used that term," I said. "Mostly about life in California, some things about when she was young. And a little about college days."

Sandi was shaking a finger, still with a smile.

"Right there. That's an example. I wanted her to go to one of at least three *other* schools. She got it in her head that Roger Williams was where she was going, and she persuaded my father. By the time acceptance letters arrived, Lisa had dad convinced."

For the first twenty minutes of the drive, Sandi, in a humorous and affectionate tone, segued from one example to the next of how their father couldn't do enough for Lisa. Little of what she related was about material 'things'. It was more a thirty-year series of Lisa deciding something, then their father agreeing with her.

"After our mother died, Lisa was *so young*, my father's life revolved around his business and his little girl." Sandi said. "Sofe and I laughed about it most of the time. We were years older. And for a long time, *I* was Lisa's mother."

"She moved to California not long after college?" I said. Sandi hesitated before answering.

"Yes. I didn't think that she would *stay* out there. But she did. And when dad was alive, he went out to visit all the time."

"It's my impression," I began, choosing my words carefully, "that Lisa has never been... crazy about your nephew, even before your father died."

Sandi was shaking her head, at the same time putting on the signal indicator to show that she was about to make a turn. She glanced at her mirror to check on Lisa.

"Nope. Any time they ever spent together, there was always tension," she said.

Picking up on the earlier conversation with Lisa on our drive from the hotel, I shifted away from 'Natty' questions to ask more about Sandi.

"Before your father died, Lisa said that you worked with him at the construction company," I said.

"Yes. I retired from my work with the school district. I'd been there for 25 years. Then, part-time, I helped dad and his estimators preparing bids for new contracts," Sandi said. "A lot of those folders you may have seen in my den, they're left over from when dad was still alive."

I was about to inquire of her work with the Taunton School District but Sandi cut me off.

"We're just two minutes from Sophia's house," she interjected, making a right turn off the highway.

Shifting in my seat to look back, I saw Lisa right behind us.

Sixty Five

It was 6:05 when Nathaniel got out of his car for what must have been the tenth time in two hours. So far, he'd managed to resist just bolting through the woods to his mother's house. It would be dark soon, at least dark enough to chance it.

The East Greenwich patrol car had passed twice when he'd been in the woods observing. It was possible they had come by while he was back in the car, too. He calculated that they were cruising the neighborhood on hourly intervals.

The location of all the homes was back away from the street, which required that visitors and parcel delivery trucks come the full length of a driveway to the residence.

Standing behind a tree, watching the street, Nathaniel focused on the mailbox at the end of the drive. It dawned on him that there could be accumulated mail. He'd left three days ago. His mother had been gone for more than a year, but junk mail still came, especially catalogs. He thought about emptying the mailbox before taking his mother's car.

As he was about to go back to his car and wait a few

minutes longer, a car turned into the driveway. He got behind a tree. He was sure that he recognized the car; it belonged to his Aunt Sandi.

Then, a second car turned in. A white Toyota pulled next to Sandi's car.

He waited.

There were lights on inside Sophia Crane's home as we approached. Sandi pulled around the side of the house and stopped in front of the garage. Lisa came up the driveway and pulled in next to us. Sandi and I got out.

"Well go in over there," Sandi said, pointing to her left at the back of the house.

We waited a few seconds, but Lisa remained in her car. Sandi turned to look at me, said nothing, then walked around the back of Lisa's car. I was standing next to a wooden gate surrounded by a fence with some type of ivy growing over much of it. There was a swimming pool, leaves scattered across its protective cover. Sandi was talking to Lisa.

"It's just so *eerie*," Lisa said, speaking to her sister through the lowered driver's door window. "The lights in the living room."

"They're on a timer," Sandi said, folding her arms and looking toward the front of the house.

Lisa sat in silence, slowly moving her gaze from the

garage door to the fence where I was standing. She looked up at Sandi.

"The day that I was here in August, it was a sunny afternoon, just before my flight back home," Lisa said.

"When you had the confrontation with Natty?"

Lisa nodded. Sandi unfolded her arms, reached into a coat pocket and pulled out a key on squiggly red plastic lanyard. She stared at the key for a second, then looked back at Lisa.

"C'mon. Let's go inside," Sandi said.

Sixty Six

Dyer was checking the investigation notes on a case that had remained open from the previous winter. It involved a stabbing incident. There wasn't anything new about the case, but a detective from the third shift had asked Dyer to take a look at the file and he was doing that when detective Ted Nichols called.

"I'm leaving in a few minutes," Nichols said. "In court tomorrow, maybe all day."

"Okay," Dyer said. "Thanks for the help."

"Angelo knows what to do. Any new activity on that phone, Jess will tell him as soon as it happens."

"Is she as good as you, Teddy?"

"Almost. Won't be long. You young guys will be working with her when I retire. Get used to it."

"You're way too modest," Dyer said.

"Text me if you really need to talk."

"Will do."

After the two pings from Nathaniel Crane's phone earlier in the day, one in Massachusetts followed by a later one in Coventry, Rhode Island, Dyer requested that a repeat BOLO alert be sent with additional info that the car was believed to be in southern New England. That was early afternoon, five hours ago. So far, no response.

Time to get something to eat. Dyer decided that he would try to have dinner with his wife. He sent a text to Angelo to tell him that he would be at home, then made a quick call to the East Greenwich PD to follow-up the BOLO.

The Sergeant on duty told Dyer that they had seen the second alert, had again checked the Crane home with nothing to report. Hourly patrols in the neighborhood would continue.

"Appreciate it," Dyer said. "He's around somewhere. Not sure he'll go back there. Taunton is another possibility and we've been in touch."

Angelo saw the message from Dyer. They had split follow-up tasks, Angelo handling the call tracking that Ted Nichols and his assistant were running, and communication with the Taunton PD. Dyer stayed in touch with Crane's aunt and the other police departments, specifically in New Jersey, and 15 miles south of Providence in the town of East Greenwich.

After bantering with detectives from the evening shift, Angelo thought it was a good time to get some air and maybe some food. He took the stairs down to the first floor and went out to his car.

Through the streets and buildings off to the west of the Public Safety Complex, Angelo could see a sliver of pinkish red sky on the horizon behind gray clouds. He held up his phone and snapped a couple photos, looked at them, then walked to his car.

Maybe good weather was coming. Angelo hoped that it would stay through the weekend. URI football at home on Saturday against Maine. Pretty even match-up.

The East Greenwich dispatcher was on the phone with a man from Courtney Drive. The man said that he was a neighbor of the late Sophia Crane and that he'd previously spoken with one of the department's patrol officers over the weekend.

"I know that you're cruising out here. I've seen the cars the past couple of days," the man said. "Thought I should tell you that I just saw two cars turn into the Crane driveway. Five minutes ago."

The dispatcher took his name and phone number and thanked him for calling in.

After hanging up, the neighbor remembered that he'd seen a vehicle in the woods on a building lot adjacent to his property, as well as the Crane property. That was two hours ago. He hadn't told the dispatcher about that.

Removing a retractable leash from a hook near the back door, the man called to his old English Sheep Dog, "Tilly. Come on girl. Let's take a walk."

Sixty Seven

Sandi unlocked the door at the back of the house. Lisa was standing next to me. Of the occasions when I'd been in her company during the past 72 hours, I had not seen her as dejected as she now appeared.

"It is really *just so sad*," she whispered. Sandi had gone into the house and left the door open for us to follow. "I didn't feel this when I was here two months ago," Lisa added.

Placing an arm on her shoulder, I took in a deep breath and could only imagine the emotion she must be feeling. She looked at me. I could see tears welling in her eyes.

"Go ahead," I said softly. Lisa stepped in front of me and went through the door.

Having turned on the lights, Sandi was standing next to an island that had a black ceramic cooktop and a small sink. It was a large kitchen, cabinets along both sides, a deep farm-style sink and a double-door, stainless steel refrigerator. Three contemporary light fixtures were evenly spaced over the center island with additional recessed lighting above the sink and along the cupboards.

We followed Sandi through a dining area to a hallway that led to the bedrooms. Lisa, head down, walked in front of me. I was looking at the paintings and art prints on the walls, and a faux Tiffany lamp placed on a table at the end of the hall.

The bedroom we entered was huge, probably 24 x 24 feet, with a walk-in closet and a bathroom opposite the queen size bed. At one end of the room was a desk, a chair and two small file cabinets. A banker's style lamp sat in the center of the desk. There were two upholstered Queen Anne style chairs next to a window looking out to the back lawn and gardens.

"Sophia's letters are in the bottom drawer," Sandi said. She walked to the desk and switched on the lamp, then opened the bottom drawer and removed two thick folders. She placed the folders side by side on the desk. "You take one and I'll take one," she added.

Lisa went to pick up a folder.

I felt like perhaps I should excuse myself from the room. Instead, I walked to one of the chairs by the window.

"*What* are you doing here?" a voice said. I turned around to see a clearly agitated man standing at the bedroom door. Eyes bulging, face flushed, clenched fists at his side.

"Hello, Natty," Sandi said.

Lisa turned to look at her nephew. She took a step

forward, stopped, and said nothing. I could see Lisa clenching her fists.

"*Who* are you? He said, voice shrill and jabbing a finger in my direction. "Is this your *lawyer*, Lisa?" he added.

I was about to tell him who I was, when Sandi held out an arm in a motion for me to 'wait.'

"Natty, I am the executor of your mother's estate. You *know* that I can come here. We're…"

"My name is Nathaniel. *You* know that!" he said.

Sandi extended her hands, palms down, in a gesture of apology.

"Nathaniel. I'm sorry. We are here to look at your mother's personal correspondence. I told you about her friend Cliff Torres being murdered. We hope that we can find something your mother may have had that will help us find someone in Cliff's family."

"Did *you* kill Cliff, Nathaniel?" Lisa blurted, taking another step in his direction. He turned, his eyes went from wide open to narrow slits. I could see his jaw clench. He hesitated a beat before responding.

"No, Lisa. I did *not* kill him. And I did *not* kill my mother," he said, stepping close enough that they could touch. I could see his body was shaking, his fists now raised from his side.

Lisa slapped him, a hard slap. "You are a *liar*, Nathaniel," she said.

His right arm came up reflexively, but he didn't strike

back. I was across the room in three steps.

Holding back from hitting Lisa, his fist remained in the air, arm trembling.

She didn't move. I got between them, jostling Lisa backward without making physical contact with him. I held both of my hands up in a stop signal, shook my head and said, "No."

In another part of the house, a door chime sounded.

Sixty Eight

The East Greenwich policeman stood at the front door. His partner, positioned between the patrol car and the two cars parked in front of the garage, waited. The cop on the porch pushed the doorbell a second time.

A few seconds passed. He looked through a glass panel that was vertical to the door frame. Someone was approaching, a woman. He took a step back before she opened the door.

"Mrs. Crane?" the cop said.

"No, I'm Mrs. Crane's sister," the woman replied. "Mrs. Crane is deceased."

"I'm sorry," he said, awkwardly. "Officer Savard, East Greenwich Police. We're trying to locate Mrs. Crane's son," he said.

Holding the door ajar, the woman looked over her shoulder. The cop tilted his head left to get a better angle into the house.

"Yes. My nephew is here," she said, turning back to face the policeman. She pulled the door open wider.

Savard gave a glance to his partner in the driveway

and made a slight motion with his head. He turned back to the woman and said, "May we come in? We'd like to talk with your nephew."

She stepped aside to allow the Savard to enter. His partner was walking toward the porch.

There were people in another room. Then the noise of something breaking, sounded like glass. A woman's voice shouted, "Nathaniel."

Savard couldn't see where the voice was coming from, farther back into the house, somewhere off to the right. The woman at the door looked at him. The other woman shouted again.

"You won't get away, Nathaniel."

Savard pulled his gun, at the same time waving his left arm to his partner and pointing in the direction of the garage. The other cop had his gun out and was running back to where the cars were parked.

Lisa tried to step around me, toward her nephew. He'd backed to the bedroom door, now slammed it closed as he went out. There was a crash of something breaking.

"You won't get away, Nathaniel," Lisa yelled.

Opening the door, I saw colored fragments of glass from the lamp scattered on the hardwood floor and rug in the hallway. There was a commotion somewhere near the kitchen and the sound of another door slamming.

Lisa was right behind me. We got to the kitchen just as a policeman, gun gripped in both hands, came in with Sandi behind him. The cop looked at us.

"He's trying to run," Lisa said, pointing to the back door where we had entered the house a few minutes earlier. The cop's eyes flashed in that direction, then back to us. He headed for the door, gun raised.

A man was entering the woods when the second cop shouted. He kept running, the cop now coming through the backyard, yelling the same command again.

"Stop. Police."

The man trying to escape slipped, fell to his hands and knees, then got up. But he didn't stop running.

The cop had his gun aimed as he closed the distance. Going through the woods, both arms flailing at his sides, the man showed no sign of having a weapon. He fell again, got up, but ran slower.

Just ahead, the cop could see a car. The man was heading for it.

Repeating a third time, "Stop," the policeman was gaining ground. He added, "*Now.*"

Falling against the car, the man pulled the driver's door open and nearly fell into the seat. The car looked like the Mitsubishi described in the BOLO alert.

Anticipating that he was about to drive off, the cop was ready to shoot tires.

The car didn't start.

Raising his arm and aiming the gun at the window, the cop carefully approached the driver's door. The car still was not moving.

Inside, the man's head and upper body rocked back and forth. He was pounding both fists against the steering wheel. He didn't look at the cop.

Savard came through the woods to the passenger side of the car, gun ready.

Jerking the door open and taking direct aim, the cop who'd been chasing him ordered the man to place both hands on the steering wheel and keep them there.

"Do it now," the cop yelled. The man stopped rocking and slowly gripped the steering wheel.

"Good move. What you do *next* is to get out of the car *very slowly*. Keep both hands in front of you." The man did as he was told, extending his arms, lifting one leg, then the other to get out. Both cops had direct aim on him.

Once he was out and standing upright, body turned to face the car, he was ordered to put his hands behind his back. That's when he tried to break away.

Savard was able to grab the man by his shirt and hook a foot out far enough to trip him. The man went down. The other cop was on his back immediately, pulling the man's right arm behind him.

The two policemen got him under control and his hands restrained with plastic flex cuffs. As they were lifting him off the ground, someone carrying a flashlight was coming through the woods from the other direction.

"Hello. Officer Savard," a man said. The second cop kept his gun ready.

"I'm the neighbor you talked to a couple days ago," the man said. He had a large gray and white dog on a leash. The dog stayed next to him. "I called in about the cars little while ago," he added.

Extending his free hand to Savard, the man held out a key fob.

"It was in his car," he said. "Thought I oughta' hold onto it 'til you got here."

Sixty Nine

Eating dinner with his wife when his phone buzzed, Dyer looked at the screen. It was a 401 call, but not a number that he recognized.

"Phil Dyer," he answered. It was the East Greenwich police sergeant, Ballan, who'd previously taken him to the Crane home.

"We have your guy," Ballan said. "Brought him in ten minutes ago."

"You don't say? Tell me about it."

"Showed up at his mother's home. Tried to hide in the woods. A neighbor called in about some cars being in the driveway," Ballan said. "Two of our men had to wrestle with him a little. But we have him, locked up."

"Did he have a gun?" Dyer said.

"Not armed when they arrested him. The Mitsubishi was parked close by. We'll bring it in, see if he has weapons in the car."

Dyer gave a thumbs-up to his wife, got up from the table while switching the phone to his right ear and held up a finger to indicate that he would be a minute.

As soon as the conversation with Ballan ended, Dyer hit speed dial to call Angelo to give him the news on Nathaniel Crane.

After police captured their nephew and took him away, Lisa and Sandi went back to the bedroom to get their late sister's personal letters. Sandi brought the two folders to the kitchen and placed them on the island.

"Do you still want to do this *now*?" Sandi said.

"Are you okay with that?" Lisa said. "I would really like to see if we can find something about Cliff's family."

"Sure." Sandi looked at me. "It might take a while," she said.

"Michael," Lisa said. "I think if you look around, you might be able to find a bottle of wine."

"The tall cupboard on the left," Sandi said, pointing. "Next to the refrigerator. There's a wine rack in there, on the bottom."

While I opened a bottle of Sakonnet Rhode Island Red, Sandi got three glasses from a cupboard. I poured the wine. We agreed that any thoughts about getting something to eat could wait.

Lisa sat on one of the stools at the island. Sandi stood, put on a pair of reading glasses, and the two of them started sorting through their sister's letters. Neither spoke as they began reading.

There was a broom and dust pan in a closet next to

the back door. I went into the hallway to clean up the shattered lamp.

Picking up the larger pieces from the broken shade, I examined a mottled blue colored fragment, about the size of clothes pin.

Surely this is a *fake* Tiffany?

Seventy

The crowd noise inside Dunkin Donuts Center was louder than Billy had ever heard. Only two nights earlier, the Providence Friars had beaten Holy Cross 71-67. Fans were ecstatic. But, in *this* game, the Friars were up against their in-state rival, the Rams of URI.

Both teams were expected to advance to the NCAA Tournament regardless of tonight's results. Final score, URI 65/Providence 62.

Billy could see Dave Gavitt courtside. And Jack Kraft, the winning coach for URI. All the players for URI, along with their fans, were jubilant in celebration. The young men playing for Providence and the people there to cheer for them, not so much.

The next image Billy had was of himself, uncertain exactly where he was. Or the year. He had this canvas bag over his shoulder. It was raining, hard. The bag was very heavy, and he was tired. He wanted to complain to someone. The words wouldn't come.

Then Billy could see his wife. And his son. They were smiling.

Father Mike got the phone call. Listed as an emergency contact, he had already met Doctor Elizabeth Oman when she explained the possibility of surgery. Now she was calling to tell him that Billy had died in his sleep.

Few people would know about Billy Woodson. Yes, the men from the pick-up basketball league would mourn his passing. It was unlikely there would be much of an obituary, online or in the newspaper, so it could be weeks before anyone who'd ever seen him on his daily walks would realize he was gone. And most people had no idea who Billy was, or, who he had been.

Some parishioners would mourn. A handful of the kids who'd spent hours and hours and hours inside the church gym, Father Mike knew, *they* would miss Billy. Perhaps some old coach, maybe some players, or a retired ref *somewhere*, if they ever learned of his passing, they too would remember Billy from his better days.

But all the stories were gone now. None recorded, none written down.

The Providence Police took custody of Nathaniel Crane. When his car was hauled in, a 9 milimeter Ruger semi-automatic pistol was found in the map compartment. He was placed under arrest in connection with a shooting that took a man's life on a downtown street on a rainy Friday night. Further investigation is pending.

The suit filed against Crane by his two aunts, claiming that he killed his mother to collect her inheritance, has now been sent to a district court judge. No hearing date has been set, no official charges have been made by the police.

Simultaneously, Crane's attorney, filed a suit in probate court to gain access to funds to help pay his client's legal fees. The probate judge has not ruled in that matter.

Sophia Crane's sisters found nothing in the personal correspondence that could provide additional information about Cliff Torres.

A life insurance policy discovered at his home in New Jersey listed a woman in Florida as the sole beneficiary. Authorities have yet to establish contact with the woman, her relationship with the murder victim is unknown.

The sisters did inform the City of Providence that they would be responsible for expenses related to Torres burial upon release of the body.

Driving back to Vermont the sky had cleared, still some foliage despite the early season storm. Not much traffic, so it was easy to take my time.

Listening to a CD featuring a classical pianist named Minkyung Oh, the volume turned down low, I watched the landscape. My brain was still trying to analyze events and the *people* of the past few days.

Thinking about Billy Woodson and the conversation I'd had with Father Mike when he called to tell me of Billy's death, I kept trying to get my head around the fact that every day, all over the world, people die and all too often their story is just *gone*. That's it. Unless the person had achieved some form of recognition, or had relatives, maybe friends, who preserved any milestones of their life, no one will ever know.

Then there was the stranger I'd exchanged a few words with about the weather, dead ten minutes later. Who *was* Cliff Torres, what was *his* story?

Two sisters, not related by blood and separated by a generation and geography, trying to get on with their lives, despite the tragedy of a family drama now being featured daily in the media. How long is it going to take for that to play out?

Still an hour from home, I hit the OFF button to stop the music on the CD player. Better to have less distraction while I tried to process thoughts and feelings that I was now experiencing about Lisa Bryan.

Our exchange in the parking lot was border-line soap opera. She was getting ready to fly back to San Diego and her work, I was going home to my dog and 'yet to be determined' plans and activities for the coming winter. We had agreed, without belaboring it, that a long-distance friendship was certainly possible, specifics also yet to be decided.

We also agreed that our brief 'personal' time together had been both a surprise and a pleasure, details for us only, thank you. Touching on that subject produced her smile.

"I will be back here a lot," she'd said. "Unfortunately. Until all of this is finished. Vermont isn't really that long of a drive, is it?"

"Not really. Maybe come back down sometime when they're doing Waterfire on the river," I said.

"You'd like it," she said.

We didn't discuss the lawsuits, the possible trial of her nephew, and the anguish and lingering tension that I knew she and her sister would struggle to resolve. We just held a gentle embrace for a long minute, then Lisa gave me another soft kiss.

Once I'd helped load her eight-wheel suitcase into the rental, she got behind the wheel and put the window down. I stood next to the car.

"I took Louie's advice to heart, by the way," I said. "I looked it up. Albert Hammond."

She stared at me, clearly no idea what I was talking about.

"1973. Found it on YouTube. It Never Rains in Southern California."

"No, it *doesn't*," she said. "Remember that." Again the smile. "You should visit sometime."

Acknowledgements:

- *On Broadway* – The Drifters (3/63 – Atlantic) and
                                George Benson (3/78 – Warner)
- *Reason To Believe* – Tim Hardin (7/66 – Verve)
- *If I Were A Carpenter* – Bobby Darin (9/66 – Atlantic)
- *Simple Song of Freedom* – Tim Hardin (8/69 – Columbia)
- *Buddy Cianci: The Musical* – Jonathan Van Gieson and
                                Mike Tarantino (off-Broadway, 2003)
- *Rhiannon* – Fleetwood Mac (3/76 – Reprise)
- *Honky Cat* – Elton John (8/72 – Uni)
- *The Scarlatti Doubles* – Minkyung Oh (11/13 – Jon Appleton
  The Couperin Doubles   and PHOENCIA Publishing)
- *It Never Rains in Southern California* – Albert Hammond
                                (10/72 –Mums)
- *The Art of Racing in The Rain* – Garth Stein (2008 -
                                HarperCollins)
- *Encyclopedia of Radio and Television Broadcasting* –
                                Robert St. John (1967 Cathedral Square)
- *Barking to the Choir* – Gregory Boyle (Simon & Shuster 2017)
                        also *Tattoos on the Heart* (Free Press 2010)
- *Talking To Ourselves* – Charles Fernyhough
                                (Scientific American – August 2017)
- *The Providence Journal* – www.providencejournal.com

Thank you for the music *and* the writing!

- Hilton Providence – www.reservationdesk.com/Providence
- Los Andes – www.losandesri.com
- The Parlour – www.theparlourri.com
- Dunkin Donuts – www.dunkinathome.com
- Il Massimo – www.massimori.com
- Marchetti's – www.marchettis.com
- Children's Home Society of California – www.chs-ca.org
- The Salvation Army – www.salvationarmyusa.org

ABOUT THE AUTHOR

The author is an award winning former broadcaster living in Vermont. He began his radio career as a news reporter covering both municipal and state government meetings, political campaigns, everyday community events and the incidents which frequently made the lead story of the day.

Many characters, conversations and real life experiences have inspired much of what you read in these books, but **the stories are fiction**.

www.nemysteries.com

Next up in the New England Mystery series:

- *A Blue Moon in VERMONT*

(Fall 2020)

Preview on pages 329-333.

Excerpts from

A Blue Moon in VERMONT

Probably never heard the shot and doubtful that he felt any pain from the impact of the bullet.

Now, he would not feel anything ever again.

At the age of sixty-five, retired only a month, a career US intelligence officer was dead. A 'hunting accident' in northern New Hampshire. The shooter turned himself in to Fish and Game authorities, paid a $500 fine and lost his hunting license for ten years.

Media coverage lasted about as long as it takes for the last autumn leaves to drop from the trees and the first accumulation of snow in the White Mountains.

The victim's family 'accepted that it was an accident,' so wrote a colleague in a memoir privately published after his own death.

A lifelong friend of the shooting victim has a different view. He believes that he has a way to prove that it was a 'contract hit'. He has *almost* enough information to identify who arranged the contract.

It was a pleasantly warm evening and we were sitting on a wooden bench in a small park in Williamstown, Vermont.

I watched the man reach down and pick a speck of lint from one of his socks. He flicked it away into the grass, made two quick inward swipes with his right hand across the bottom of a pant leg, then sat up straight and looked directly at me.

"Much better here than back at Camp Keyhole," he said, followed with a short chuckle.

"You're not crazy about living there?" I said.

He shook his head, quickly raising both hands as in a gesture of 'hold it a second.'

"Truth is, I like it there very much. Didn't think that I would. Knew I couldn't live alone any longer," he said, gazing at the few cars travelling along Route 14 through the center of town.

"And I've been coming to Vermont practically every summer since I was ten years old." He watched me take this in, then added, "If you want some help with the math, that's seventy-five years now."

"On the phone last week, when you called to ask me to come meet you," I said, "you implied that you needed some help with a project."

He nodded. "That I did. And I do."

I waited. He waited. It took me all of five seconds to accept that I would lose at playing poker with this man.

"So, can I ask for the Executive Summary" I said.

He studied me for a beat, leaned backward, stretched a long left arm along the top of the bench, crossed his legs and raised his right hand up to his chest as though he were about to pledge allegiance. Instead, he softly patted his hand a couple of times on his breastbone while still watching me.

If we're playing cards here, I was going to stick with the hand I'd been dealt. I said nothing.

"It's a project about getting at the truth of something that happened more than 40 years ago," he said. "Really, it was something set in motion *long* before that."

This was my second visit with Frank Marino. Instead of walking to the park bench we'd used a week earlier, we sat in two composite wicker chairs on the back lawn of the retirement community where he now resided.

"I found some of the articles you mentioned," I said, moving my chair around so I could face him. He held a hand up to stop me.

"Before we discuss any of that, Mister Hanlon, may I ask, do you have a passport?"

I nodded. "Yes."

"That's good. If we can agree on what I'm about to propose, there will be some travel."

"**What's the *name* of this dish?**" Ragsdale said. I half expected to see him start licking his fingers.

"Imam Bayildi," I said. "The Prof says it's also known as 'the sultan fainted.' Not bad, huh?"

"I might faint," he said. "This is really something."

"Glad you like it." I looked around the room at the other patrons. Those eating seemed to be enjoying their meals, perhaps not as much as Louie was enjoying his. I couldn't recall *ever* having heard Louis James Ragsdale actually rave about food.

The waiter returned with a second carafe of wine, topping off our glasses.

"Efharisto," I said. The waiter nodded, smiled and went to another table. Louie stopped chewing long enough to give me a smirk.

"It's all Greek to me," he said.

"Yuk, yuk." I took a sip of my wine.

"So, tell me again when we get to see this pal of yours," Louie said. He took a sip of his wine, then added, "And do you think he knows anything about Vangelis?"

Two-hundred-fifty-one towns and cities in the state and I wondered why Marino had chosen Williamstown to spend his final years.

After scrolling through the photos on my camera to refresh my memory, I popped the SIM card so I could insert it into my laptop and be able to show the photos to Frank on a larger screen.

It was twenty after ten. He'd said that I should get there at Noon and that he would be ready. The drive from Quechee normally took about 45 minutes. Then on to Burlington would take another hour.

Depending on what he thought of the photos, and my report from the conversations with Selene, would influence what he asked me to do next.

I had a pretty good hunch about 'next'. If I was on target, all of this could wind up involving more than a few cops and possibly the FBI.

Didn't matter. It would not be my call.

A Blue Moon in VERMONT – book seven in the New England Mystery series – to be published in the fall of 2020.

Visit the website – www.nemysteries.com